Seth was still ~~staring at her, and~~

~~have stopped if she'd wanted to. The hurry in~~
her stomach turned into a heavy glob. "Oh...?"

"Yes, Millie."

Every muscle in her body froze.

"Why ~~are~~ ... ~~library.~~ My
wife. Yo...

AUTHOR NOTE

Other countries have had their wild, rowdy or scandalous times, but only America can lay claim to the 'Old West'—the vast, unclaimed land west of the Mississippi that held promises of change, beauty, wonder and riches. The American Frontier lured people westwards in droves, and I for one never tire of reading and writing about those brave, wonderful souls.

This time I bring you to the Oklahoma Territory, once known as the roughest place in the nation.

Major Seth Parker believes there is no place for women at Fort Sill. Besides Indian uprisings there are whisky pedlars, Mexican traders, desperados, horse thieves, cattle rustlers, prostitutes, and men just bent on killing. But Millie St Clair has no choice.

I had a wonderful time putting Seth and Millie's story on paper, and it is my sincere hope that you will enjoy their journey to finding happy-ever-after in the wilds of Indian Territory.

Cheers!

THE MAJOR'S WIFE

Lauri Robinson

MILLS & BOON

Published in Great Britain 2014
by Mills & Boon, an imprint of Harlequin (UK) Limited,
Eton House, 18-24 Paradise Road, Richmond, Surrey, TW9 1SR

© 2014 Lauri Robinson

ISBN: 978 0 263 90942 5

Harlequin (UK) Limited's policy is to use papers that are natural,
renewable and recyclable products and made from wood grown in
sustainable forests. The logging and manufacturing processes conform
to the legal environmental regulations of the country of origin.

Printed and bound in Spain
by Blackprint CPI, Barcelona

Lauri Robinson's chosen genre to write is Western historical romance. When asked why, she says, 'Because I know I wasn't the only girl who wanted to grow up and marry Little Joe Cartwright.'

With a degree in early childhood education, Lauri has spent decades working in the non-profit field and claims once-upon-a-time and happily-ever-after romance novels have always been a form of stress relief. When her husband suggested she write one she took the challenge, and has loved every minute of the journey.

Lauri lives in rural Minnesota, where she and her husband spend every spare moment with their three grown sons and four grandchildren. She works part-time, volunteers for several organisations, and is a diehard Elvis and NASCAR fan. Her favourite getaway location is the woods of northern Minnesota, on the land homesteaded by her great-grandfather.

Previous titles by Lauri Robinson:

HIS CHRISTMAS WISH
  (part of *All a Cowboy Wants for Christmas*)
UNCLAIMED BRIDE
INHERITING A BRIDE
THE COWBOY WHO CAUGHT HER EYE
CHRISTMAS WITH HER COWBOY
  (part of *Christmas Cowboy Kisses*)

Also available in Mills & Boon® Historical *Undone!* eBooks:

WEDDING NIGHT WITH THE RANGER
HER MIDNIGHT COWBOY
NIGHTS WITH THE OUTLAW
DISOBEYING THE MARSHAL
TESTING THE LAWMAN'S HONOUR
THE SHERIFF'S LAST GAMBLE
WHAT A COWBOY WANTS
HIS WILD WEST WIFE
DANCE WITH THE RANCHER
RESCUED BY THE RANGER
SNOWBOUND WITH THE SHERIFF

To my wonderful nephew Kris and his beautiful wife
Vikki, who so graciously assisted in researching Fort Sill.
All my love, and hugs and kisses to Evan and Bear!
Aunt Lauri

Chapter One

1878
Oklahoma Indian Territory

Naked?

A bout of tremors attacked her knees and Millie St. Clair grasped the handrail of the train that had jostled her for miles on end. Swallowing hard and blinking, she hoped the scene before her might change.

It didn't.

They were naked.

Leastwise from the waist up—a sight she'd never seen before—yet they milled around the railway platform as freely as others who were fully clothed.

"Ma'am?"

"Good heavens," she muttered.

The porter took her arm. "Ma'am. Step down, please. There are other passengers behind you."

"Oh, yes, of course, forgive me," Millie stammered. It took considerable effort to unlock her knees and lower her feet to the metal steps and then onto the wooden platform, for all that skin was shocking. It couldn't help but hold her attention. Fortunately, the porter, with a solid grip on her elbow, aided her the entire way.

He'd been a kind man, offering smiles and asking about her comfort several times since she'd boarded the Missouri-Kansas-Texas rail line back in Missouri. His elderly face, complete with bushy gray brows and deep wrinkles that reminded her of a garden gnome, held compassion now as he pointed toward a small building at the edge of the wide wooden platform. "Your baggage will be placed along that wall."

A goose egg formed in Millie's throat as her gaze once again snagged on the shirtless men mingling in the crowd. This was known as Indian Territory, so encountering some was expected, but she'd had no idea they walked around half-dressed. In public no less.

"Is there someone to meet you?" the porter asked, tugging her farther out of the way.

"Y-yes, yes, my br—husband was to send someone," she managed to say. Husband. No matter how odd it was, she had to remember to refer to Seth Parker as her husband, not her brother-in-law, as he truly was. One slip of her tongue would send her back to Virginia, and that couldn't happen. Leastwise not before she settled things. For years she'd dogged Rosemary's footsteps, righting wrongs and cleaning up after her older sister, but this was by far the most imperative. Perhaps the one that would convince her sister that life was worth living.

Willing her nerves, and the familiar sorrow sitting heavy in her heart, under control, Millie did her best to pull up a smile for the porter, as well as tug her gaze off all the dark-shaded skin of the bare-chested Indians. "My husband's sending someone from Fort Sill to pick me up."

"Fort Sill?" The bobbing of the porter's Adam's apple above his smartly buttoned-up collar sent a shiver all the way to her toes.

"Yes." The air was so hot and dry her lips cracked as soon as she wet them, and a chill settled around her spine. "Fort Sill," she repeated. Her home for the next three months. A mere snippet of time, considering it would save a child from becoming motherless. That's what had kept her putting one foot in front of the other since this trip had started.

"Rosemary's just like your mother was," Papa had always said, which was a fear Millie had lived with for as long as she could remember.

She didn't have a single memory of the woman who'd given birth to her. Other than a few stories others had shared, her mother was nothing but a name. One that filled Millie with sadness, and only intensified when she thought of her sister following in their mother's footsteps.

The porter had disappeared among uniformed men, women dressed in everything from common calicos to eastern gowns as stylish as those in Millie's trunks, and of course, the Indians with little more than tight-fitting britches and soft-soled, knee-high moccasins. Some, she noted, now that she could see beyond the bronze-colored skin that had been so shocking, had on army jackets and pants, but even they had very long hair and feathers in their hats, as well as ornate necklaces hanging around their necks.

A weary pressure settled inside her chest. Seth Parker might not have sent someone to escort her. There was no way to know if he'd received the message of her impending arrival. It had been sent; she'd seen to that herself, five days ago, before boarding the first of several trains with so many separate railroad names she'd long ago lost track.

Someone jostled her elbow, almost pivoting her in a circle.

"Excuse me," a man muttered, rushing past.

She nodded, but he was gone, one among many

bustling about. The noisy surroundings, as well as the town—from what she could see of it—did suggest things were somewhat civilized in Indian Territory, which provided a bit of a comfort. She'd harbored considerable fears about residing at the fort, bearing in mind she'd never left Richmond before this trip.

Setting her traveling valise on the ground, Millie pulled down the hem of her waist-length jacket. The coal smoke and dust from the trains had turned the pale green traveling suit grayish, and her hair was so stiff she didn't dare remove a comb for fear every last strand would break off. But in a few miles, her travels would be over.

Then the real work would begin.

Work indeed. Pretending to be her sister would be the most challenging thing she'd ever done. Not in looks—people had been confusing the two of them forever, and she had cut her hair. It no longer hung to her waist in the simple braid she'd favored for years. For this journey she'd had to twist it around the hot prongs of a curling iron, then pin it up in a fashionable way. Rosemary had shown her how, though Millie still didn't have the knack her sister did. Maybe because it was a frivolous waste of time. Rosemary had changed her hairstyle so many times over the past years Millie sincerely doubted her sister remembered how she'd worn it when marrying

Seth. Besides, Millie had larger worries. Such as hoping she'd recall what Seth Parker looked like. It had been five years, and she'd seen him only once. Mistaking someone else for her so-called husband could prove disastrous.

Yes, when played against everything else, her hair was truly the least of her concerns. Picking up her satchel, Millie moved forward, elbowing her way to the little building with a sign proclaiming *Tulsa* in faded red letters.

Two of her trunks sat there. She set her traveling bag on one and stretched up on her toes, attempting to peer over or around heads sporting every type of hat imaginable for a glimpse of her additional luggage—or rather, Rosemary's.

The high-pitched screech of the train whistle and the shout "All aboard" echoing over the crowd had her searching harder.

People rushed by, bounding up the metal steps, and steam started hissing from beneath the locomotive. Surely the train wouldn't leave before all her belongings were unloaded. The distance between most of the previous stops had been lengthy; even when she wasn't switching trains there'd been time to walk about, stretch her legs.

Bubbles of anxiety filled her stomach and Millie scrambled on top of one trunk. Using a hand to shield her eyes from the sun, she scanned for a round bald head ringed with gray hair. Sighing in relief at the sight of the porter dragging a trunk behind him, she climbed down. The crowd diminished a bit, leaving more room for the man and his assistant to deposit her other trunks next to her.

"Thank you," she said earnestly. "I was getting worried."

The porter, wiping at the beads of sweat running down the sides of his face, eyed her quizzically. "Ma'am," he said, "you do realize how far away Fort Sill is, don't you?"

She smiled and nodded. "Yes, the train agent in Richmond—Virginia, that would be—informed me I'd have to take a wagon the last few miles." Patting the varnished trunk he'd set down, she continued, "That's why I was getting worried when I didn't see this trunk. I'll need a parasol out of it."

"A parasol?" The porter shook his head. "It's pert' near two hundred miles to Fort Sill from Tulsa, ma'am."

"Surely not t-two *hundred*."

He nodded.

Stunned, she sank onto one of the trunks behind her. Air refused to catch in her lungs despite several tries. Once able to speak, Millie asked, "Surely there's another train—"

"No." The porter paused momentarily as the

locomotive whistle sounded again. "Trains from here head straight west and straight south. Nothing goes through the center. That's the heart of Indian Territory."

Stretched out in bed, with nothing but a sheet covering his lower body, Seth Parker watched the sun crest the pointed tops of the stockade walls out the window of his loft bedroom. Tension had ahold of his spine like a snapping turtle latched on to a stick. Had for the past ten days. Ever since he'd dispatched a wagon to pick up his wife.

As the sun inched higher, disgust, dread, anger and a plethora of other things boiled together inside him, leaving a taste in his mouth so bad no amount of rinsing would help.

Today was the day. It could have been yesterday, so he should at least find gratitude in having had one more day of peace in his life. But yesterday was over, and that meant she'd arrive today.

Unless, of course, she'd changed her mind. That possibility would suit him just fine. It would mean he'd sent two men and a wagon to Tulsa for no reason.

Shaking his head, Seth stared at the beamed ceiling. Cutter and Wilson were good men, but they'd probably never forgive him for hauling Rosemary St. Clair—or Parker, if she was using his name—across Indian Territory. Five days of her attitude…

What did she want? They hadn't seen each other for five years. Their so-called marriage had been a sham from the start. His ire hadn't lessened in the years since she'd crawled into his bed and lied about what had happened the next morning, and it grew now as he lay here remembering it.

The conniving little wench. He'd been so exhausted a herd of buffalo could have stampeded through the room and he wouldn't have awakened that night. Since then, though, he slept with one eye open.

Lesson learned.

Throwing back the covers, Seth swung his legs over the edge of the bed. What could she possibly hope to gain by coming out here? Why hadn't she just signed the divorce papers and put an end to this misery? He'd sent her five sets. One a year. Every time an army lawyer visited the post, he filed another petition, and not once had she sent them back—signed or unsigned.

He pushed off the bed and crossed the room, lifting his clothes from the chair and pulling them on with all the joy of a man heading to the gallows.

Marriage was the last thing he'd ever wanted,

and he wanted this one dissolved. Had since the day it had happened.

She should, too. Her father, General St. Clair—a man Seth had held in high esteem—had passed away four years ago, so she had no reason to continue the pretense.

Dressed, Seth made his way to the ladder and climbed down the rungs. She wasn't going to like the living quarters, that was for sure. Besides the simple accommodations, a rough-hewn three-room cabin with a loft, there was the desolation of the fort, the weather, the landscape. None of it was going to be to Rosemary's liking. She'd lived in the general's posh Richmond home her entire life.

"Morning, Major," Corporal Russ Kemper said, carrying two cups of coffee through the open doorway.

"Morning." Seth took a cup and went to lean against the doorjamb as the rising sun erased the darkness of the cabin. His office had a window, but neither this room—the kitchen, dining room and parlor all rolled into one—nor the bedroom behind it did.

The living quarters, or barracks, as the army called them, were two rows of cabins facing each other, with the large open courtyard of the fort between them. As a major, the man in charge, Seth was assigned officers' quarters, one of the four houses flanking the fort's headquarters building, and was entitled to move in there, especially now that his wife would be living with him. But hell would freeze over first. If Rosemary wanted to live here so bad, she'd have to do it right here, in this little cabin, with Russ Kemper snoring the roof off every night.

A shiver zipped up Seth's back, so sharply he stiffened, and he had to step onto the covered wooden walkway running the length of the row of cabins to shake it off.

Russ slept in one bed, him in the other. Where would Rosemary sleep?

A smile formed, the first one he'd felt in days. The first one he'd felt since getting the telegram telling him to pick her up in Tulsa.

She'd have to figure out her own sleeping arrangements. His house was full.

Seth finished his coffee and walked back into the cabin. "Ready for some breakfast?"

A young man, barely eighteen, with big eyes and long legs, Russ nodded. "Always."

Together they angled across the courtyard to a building along the back where all the single men ate. Which was most of the forty-five men at the fort. Only four had wives, not counting Seth, of course. Six more had Comanche wives, but they lived outside the compound. The only Indians allowed to reside inside the fort on a regular basis were the four Comanche maidens who assisted the cook, Briggs Ryan. That was four more than army rules allowed, but Seth liked to keep his men happy, and hungry men weren't happy. And Briggs, a six-and-a-half-foot-tall Swede with hands that could wrap around a cannonball as if it was a marble, wasn't happy without his maidens.

After breakfast, a hearty meal that sat in Seth's stomach like lead with all the commotion going on inside him, he ordered the M troop to mount up for drills. It would suit him just fine to be gone when Rosemary arrived. It'd suit him fine to be gone the entire time she was here.

That wasn't his luck. He'd barely arrived back at the fort, having spent three hours in the hot September sun—which in Indian Territory was as hot as the August sun most days—when the sentry in the guardhouse signaled a wagon was approaching.

With his jaw locked and his temples pounding, Seth turned his mount over to Russ, and after splashing water on his face, planted his hat on his head and made his way to his cabin. Meeting her in his office would be the best thing for everyone.

It was there, at his desk, that he got the first glimpse of her. Frowning, for it was a perplexing sight, he pushed his chair back and stood to get a better look out the window. Mirth was a good feeling, and when it bubbled up the back of his throat, he let it out. This he had to see in person.

Leaning in the open doorway, shadowed by the overhang, Seth watched the wagon roll to a stop several yards away. A chuckle still tickled his throat, and he covered it with a cough as people started gathering, catching their first glimpses of his wife.

She was holding a once-fancy umbrella the wind had reduced into a misshapen frame of sticks waving several haphazard miniature flags, and her hair was bushed out as if a porcupine sat on her head. The skirt flapping around her ankles sent up puffs of dust as she climbed down, aided by Ben Cutter, who gestured toward the cabins. Throwing her shoulders back, she started walking across the hard-packed ground.

Seth was biting the inside of his cheek, for she certainly looked the worse for wear, but then a frown formed, tugging hard on his brows. He didn't remember her having a limp. Then again, they hadn't spent more than a couple hours together, and most of that time had been used up with her father convincing Seth to say I do.

Millie's backside was numb and her legs were stiff, to the point every step had her wondering if she'd become a walking pincushion. But head up, she started directly toward the man she knew to be Seth Parker.

He was the one smiling.

No, not smiling…smirking.

Holding in a great bout of laughter, she'd bet.

At her expense.

Frazzled, tired, weather-beaten and sore, she marched onward. Well, limped. The heel had broken off her boot back in Tulsa. Five days ago. On the other side of the world. For the first time in her life she felt as ornery as Rosemary.

A gust of wind caught her parasol, and this time Millie let it go. There was nothing left of it, anyway. People were gathering around, but she couldn't care less. She needed a bath, a cup of tea and a bed. In that order.

Never in all her born days could she have imagined what it was like traveling in a buckboard wagon with no canopy, across land that was little more than a desert, with two men who ate beans for every meal.

Beans.

Beans with no ginger. Everyone knew ginger helped eliminate human gases produced when people ate a lot of beans.

She hobbled onto the boardwalk, and without a pause in the clip-thud of her uneven footwear, she pointed toward the door behind her supposed husband. "Is that our house?"

"Yes."

The grin he held back made her jaw sting as her teeth clenched. She ignored it, and him, and crossed the threshold.

A rusted, mini parlor stove, a crude table with two chairs, a tall cupboard, two doors and a ladder leading to an open area overhead… The open door on the right showed a desk, so she went left.

"That's Russ's room."

The stabbing sensation between her shoulder blades stopped her movements. With only one heel, standing straight was impossible, so, as crooked as a scrub oak, she spun around. "Who is Russ?"

"Corporal Kemper," Seth said. "My assistant."

"He lives with us?"

"No, he lives with me."

Millie pulled in air through her nose until her lungs were full all the way to her chin, but it didn't help. Rosemary would have an opinion on that, but Millie really didn't. Letting the air out, she asked, "Where will I live?"

Seth shrugged.

Her last nerve was gone, and she really didn't know what to do about it. Not that there was a whole lot she could do. Between the train and wagon rides, her well of self-encouragement had gone dry. Finding the fortitude to pretend to be Rosemary was impossible. Yet she was here, had arrived and needed to regain her composure to make it through the next three months. Taking another breath seemed to be her only option. So she did that. Long and deep.

Mr. Cutter and Mr. Winston chose that moment to appear at the door with two of her trunks. Both men had done all they could to make the unpardonable journey across the most desolate land in the nation as comfortable as possible— despite their predictable but unfortunate reactions to the beans.

"Where do you want these, Major?" Mr. Cutter asked.

Seth moved away from the door, stepping into the room, which made the tiny space ten times smaller. She didn't budge. She remained standing next to the little stove, which emitted a scent of creosote. Her nostrils would never be the same. They seemed to thrive on obnoxious smells now.

"Just set them down anywhere," Seth instructed, never taking his eyes off her. With a wave of one arm, he said, "I'd like to see you in my office."

"No," she answered, returning a gaze just as bold as his. The clump of hair hanging over her right eye probably took some of the sting out of her glare, but she kept her chin up, mentally telling her hand not to tuck the hair behind her ear.

"No?" His expression suggested he rarely heard the word.

She didn't have a chance to respond before someone said, "I'll get my things."

A young man with the longest legs she'd ever seen set her traveling bag on the table and then sidestepped around her toward the room with the closed door. Two other men set down her additional trunks and ducked out the front, while clanging and banging erupted behind her.

"Russ, your corporal, I assume?"

Seth nodded.

Had his eyes always been that blue, that piercing? Perhaps. She'd seen him only once. The day he'd married Rosemary. A few minutes ago Millie did recall his hair had been so black it looked blue, but he appeared taller than he had years ago, broader across the shoulders, and more unapproachable than her feeble memories recalled. Maybe it was the blue uniform. The tailoring of the outfits could do that to men.

The gangly corporal nodded as he scurried past her with his arms full. "I'll bring over some clean bed linens."

"Later," Seth responded curtly.

The man shot out of the cabin, and Seth shut the door behind him. The sound, as well as the darkness—for only a small amount of light filtered into the room from the open office door and alcove above—had Millie holding her breath. She'd best get used to it…being alone with him. Three months was a long time.

Once again he pointed toward the office.

Emptying her lungs with an audible sigh, specifically for him to hear, she held her ground. "I need a bath, I need a cup of tea and I need a bed. In that order. Then I'll meet with you in your office."

Saying it aloud increased her longing. There was such an indecent amount of dirt in her hair that her scalp itched, her entire body felt sand-pitted and crusty, and her traveling suit was no longer either pale green or gray. It was now a pitiful shade of orange. The entire territory was made up of red-hued dirt that clung to everything. But it was the bed she wanted most. Just a few quiet moments, without wheels turning beneath her, to gather the energy to become her sister.

Seth leaned a hip against the table. "There's a community bathhouse at the end of the barracks. I don't have any tea, and I guess Russ just gave you his bed, but I'd advise you to change the sheets. I don't how long it's been since he did."

A smirk still sat on his face, and it increased his genuine handsomeness, so much that she wondered if Rosemary remembered what he looked like, for looks meant a lot to her sister.

Then again, perhaps Rosemary did. He was the one, after all, demanding the divorce. A weight settled on Millie's shoulders. It was her job to make sure it didn't happen for three months—until Rosemary delivered her baby.

Holding in the sigh welling in her chest, Millie concluded that, whether she was ready or not, it was time to start acting.

"Seth," she said. A wife should call her husband by his given name, yet it felt very strange. "I understand you're curious about my arrival, but I've been traveling for almost two weeks, and I'm more than exhausted."

He folded his arms, and the way his eyes traveled from her broken boot to her itching scalp made her need for a bath and clean clothes intensify.

"Curious?" he asked with a hint of cynicism.

She nodded.

"Oh, I am curious," he said, with a direct stare. "Even more now that *you've* arrived."

The way he said "you've" sent a tingle coiling around her spine. Rosemary had said they'd never been together, as in man and wife, so that was not something Millie needed to worry about, but that's what settled in her mind. Men grew amorous when they were alone for long lengths of time. Women, too, or so her friend Martin said. Not that she'd actually understood exactly what he'd meant.

Seth was still staring at her, and the least she could hope was the muted light of the room made it too dark for him to notice the way her cheeks blazed. Of all the things to think about, Martin's explanation should not be one of them. The fluttering in her stomach had her trying to reroute her thoughts. Rosemary was married to this man. He just wasn't the father of her child. It was truly a jumbled mess—which now, unfortunately, Millie was right in the midst of.

She was here for the child's sake, would do whatever it took to keep Seth from learning about the baby. Once things were settled—back home, that is—she might travel to Texas. Martin was there, and after this escapade—pretending to be married to a man she wasn't—she'd need her best friend. Her only friend. Few others would forgive such a scandal. But a life—no, two lives—were worth more than her reputation. Especially the life of an innocent child.

Seth shifted his stance, leaning farther back, and the smirk grew to resemble more of a smile as he looked her up and down again. It was unnerving, yet she couldn't think of a thing to say that might make him stop, nor slow the outrageous fluttering inside her.

"Matter of fact," he finally said, slowly, thoughtfully, "I'm so curious I want to know the truth right now."

She gulped, a nervous reaction she couldn't have stopped if she wanted to. The flurry in her stomach turned into a heavy glob. "Oh?"

"Yes, Millie."

Every muscle in her body froze.

"Why are you here? Instead of Rosemary. My wife. Your sister."

Chapter Two

"I. . .I...I—" This couldn't happen. Closing her eyes for a moment, Millie imaged how her sister would react to the accusation. It appeared instantly, for Rosemary never accepted fault. Huffing out a breath, she sent across the room a bitter glare akin to ones she'd witnessed on several occasions. "Millie?"

"Yes, Millie," Seth repeated. The ire zipping beneath his skin was mixed with a goodly portion of mirth. She was a sight, not just her travel-worn outfit and windblown hair, but her beet-red cheeks and eyes as big and round and startled as a doe's at the end of a gun barrel.

"I'm not Millie," she insisted. "Goodness, Seth, I'd have thought you'd remember your own wife."

"I do. And you're not her." There wasn't anything he could put a finger on, for he didn't know the sister any better than he knew his wife. But this woman was not Rosemary, therefore she had to be Millicent, the younger sister. Why— the foremost question that had been bouncing around in his head for over a week—intensified.

"Seth," she said, pressing both hands to the base of her throat. "I realize it's been five years, and I understand how easy it is to question my youthfulness. Yes, Millie is younger than me, but please…" Her sigh was accompanied with a steady batting of her eyelashes. "She's shorter than me, somewhat chunkier and not as attractive—her eyes are too close together. People have said that for years. Since the day she was born, actually." Patting the hair sticking out in all directions, his visitor continued, "Now, I know I must not look myself right now, but once I've had a bath, you'll see it's me, Rosemary."

Now, that sounded like Rosemary. Matter of fact, those were almost the exact words she'd said the first time they'd met. General St. Clair had just introduced them, and commented that the youngest sister wasn't home, but the two were practically identical. Rosemary had piped in then, stating that she was much more attractive than her sister. Seth recalled it so clearly because at the time, he'd thought her the snootiest girl he'd ever met. The next morning he'd decided she was a lot more than snooty. Downright mean and nasty was more like it.

Maybe she had changed. The Rosemary that had climbed into his bed back in Virginia, the same one that insisted he'd taken advantage of her, and convinced the general her reputation was ruined, would not have been as calm and patient as the woman standing before him. The girl from that night would have been screeching and stating a list of demands before she got off the wagon. Actually, she'd never have gotten on the wagon.

Frustration gurgled in his stomach. The two girls looked enough alike to be twins, he remembered that, and Rosemary was older by three or four years, if he recalled correctly. She'd be twenty-four now. He shoved away from the table. Why was he concerned with any of it? All he wanted was a signed divorce decree.

A knock sounded and the door opened before he responded. That wasn't unusual; his men knew he was always at their disposal.

"Excuse me, Major," Ben Cutter said, barely glancing his way. "Ma'am, the bathing house is ready. I saw to it myself."

"Oh, thank you, Mr. Cutter. Your kindness is never-ending."

Seth's back teeth clamped together and had his jaw stinging. Not just at her fawning, but at how Cutter was looking at her. One would have thought the man was gazing at an angel. Seth, of course, knew differently.

"If you tell me what you need, ma'am," Cutter said, "I'll carry it down there for you."

An uneven click and thud echoed against the rough-hewn walls as she walked across the room toward the table.

"Her heel broke off in Tulsa," Ben said directly to him. "It got caught in a knothole on the train platform. Ralph fixed it, but it broke off again yesterday."

Seth didn't need an explanation; it made little difference. Yet because in most instances he did expect full reports from his men, he nodded to Cutter before he asked her, "Don't you have another pair of boots or shoes?"

The sideways glance she sent his way was full of intolerance. "Do you honestly think I'd be wearing these if I had another pair?"

That, too, sounded like Rosemary.

She lifted the tapestry bag Russ had set on the table. "I have day slippers I can wear now, but they wouldn't have held up while traveling." Turning to Ben, she smiled. "I packed everything I'll need in here last night, after you and Mr. Winston explained the layout of the fort."

"Here, then, ma'am, I'll carry that for you," Ben replied, taking the bag and holding the door wide with his other hand.

"Thank you." Chin up, she marched—with her awkward high-low steps—out the door, without a single backward glance.

Seth was just fine with that. Though he did follow as far as the opening. A crowd had formed, which was to be expected. The fort was close-knit, more so than some families, and there were a few men who'd probably been standing right outside the door, attempting to hear every word. They were off to the sides now, watching curiously. Only a select number of people had known he was married, but once the telegram came in, announcing her arrival, word had spread fast. A twinge pulled at his forehead. He'd have to tell his mother now, and better send the letter soon. If someone else mentioned it, she'd never forgive him.

"Major, sir," Ralph Winston said, clicking his heels together as he stopped next to the open doorway. "Did Ben explain your wife wasn't hurt, other than a broken heel, when she fell? I did fix her boot, but without the proper tools, it broke again."

Seth was grinding his teeth again; he had to pull them apart to answer. "Yes, he did."

"She was attempting to help us load her luggage, sir. We told her it wasn't necessary. Half the town thought it was a gunshot, the way the sound echoed beneath the platform." Winston wiped his brow and replaced his hat. "My heart danged near stopped working, seeing her sprawled out on the ground."

Seth was a touched surprised by the concern that raced over him—and irritated. One more person to be concerned about. Responsible for. Army men were one thing. Women and children another—and something he never wanted to have to worry about again.

The giggle that sounded a short distance down the walkway snagged his attention, but through will alone, he kept his gaze from turning that way. He was about to dismiss Winston when the man continued.

"She's a trooper, Major. Was laughing to beat the band when I helped her to her feet. Never saw a woman laugh at herself like that."

Seth's spine stiffened all over again. The Rosemary he knew—or the one he thought he knew—would never have laughed at herself. True, he'd left Richmond less then twenty-four hours after meeting her, returned here to the Indian Wars, but her attitude, her persona, had imbedded itself within him the first hour he'd known her.

"I'll see the heel gets repaired properly this time, sir."

After a nod, Seth waved a hand, dismissing Winston. His eyes then went to where *his wife* entered the door to a room with tubs and water barrels. The officers' quarters were separate homes with space for private bathing, and Rosemary would have demanded to know why he didn't live in one of them.

He turned and reentered his cabin. Even after becoming a major, he'd gone on living in the barracks. Back then things had been so busy, he hadn't had time to think beyond knowing he had a bed to fall into at night.

The turmoil had calmed down considerably over the past few years, even more the past months, but he still hadn't thought about moving. Besides, the major's house, as it was known, had become a catchall. Storage for items no one knew what to do with.

As Seth spun to shut the door, the hairs on his neck stood up. People were still gathered about, some pretending to be on missions, whereas in reality they were staring at him. Watching for his next move.

That was common. By nature, and due to his position, everyone at the fort was always watchful for his command. This was different, though. It had nothing to do with army business, and… A heavy sigh escaped, one he hadn't known had built in his chest. He didn't know what his next move would be, either.

That was an oddity. For the first time in a very, very long time, he was at a loss.

"Major?" A hand planted itself on the half-closed door.

"Briggs," he said, in answer to the man pushing the door open again.

"I see your wife," the Swede said in his deep and gruff voice. "I bring food. Here to your cabin, she eat after cleaning up. No?"

It didn't matter what the man said, question or statement usually ended with no. And right now, it fit. "No, Briggs. If she's hungry she can eat at the hall like everyone else."

"But Major, a woman—"

"She might as well get used to it."

The startled look on the cook's face made something recoil inside Seth. He usually got along with his men, because of mutual respect, but the way he'd just snapped at the Swede, said he didn't like it. Seth squared his shoulders, let his stance confirm who was in charge. "Is there anything else you needed, Sergeant?"

"No, Major. Sir."

The man spun around, and this time Seth all but slammed the door. Exactly what he'd always suspected. A wife would interfere with his duties.

A reflection of the dented brass tub caught in the mirror. The accommodations were rough, but she'd never enjoyed a bath as much. Twisting, needing the mirror's assistance in placing the combs, Millie coiled each braided length and pinned them in place at the back of her head. Drying it would take an hour, and curling it even longer, and she didn't have that kind of time. Besides, just as she'd suspected, curled hair would not convince Seth she was Rosemary.

Satisfied the combs were secure in hair that was once again brown and not dust gray, Millie tidied up the area before opening her bag to stuff her boots on top of the traveling suit that would never be pale green again. It had been new at the beginning of her journey, and clothes usually lasted her years. A miniature shiver had her lifting her head, gazing toward the mirror again.

The reflection in the glass mocked her. Millie would be sad about the dress, Rosemary would not. An invisible weight pressed upon her shoulders, so heavily she sat down next to her bag. Being Rosemary was more difficult than she'd imagined. Back in the cabin, when Seth had voiced his suspicion, it had been easy to know what to say. People often confused the two of them, especially from a distance, but in reality, her sister was more attractive, and never failed to remind her of it.

After she'd pulled Rosemary into her mind and said those words to Seth, her stomach had twisted inside out. His expression had turned hard; those piercing blue eyes had gone cold enough that she'd shivered. Seeing the tick in his cheek had made her afraid for the first time since she'd left Richmond.

Millie let out another sigh. No matter how irritated *Rosemary* made Seth, that's who she had to be—*Rosemary*. She had to remember that.

It took several deep breaths, and a few minutes of concentration, but by the time she opened the door and stepped out onto the walkway, she was once again convinced she could do it. Could be her sister for the next three months—until the baby was born.

People stared, mostly men dressed in their blue uniforms with brass buttons, wide yellow neck scarves and flat-brimmed hats, and though Millie would have smiled, nodded, Rosemary would not, so she kept her nose up and moved forward. She did ignore a few things that her sister wouldn't have. There was nothing she could do about the wind and dirt, and she had to wave at Mr. Cutter. It would have been too rude not to. The man had to be twice her age, yet his cheeks shone crimson every time he spoke to her. She appreciated him, too, for all he'd done.

Those things were inconsequential, of course. Seth was the only one who had to believe she was Rosemary. She could do that.

Then she arrived at their cabin, where he stood in the doorway.

Smiling.

Oh, goodness.

"Feel better?" he asked.

Millie pressed the thin leather soles of her day slippers against the boards below her feet. Rosemary wouldn't respond—she'd ignore him pointedly or start spouting demands. But he appeared to be making an effort, and whether her sister would appreciate that or not, Millie did, and couldn't discount it.

"Yes, thank you," she said. "It's amazing what a little water can do."

Once again his gaze became so penetrating her insides sprouted wings. A stirring silence grew between them, and she clutched the satchel handle tighter, afraid it might tumble out of her trembling fingers.

"Yes, it is," he said, stepping back, clearing the cabin's doorway for her entrance.

She pressed a hand to her stomach, to calm the flapping there. The gown was a simple blue calico with short sleeves and a square neckline. It had seemed the most appropriate for the weather yesterday when she'd packed her bag, sitting in the back of the bumpy wagon.

When she lifted her gaze, the explanation died in her throat and her feet grew roots. There was a tightness in his jaw, and she could feel his contempt. Tugging her feet off the walkway, and praying she wouldn't stumble, for there was no excuse now that she was no longer wearing the off-kilter boots, Millie dipped her head and moved forward.

She'd barely stepped inside the cabin when a clanging noise echoed through the open courtyard.

"It's lunchtime," Seth said. "Are you hungry?"

Five days of beans—the thought was still horrifying—blasted into her mind like a storm. Men could release the pressure beans produced, but women couldn't, and most certainly never in mixed company. She'd requested to sit in the back of the wagon for fear she'd burst at times, and the thought of eating beans again today was deplorable. But so was the confrontation about to take place—it was right under the surface. She could tell he was ready to claim once again that she wasn't Rosemary.

He was probably going to say her sister would never have made the wagon trip—or half the train rides. She'd have returned to Richmond long before crossing the Mississippi. He'd be right, of course. But Millie hadn't had the choice of not coming—nor of leaving.

"As a matter of fact, I am hungry," she said, setting the bag down on one of her trunks.

Once again the thought of Rosemary doing what their mother had done made Millie's insides quiver. The housekeeper, Lola, insisted she mustn't blame herself. Millie tried not to, but when you're responsible, you carry blame. Forever. Papa had always feared the same thing— that Rosemary would do what Mother had done—and Millie had never told him how close Rosemary had come once. She'd never told anyone. Martin knew. He'd been the one who saved Rosemary's life, but he'd thought she'd fallen into the river.

The weight in Millie's chest grew immense. Lola had vowed no such thing would happen while Millie was gone, and if anyone could make Rosemary behave it was their loyal, watchful housekeeper. Remembering that gave her fortitude. If Lola could handle Rosemary, surely Millie could handle Seth. After five years postponing the divorce, an additional three months couldn't be that difficult.

"Shall we go then?"

Dropped back to earth like a peach falling from a tree, Millie paused mentally, gathering her wits. "Yes, lunch," she mumbled, mainly to herself. Food probably wouldn't help, but not being alone with him would. Her nerves were too jumbled for her to think straight right now.

Millie didn't attempt to concentrate on becoming Rosemary during the short walk across the compound. She was too focused on keeping up with Seth's long strides. Once they entered the building a man as large as a bear, with hair as yellow as corn, met them at the door.

"Mrs. Parker," he said, dipping his head. "My name's Briggs Ryan. Private Cutter said you like tea, no?"

"Yes, yes, I like tea," she responded.

"Good. Ja, I have some for you. This way."

As wonderful as the tea sounded, she couldn't help but pause at the way Seth stiffened at her side. He didn't take a step to follow the man, so she didn't, either.

"I set a table for you and your wife, Major," the man said, "as usual when we have company."

There appeared to be some kind of showdown between the two, and Millie had to believe she was the cause of it. "I'm not really company," she said, hoping to ease the tension.

Neither man spoke, but after another quiet moment, Seth nodded his head slightly. He then took ahold of her elbow and led her across the room, following Briggs Ryan.

The large room was crowded, but almost silent now as they made their way to the table. All men, dressed in their blue uniforms. Some were sitting at the long tables flanked with benches, others standing in line, filling their plates from huge platters set out on a high counter.

Mr. Ryan held a chair and she sat. The table

was small and set for two, complete with a tablecloth and napkins.

"I'll have your plates out in a minute and your tea, ma'am," Mr. Ryan said before walking away. He, too, was wearing a uniform, but it was covered with a long white apron.

"Is Mr. Ryan the cook?"

"Yes," Seth answered. "Keeping the unit fed is his job."

The words seemed to hold a double meaning, but it was beyond her to understand exactly what. The man was back within minutes, placing a teapot and two plates of food—stew, not beans—in front of them.

The tea was refreshing, but it didn't help as much as she'd hoped. Perhaps because the room held a thick silence, one that had her wondering if being alone with Seth would be better.

They, too, ate in silence, and though he didn't gobble his food, Seth was done long before she was. At which point he pushed away from the table. "I have work to see to. I assume you can find your way back to the cabin."

After patting her lips, she laid her napkin on the table. "I'm finished, too. May I walk out with you?"

He eyed her slowly, then gave a slight shrug. "If you want."

She wanted, all right. The eyes staring their

way had burned holes in the back of her dress. It was to be expected, her showing up out of the blue like this, yet she couldn't help but wish things were different. That animosity didn't ooze off of Seth.

Mr. Ryan met them at the door again. "The food was to your liking, no?"

"Oh, yes," she assured him. "The stew was delicious. And the tea wonderful. Thank you, Mr. Ryan."

The man grinned, but his smile faded as he glanced toward Seth.

"I'll talk to you later, Sergeant," Seth said.

"Yes, sir, Major, sir."

Needing fresh air, Millie bolted out the door as soon as Seth opened it. How was she ever going to pull this off? Someone that stern, that commanding, was sure to know a lie when he heard one.

You catch a lot more bees with honey than vinegar. One of Lola's sayings raced through her mind, and Millie couldn't help but wonder why that one came to her now. Rosemary wasn't known for her kindness. Then again, the saying did produce another thought. "You know, Seth," she said, forcing her voice not to tremble, "it's been five years. People change."

"I haven't," he said.

"I'm sure you have in some ways," she insisted, while keeping up with his fast strides again. "I know I have." That much was the truth. Five years ago she'd never have done this: traveled to Indian Territory, taken on her sister's identity, lied. Papa would have been alive and he wouldn't have let her.

Seth stopped and once again studied her thoroughly. "So much that I should believe you're Rosemary and not Millie?"

She sighed heavily, partly because lying made her feel more soiled than her travels had. "I am Rosemary."

Seth wasn't exactly sure how to respond. In some ways he couldn't think. He hadn't gotten over how a bath had transformed her into a stunningly beautiful woman, and it didn't help that the men—*his men*—were already treating her like royalty. It was how he'd expect them to treat his wife, but she wasn't his wife. Leastwise he didn't want her to be. Never had. She'd already instigated the first-ever clash of power between him and Briggs Ryan. The cook was right. Guests, moreover women, were respected at all times at the fort, and held in the highest esteem. Making her eat at the long tables wouldn't have been right, but Seth was in charge here, and his orders had to be followed.

Not that Briggs had disobeyed any, but he'd

come close, and Seth didn't allow any man to challenge his authority.

This time, he'd thank the man for seeing to Millie's comforts. For that's who she was, and what Briggs had done wasn't out of line. Anger had overruled Seth's own manners, but Briggs had to know he was walking a thin line. It had to be that way. If not, the entire regiment wouldn't have lived through the past few years. Now wasn't the time to let their guard down.

Especially not Seth.

As the thoughts conformed in his mind, and settled, his gaze roamed. Men, mingling in the courtyard, were moving closer, hoping for an introduction, no doubt. He'd have to make them, and take her over to headquarters to meet Jasper Ketchum—his second in command—and Jasper's wife, Ilene.

Seth's temper once again flared. He'd have to introduce her as Rosemary. Explaining his marriage had caused enough confusion. Introducing her now as Millie would have the questions deepening, and that couldn't happen. People would wonder if he was capable of commanding a fort when he couldn't handle his own life.

"Seth?"

Her whisper was soft, but the hand she'd laid on his arm bit through his coat and shirtsleeve, hotter than the fangs of a snake. Yet the anxiety

filling her big brown eyes had his insides collid-
ing. Whether he wanted her here or not wasn't
the issue. She was here and he had to offer his
protection.

With that, he reached over and patted her
hand. The action had him smothering a curse.
He didn't want to care about her, but he did care
about his men. They looked at him for leadership, and true leaders did whatever it took. Nodding at the first man in line, he then glanced her
way. "Rosemary…" Saying the name had disor-
der leaping inside him. "This is Quartermaster
Josiah Fallon." Turning toward the man, he said,
"Josiah, this is Rosemary Parker, my wife."

The word tasted bitter, and her fingertips dug
deeper into his arm.

"Mrs. Parker," Josiah exclaimed. "It's a pleasure to meet you. If there is anything you need,
you just let me know and I'll find it for you."

"Thank you, Mr. Fallon. It's a pleasure to meet
you, too," she responded with sincerity. "Mr. Cutter and Mr. Winston told me about you." Leaning closer, she said, "Thank you for finding the
tea Mr. Briggs served with lunch."

Fallon was as hairless as a rock, and right now
the top of his head was bloodred, while he shuffled feet the size of snowshoes until a dust storm
hovered around his ankles.

"Private Cutter told me you were hoping for

tea," the quartermaster replied. "I had a tin left over from when we had some English visitors a while back. I dug it out and hauled it over to the cookhouse as soon as Ben mentioned it."

"Well, thank you very much. I truly enjoyed it."

Seth could have sworn there were stars in her eyes, the way they twinkled.

Fallon was the catalyst that led to a list of introductions so long Seth started confusing names. Neither he nor Millie moved; people just kept filing past, to the point he wondered if some weren't coming by a second time, just to get another look at her. A part of him couldn't blame them. She was overly charming, and remarkably, had conversed enough with Cutter and Winston to know a small bit of information about each and every person he introduced her to.

The line finally ended with Jasper and his wife, who invited them to sup at their home tomorrow night.

"That will give you time to settle in, dear," Ilene Ketchum finished.

Her angular face with sunken cheeks and narrow eyes could never be noted as pretty, but Seth had never known a more benevolent woman, and he respected Ilene's knowledge and support as much as he did her husband's. Lying to her, pretending the woman beside him was Rosemary, had Seth's stomach curdling all over again. It was almost as bad as letting down his own mother.

"Thank you, Mrs. Ketchum, that's very kind of you," his supposed wife answered, but she glanced his way before accepting the invitation.

"We'll be there," Seth stated, nodding in turn to both women. He couldn't refuse the invitation, yet he needed to do some serious thinking before the event.

Jasper, a good four inches shorter than Ilene, and twice as round, gave Seth an inquisitive look. His second in command knew about the marriage and the divorce papers—had since the beginning. "I'll take care of things for a day or two," Jasper said. "You take some time getting to know your wife again."

"No," Seth replied, his insides stiffening. "That won't be necessary. But thank you for the offer." The last thing he wanted was to get to know Rosemary—or Millie. He was starting to question in his own mind who she was. Which was ridiculous. The woman beside him was nothing like the conceited little snit who'd insisted, that morning back in Richmond, that no man could resist her body.

He hadn't touched her then, when she'd claimed he had, and he wasn't about to touch her now, but he wasn't going to put himself at her side, either. She was a beautiful woman, there was no doubt about that, and he'd never been one to tempt fate.

"I'll see you over at headquarters shortly, Jasper," he said.

The Ketchums departed, and with her hand still holding his elbow, the woman beside him sighed deeply. "I never expected this."

"What?"

"It's so…" A blush covered her cheeks. "Civilized."

"Civilized?"

A tiny frown had formed over her big brown eyes. "Yes, Rose—uh, roses could grow in that garden over there." She lifted a hand, pointed toward the flower bed Ilene pampered, but the way she'd stuttered had his spine quivering.

"Rose, huh?"

"Yes, roses. They are my favorite flower."

The innocence in those doe eyes was choking off his air like a hangman's noose. "Roses for Rosemary," he said, not quite sure where he'd heard that before.

"That's what my father always said."

Her face had softened and the words were almost a whisper, lacking joy. She was missing her father, no doubt. He understood that emotion. His own father had died on the battlefield, but hers hadn't. No illness, no war. The general just hadn't woken up one morning in his bed at his Richmond home.

The facts of the death had been forwarded to the fort, as many details as possible. Millicent, the youngest sister, had found their father that morning, and per the report, had been distraught. Seth's insides jittered again—an odd sensation he recognized and listened to regularly. It was what he'd felt earlier. Intuition that held a warning.

In the few hours he'd known her, he'd understood Rosemary to be a hard woman, and he couldn't, or perhaps wouldn't, believe she'd mourn her father after four years. But Millie, though he'd seen her only once that day, sitting in attendance at the wedding, had been softer. She'd actually shed a tear when offering her congratulations after the ceremony. Yes, Millie would still miss her father after four years.

He should offer his condolences, yet he couldn't do that, either. For if this was Millie, she'd changed. Was now lying through her teeth, pretending to be Rosemary.

"So," he asked, "what kind of flower did your father relate to you, Millie?"

Chapter Three

Millie pulled her hand off his arm, but instantly wished she hadn't. His solidness had kept her stable during all the introductions, and she found herself needing that support again.

Squaring her shoulders didn't help much, but it was all she had. "I wish you'd stop calling me that."

The only movement he made was to lift a dark brow, but it said a lot. Digging deep into the dredges of her mind, she found a fraction of truth to embellish upon. "Millie is…" She drew a deep breath, hoping lightning wouldn't manifest out of the blue sky and strike her. "Engaged. Millie is engaged to an army man, too."

This time Seth frowned.

She held her breath.

He took her elbow and guided her along a well-worn pathway. "Really? An army man?"

"Yes," she answered, looking everywhere but at him as they walked.

"In Richmond?"

Thank goodness. A subject she could discuss freely. There was no reason to lie about Martin. "He's from Richmond. His family lived only a few blocks away from our house. The three of us grew up together and everyone always said we... that is, the—the two of them would get married. He's in Texas right now. At a fort there, and Millie is preparing to travel there. Their wedding will take place shortly after she arrives."

"What's his name?"

"M-Martin Clark." The conversation was making her stomach gurgle. If or when Martin learned of this escapade, he wouldn't be happy. They'd been best friends for years, and he'd been her rock when Papa died, but he wouldn't be happy to know she was saying such things. Especially not as a cover-up for Rosemary.

"Is that a trading post?" She flinched as she said it. The sign painted the length of the building said precisely that, but she was searching desperately for anything she could use to change the subject.

Seth had stopped beside her, was staring at her thoughtfully.

"Oh, I apologise, you have work to do. Forgive me." She spun, and a stone caught under the ball of her foot, making her recoil at the sting. It also gave her an answer. "I was just wondering if the trading post might have a pair of boots. These slippers are not made for outdoors."

His dark eyes went to her feet and then to several men still watching them before he said, "I can spare a few minutes."

"The fort is so large," she said, as they started walking again. "It's like a complete town inside walls." Working hard at sounding normal, she added, "Mr. Cutter said there's a hospital and a church here."

"On the other side of the barracks, along the back wall."

His answer was clipped, and Millie bit her lips. Rosemary had said they'd be living in tents and cooking over campfires. Though, in the next breath, she'd insisted it was completely safe and that Millie had to go.

Quietly, not wanting to draw his attention, she let the air out of her lungs. Pretending to be Rosemary might not have been the best idea, but after her abruptness, Seth would probably believe she was Rosemary now.

Oh what a tangled web we weave. Another one of Lola's sayings. It didn't help any better than the first one had.

Seth stepped to the side as they neared the door, allowing her to enter first. Millie showed her appreciation with a nod, not trusting her mouth to open again. Upon entering the dark and crowded store, she wanted to take hold of his arm again. The space was crammed with shelves, barrels, crates and tables full of merchandise, and Indians. Lots of Indians. Her heart started beating erratically.

"This way," Seth said, walking around several tables stacked high with merchandise.

Very few windows let light into the area, not that sunlight would have helped. She had to get over this. Nothing had happened for her to fear the Indians, yet the way they looked at her had her inching as close to Seth as possible when he stopped to speak to someone.

"Here," he said, pulling over a stool. "Sit down."

"I'll have to measure your foot, ma'am."

Millie gulped, glancing toward a burly man with a straggly gray beard hanging almost to his belly.

"I don't get much call for women's boots," the bearded man was saying as he knelt down near the stool.

She sat, and inched the hem of her dress just high enough to display her day slippers.

"I'll have to order them. It won't take much

more than a month or so." The man measured the length and width of her foot, and then stood, tucking the flat wooden ruler into his back pocket. "I could try to get them faster, but it'll cost extra."

"Get them as soon as possible, Jenkins," Seth said.

"Aye, aye, Major. I'll see what I can do."

Seth helped her to her feet, then kept one hand on her elbow. "Don't see, Jenkins, make it happen."

"I ain't got the pull you do, Major, but I'll get them." With a tip of his head, which was hairless compared to his face, the man shuffled toward the long plank laid atop two barrels, with several people crowded along it.

"Is there anything else you need?" Seth asked.

Millie shook her head, barely able to keep her eyes from going to the Indians again.

A little shudder rippled through her. "Are they friendly?"

His gaze went to the Indians for a moment. "Friendly?"

She nodded.

He led her out the door, and she sighed at both the bright sunshine and the fresh air. The smell of coffee had been overpowering in the store, yet she hadn't noticed it until they'd stepped outside.

"For the most part," he answered, glancing toward a group exiting the building behind them. "When they want to be."

She shivered again. None of them appeared threatening, but their stares were acute and left her chilled. "Isn't that why you're out here? To fight them?"

"No."

"But you would if they attacked, wouldn't you?"

He shrugged. "Guess that would depend on why they attacked."

Even her throat was quivering. "What do you mean, why?"

"They only attack when they want to steal women. Not too many women around here. We'd be better off just turning them over, rather than losing men in a battle."

Completely ignoring the stones beneath the soft soles of her slippers, she hurried to remain at his side when he started walking again. "The women? You'd just give—?"

"I have work to see to," he said. "I assume you can make it to the barracks on your own."

The cabins were only a few yards ahead, and she had no doubt how fast she could make it there and shut the door. Matter of fact, there was probably a rooster tail of dust behind her, but she didn't care. Her focus was on whether the cabin door had a lock or not.

It didn't, and Millie was dragging, pushing and shoving one of her trunks to barricade the door when a knock sounded.

"Ma'am?" Ben Cutter said, poking his head in the doorway.

"Y-yes?" she stuttered, breathing hard, mainly because her heart was still in her throat.

"Briggs wanted me to deliver this pot of tea to you. He thought you might like a bit more than you had for lunch."

"Oh, thank you." Stepping aside so he could squeeze in the small opening—the trunk was almost in place—she waited until he set the pot and a delicate china cup and saucer on the table. "Mr. Cutter, how many women are here at the fort?"

"Well, let's see, there's Mrs. Ketchum, and…"

By the time Ben Cutter was done explaining exactly who the other four women at the fort were, Millie was full of additional questions, which he readily answered.

She listened carefully as he explained that the fort had been built ten years ago, when General Sheridan was campaigning to stop Indian raids on white settlers in Kansas and Texas. He also explained Grant's peace policy. How it promised tribes provisions if they moved onto reservation land, and how special Indian agents had been assigned to oversee the activities.

Cutter went on to tell her how when General

Sherman arrived at Fort Sill several years ago, he'd found several chiefs boasting about the raids they'd initiated on wagon trains and when he'd ordered their arrests, the general had almost been assassinated.

Some tribes accepted the agreement, but others didn't, and considered the reservations safe havens. A place where no one could retaliate against them.

Millie was fascinated by all this. General Sherman and her father had been close acquaintances. During one of his visits to their Richmond home, he'd appointed her father to oversee the men assigned to this fort.

Years ago she'd learned that Seth was a West Point graduate, and had been in Richmond, the day he'd married Rosemary, to deliver a report to their father about the raids and how rations weren't being delivered.

Millie asked a few more questions, mainly about the Indians, and Cutter answered them, praising the major for his bravery and leadership in dealing with various tribes. The man made it sound as if everyone at the fort was alive because of Seth's valor.

Having plenty to think about, Millie thanked Mr. Cutter for all his information, and allowed him to move her trunks into her room before he took his leave.

Papa had rarely spoke about such things with her, but Lola did. The housekeeper insisted Indians were as misunderstood as Negros, and that white folks shouldn't talk about things they didn't understand.

Mr. Cutter had just explained that the army was the only law in Indian Territory. He'd also said their duties included protecting the Indians and civilians, while teaching the former how to farm in order to feed their families. More importantly, he'd told her Indians didn't steal women.

Pacing the floor of the dreary cabin, Millie imagined just how irritated Rosemary would be by all this. Her sister wouldn't just be frustrated with the surroundings, she'd be furious at the way Seth had purposely frightened her.

A hint of a grin formed. Maybe being Rosemary could be fun, after all.

The report Jasper was reading aloud—about how the declining cattle drives would leave more tribes without food for the winter—wasn't holding Seth's attention. It wasn't anything he didn't already know. At one time the cattle drives had run directly through Indian Territory, and the ranchers had been more than happy to exchange a few head of cattle for safe travels, but the growing rail lines were replacing the drives. They'd had only half as many this year as last.

The window was what held Seth's interest. More so, the activity happening across the court-yard. His so-called wife had beckoned to Ben Cutter a short time ago, and shortly afterward the man had led two of Briggs's maidens to the cabin. Since then Seth had barely been able to keep up with the comings and goings. Clean linens were carried in—he'd noticed them in one of the bundles—but for the number of trips the women made there would have to have been a dozen beds instead of one. Well, two if you count his, but he highly doubted she'd have his bedding changed.

Intuition was gnawing at him again. If this was Millie, as he still believed, why was she here, if she was engaged to Martin Clark? Or was Rose-mary engaged to the man? Then why hadn't she just signed his divorce papers? Or was this Rose-mary, and now that Millie was engaged...

His mind was churning faster than the crank on a Gatling gun as he watched the door of his cabin. Over the years, remembering only his wife's personality, he'd forgotten her looks. Every man in the fort had noticed her beauty. That had been overly apparent during the introductions.

What he did clearly remember was that the woman he'd married was too full of herself to be concerned about anyone else. Yet the one he'd introduced to his men had taken the time to learn about the people living at the fort.

Frustrated, Seth ran a hand through his hair. Had he been out here so long, gotten so used to deciphering the cause behind every action, he could no longer accept actions—or people—without overanalyzing them?

A sour sensation curdled in his stomach. Martin Clark. She'd smiled when she'd said the name. Briefly, but enough that it had displayed her white, even teeth, and showed she cared about the man.

The name could be familiar, but Seth had met many soldiers over the years. For all he knew, Clark could have been one of the soldiers from Texas escorting the drives that came through this spring.

Seth scanned the area out the window once more, and frowned when he spotted the quartermaster carrying a large crate across the courtyard, toward the cabin. His teeth clamped down. He'd lied to her about the Indians, but there were dangers here. Plenty of them. The Oklahoma Indian Territory was the roughest place in the nation. Besides the very real possibility of an Indian uprising at any time, there were whiskey peddlers, Mexican traders, desperados, horse thieves, cattle rustlers, prostitutes and men just bent on killing. It was no place for women, and no matter which sister it was, he should send her back as fast as possible.

Yet he didn't want to. Instead, he wanted to know why she'd traveled weeks to get here. Her telegram had confused and irritated him, but now she had him out of sorts. She was the exact opposite of what he'd expected. What he remembered.

"You know, Seth, sometimes what we claim not to want is the exact thing we need." Jasper had moved, and now stood staring out the window on his right.

Seth gestured toward the activity happening around his cabin with a nod. "That is nothing but trouble, and I don't need any more troubles."

"Maybe she won't be trouble," Jasper said. "Maybe the changes she brings are what the men need."

Seth took pride in commanding a well-run fort, but knew the counsel he received from his second in command was a driving force behind all his actions. Still pondering what Jasper could be referring to, he glanced toward the other man when he shifted, pointed out the window.

"Things have changed out here the past few years, Seth, and they're good changes. Towns are popping up, settlers moving in, the population is growing. Including women. And I'm not referring to the soiled doves that have made the rounds for years. The army sees it, too. More and more wives are living with their husbands at the forts rather than staying back East. The men here want that, too. Most men, whether they're soldiers or not, don't want to remain alone forever."

Seth turned from the window, walked to his desk and picked up the report Jasper had been reading, but it was just to give him something to do. "You know how I feel about soldiers being married."

"Yes," Jasper answered. "And you know how I feel about it."

He did know how Jasper felt. Four years ago, when the man had been assigned to Fort Sill, Seth had refused to allow Ilene to accompany him out here. Neither the man nor his wife had accepted that command. It had made for some tense meetings, but, now, Seth had to admit, Ilene was as much a part of the fort as Jasper was.

Spinning so he leaned against the wall, Jasper folded his arms. "You're one of the best commanders I've seen, Seth. Men not only respect you, they trust you. When are *you* going to learn to trust?"

"Trust who?" he retorted bitterly. "Her?"

Jasper shrugged. "Maybe, but I'm referring to life in general."

Tension was eating at him, mainly because his second in command was much more than that. Over the years, Jasper, with his mellow ways that

were the opposite of the urgency Seth often felt,
had become the tutor he needed, often sought.

"You can't hide it from me. I've noticed you
struggling ever since that telegram arrived."

Seth threw the report back on his desk. "Of
course I've been struggling with it. I can't imagine what she wants."

"Then ask her."

He let his glare show what he thought of that.

Jasper cracked a dry grin.

Seth ignored it.

"I know you only married her to appease her
father. No one said no to the general. Ever. Including me. But—"

"Army men shouldn't be married," Seth interrupted.

"In your experience," Jasper said. "I understand why you feel that way. Losing your father
in battle, taking over his responsibilities for your
family at such a young age… But it's not always
like that."

"No?" Seth snapped. "I've seen it here, too. How
battles take lives. Leave loved ones alone." Perhaps he'd look upon things differently if his mother
had been weaker. Amanda Parker-Wadsworth had
cried over the loss of her husband—silently and
behind her closed bedroom door. But in front of
her children, she'd displayed strength and determination. Seth had seen through it, to the pain

his mother harbored while comforting him and his siblings. To this day he lived on the tenacity her resolve had imbedded in him. Every day after school, he'd gone to work in the shipyards until dark, wanting to ease the burden that had fallen to his mother. Once old enough, he'd continued overseeing crews building ships, until his mother had ordered him to stop.

She'd always known his wish was to become a soldier, but considering he'd lost his father and two uncles at the Battle of Shiloh, Seth had given up on the dream. Not only for his mother's sake—she'd lost her husband and two brothers on the same day—but for his, too. He needed to continue the shipbuilding business his father and uncles had started before the war, make sure his family was financially secure.

Even now, years later, he wondered if she'd truly wanted her sons to go to West Point, as she'd said, or if his mother had pushed him to because she'd known it was what he'd still wanted. It had been, and by then, money hadn't been an issue. So he'd gone. Not just to make his mother happy. It had made him happy, too. By then he'd carried the weight of responsibility for his family and the shipbuilding crews for several years, and he'd found he liked commanding men. It came naturally to him. What he'd decided he didn't want was the responsibility of having a wife and children. He loved his family, but the loss of their father had affected them all deeply.

"Yes," Jasper said. "It's here, too. There's no avoiding death."

Seth didn't respond. Death was inevitable, but there was no reason to leave broken hearts and shattered homes when it happened. He saw it on the battlefields, but he shouldn't have to see it in the faces of the wives and children left behind. It was too much.

"Someday, Seth, you'll understand that living is as much a part of life as dying is." Jasper crossed the room and left, closing the door softly.

A shiver settled deep in Seth's spine, making his back stiffen. Living didn't need to include a wife. Snatching up the report, he forced his mind to concentrate on it, as well as several other tasks that needed to be completed. So it wasn't until the dinner bell echoed over the compound that he rose from his desk.

From the front steps of the headquarters building, where he was stretching muscles that had stayed idle too long, his gaze went to his cabin. The right thing would be to go get his wife, escort her to dinner. Then again, she had ears, and as he'd told Briggs, she might as well get used to fort living.

He was toiling with his decision when he entered the hall, almost feeling guilty. That instantly changed. She was here. Not sitting at a table set for two, but at a long bench, talking merrily with several men already seated around her.

A growl vibrated at the back of Seth's throat. That definitely reminded him of Rosemary. As did the way she turned and lifted her brows at the sight of him.

Men moved, gesturing for him to take their seats, and Seth, accustomed to making snap decisions, faltered. He couldn't ignore her in front of all his men, yet he couldn't pretend they were happily married.

Or could he? That might prove to be the one thing that would irritate Rosemary—or Millie, or whoever she was. After five years, an amorous husband would be the last thing she'd expect, and perhaps the one thing that would send her on her way.

It was a twist he hadn't thought would thrill him, but it did, and he almost cracked a grin as he walked across the hall. "Hello," he murmured, gently placing a hand between her shoulder blades, where he felt the tiniest quiver beneath his palm.

Shock shimmered in her eyes as she answered, "Hello."

"I trust you had a nice afternoon," he said, taking a seat and scooting a bit closer to her side than necessary.

"Y-yes, thank you," she stammered.

The twitching of her lower lip did make him want to smile. Oh, yes, this might be the perfect plan of attack. He should have thought of it earlier. Not doing what his enemies expected had kept him alive for years.

When Briggs opened the food line, Seth escorted her through it, with his hand riding low on the small of her back. He noted how her feet kept stumbling, and her nervousness had triumph rising inside him. They ate with the men at the long table, and Seth encouraged her to answer the slew of questions the soldiers posed. Many of them hadn't been outside Indian Territory for years, and they were hungry to hear what was happening in other parts of the country.

The attention was more than she'd bargained for—her trembling fingers said that. And the edgy glances she sent his way told him she hadn't expected him to be so accommodating.

Seth simply smiled, and asked a few nonessential questions of his own. When the meal was over, he took her hand and folded her arm through the crook of his while leading her to the door.

Things were slow at the fort right now. The cattle drives were over for the year and most of the crops harvested. That had bothered him this morning, knowing he wouldn't have other duties consuming his time, but now he realized it was a good thing. Dedicating a few days to a plan that would ultimately hasten her departure was exactly what he needed.

The way he'd linked her wrist around his elbow had her breast brushing the upper part of his arm, and she was straining to keep the simple contact from happening. Telling himself it wasn't affecting him, Seth asked, "Would you like to take a stroll through the compound?"

Her gaze bounced to the cabin and she pinched her lips together, which made him suddenly want to see what all the commotion had been about. "But you must be tired," he said. "It's been a long day. Let's just go home."

"No," she said nervously. "We could take a stroll."

"It's all right, you'll have lots of time to explore the fort," he cajoled. "Right now, you need some sleep."

"No, really—"

"I insist." Seth let go of the hand he'd kept hooked on his elbow, and looped his arm around her shoulders. "You must be exhausted."

She let out a sigh that held a tiny groan, but didn't struggle as he guided her forward.

The sun hadn't set yet and the warmth intensified Seth's sense of smell. They were across the compound from Ilene's flower beds, but he caught the scent of flowers. Or maybe it was perfume, because it smelled more like roses. Actually, he'd noticed a hint of it when he'd sat down next to her back in the hall.

A shiver rippled his spine as he turned his head, glanced down at the woman standing next to him. Her grin was much more of a grimace as she stepped aside for him to open the door to their cabin.

The warm, closed-in air rushing through the open doorway was downright overpowering. Blinking from the sting in his eyes, Seth asked, "Did a vial of rosewater burst in one of your trunks?"

"No," she said, stepping past him to enter the cabin. "I washed the floors with it."

"Washed the floors with it?"

Millie drew a deep breath, almost choking. The rose oil Lola made was quite potent and she may have used more than necessary. But it was what Rosemary would have done. "I also had To-She-Wi and Ku-Ma-Quai help me wash the walls." She flinched slightly, not wanting to get two of Briggs Ryan's maidens in trouble. The Indian women had proved to be not only friendly, but most helpful in assisting her with transforming the cabin.

"Wash the walls!" he exclaimed. "That oil will soak into the wood. It's going to smell like this forever."

"One can only hope," she replied, sounding so much like her sister she wanted to bite her tongue. "It smelled of sour men before."

The tick that appeared in his cheek should alarm her, but from what she'd learned today, Seth was not unfair. Though she might have decorated things a little more than she should have. It had been fun at the time, thinking she was getting him back for frightening her.

"My eyes are watering," he said.

"You'll get used to it."

"What's this?" He gestured toward the table.

"I know you've seen a tablecloth before."

"Not in an army barrack."

Making her best attempt at being nonchalant, she shrugged.

"And pillows, and cushions, and rugs." He was walking through the tiny area, pointing things out, and stopped in the doorway to his office. "Curtains? Curtains in my office? Where did you get all this stuff?"

"Mr. Fallon. You must be quite proud of him. He has a bit of everything."

Seth gave her a glimpse full of disdain before he spun to take a second look at the space that had been his office. Once again Millie flinched inwardly. She'd never done anything like this before, and pulling up the courage to finish what she started was not easy.

"Where. Is. My. Desk?"

His cold tone had Millie gulping, but she managed to find the nerve to step into the room and point toward the far corner. With the desk up against the wall, covered with a tablecloth, and the chair positioned in front of the window, decorated with two tiny pillows, plus a rug covering the floor, the room looked much bigger and more homey. To her. What Seth thought was probably a bit different. Obviously was.

He glared at her with those piercing eyes for several long moments. "You are Rosemary, aren't you?"

She held her breath, hoping the churning in her stomach wouldn't erupt.

"Put it back," he growled. "Put it back the way you found it. All of it."

Millie scurried aside as he left the room.

"And get rid of those stupid curtains!"

The door thudded shut and Millie let out her breath in a gush. Rosemary wouldn't put any of it back. So Millie wouldn't, either.

Chapter Four

$\mathcal{CQ} \mathcal{Q} \mathcal{Q} \mathcal{Q} \mathcal{Q} \mathcal{Q}$

Millie did walk over and open the office window she'd closed earlier, having known the heat would intensify the smell of the rose oil while they were eating supper. Lola had said to use it sparingly, just a drop or two in a bathtub of water. Millie had used an entire bottle scrubbing the cabin.

Exhausted inside and out, she plopped onto the chair. What would Rosemary do now?

Millie couldn't remember when she'd learned her mother had died; it had happened when she was just an infant. But she did recall the moment she'd learned *how* her mother had died. It had been her eighth birthday. Papa had given her a new saddle, black with silver conchas, and a seat as plush as velvet. She'd ridden all afternoon. It was that night, when she was in bed, that Rosemary had entered her room and said if she didn't give her the new saddle, she'd jump in the river. Drown. When Millie said she wouldn't give it to her, her sister had told her the family secret.

No one was ever to know, Rosemary had said, but their mother hadn't died from complications of childbirth. She'd taken her own life when Millie was six months old, with one of Papa's pistols.

Papa hadn't been home—he had been off doing army business, as he had been most of their childhood. The saddle had been ordered and delivered with a note from him. So Millie had asked Lola about their mother the next morning.

The housekeeper confirmed what Rosemary had said was true, that their mother had shot herself when Millie was a baby. She'd also said no one but their dear mama, God rest her soul, knew why she'd done it.

Months later, when Papa had come home and asked Millie about the saddle, she'd told him she loved it so much she was sharing it with Rosemary. Papa had said he was proud of her, how she understood Rosemary was different, and needed to be assured constantly that she was loved, just like their mother.

Millie closed her eyes. It was true. For as bold and brassy as Rosemary was on the outside, inside she was fragile, as delicate as glass, just as their mother had been. Rosemary had said she'd take her own life, and that of the baby, before allowing Seth to discover the truth. He would ruin her if he found out. Millie didn't believe there was much left of Rosemary's reputation to ruin, considering the number of men her sister's name had been linked with, but she did believe her threats. She feared the baby would be in danger, for Rosemary did appear to be as desperate this time as she'd been over the saddle, when she had jumped into the river.

The weight on Millie's chest increased tenfold. She didn't believe her sister capable of murder, but she did know there were things worse than death. And knowing that had left her with no option but to agree to travel to Fort Sill to keep Seth from going to Washington, and possibly Richmond, as the letter he'd sent implied, until December.

Her gaze roamed the room. Seth didn't deserve the deception, neither Rosemary's faithlessness nor Millie's lies. And he didn't deserve her painting his cabin with rose oil, either. But Rosemary was her sister. There was nothing she wouldn't do to protect her, and the life growing inside her.

If Millie was more daring and courageous, this would be easier. Actually, if she'd told Papa the truth five years ago, she wouldn't be here now. She'd known about Clifton Wells, that Rosemary was planning to run off with him, but instead of saying something, fearful there'd be a row when Papa discovered it, Millie had gone to a friend's house to avoid being dragged into the argument. The following morning, when she'd been summoned home, she'd been confused to hear Rosemary was marrying Seth instead of Clifton. Until Papa told her Clifton was already wed, and marrying Seth was the only thing that would save Rosemary's name.

A knock on the door had Millie pushing off the seat and squaring her shoulders. She couldn't stop protecting the family secrets now, nor could she give up on this mission.

"I hope I'm not intruding, Mrs. Parker," Mr. Winston said when she opened the door, "but I wanted to drop off your boots. They should be fine this time. Good as new, actually."

A lump had formed in her throat at how he'd addressed her. Others, when making her acquaintance, had called her Mrs. Parker, but right now, after contemplating the past and the events that had led her to here to Seth, the deceit seemed uglier. Heavier. Taking the boots, she found a simple smile. "Thank you, Mr. Winston. I do appreciate all you've done."

"It's been my pleasure, ma'am," he said, bowing his head as he backed out the doorway.

Not so much as a single scuff mark signaled

that the heel had once been separated from the boot. Brand-new at the start of her journey, the black leather was still relatively stiff and the breakage had been disappointing. To Millie. Rosemary would have thrown them away and bought a new pair in Tulsa.

"Good night, ma'am."

"Good night," she repeated, closing the door.

Seth watched the door close from where he stood across the compound. The smell of roses still filled his nostrils, leaving his insides hard. The flower's aroma might be pleasant in small doses, but what he'd just experienced was sickening, mainly because it reminded him of Rosemary. The overpowering smell had taken him back in time.

"Marry her and I'll make you a major," General St. Clair had said that fretful morning five years ago.

Seth's stomach recoiled all over again.

He'd refused the offer, more than once, but ultimately, before the day was done, he'd become a major and married her.

It had been a goal he'd set for himself, to become a major, and to do so at the age of twenty-three had been enticing, but that was not why he'd given in. The reason had been the general. The man had been afraid. Seth had assumed it was because of his daughter's reputation, but St. Clair's fear had been deeper, more distressing than one might experience over a reputation. The general had talked as if Rosemary's very life was in danger, and eventually shared the truth that Rosemary was seeing another man, one she shouldn't have been associating with, but was.

None of that had truly been Seth's concern, but knowing how the general had numerous times put his own life in danger to save the men he commanded, he hadn't been able to ignore the man's plea for assistance. When the general had assured Seth that he could still return to Indian Territory, and that when things calmed down in Richmond, he'd see to the divorce himself, Seth had finally agreed to marry the girl. In name only. He'd left shortly after the ceremony, with the general's promise of a divorce within the year ringing in his ears.

St. Clair had died less than a year later, and that's when Seth had started pursuing the divorce on his own. It galled him, how he'd accepted the man's deal—saved her reputation, and then worked twice as hard to prove he was capable of the position he'd been granted—only to have her ignore his requests. Not so much as a note had been sent his way, verifying she'd received his letters.

Why was she here now? The question jarred his insides. She had nothing to gain, and though he lived half a world away from Richmond, word traveled. He knew Rosemary wasn't sitting in her father's parlor, pining for her husband.

His gaze followed Winston as the man walked almost the entire length of the compound, his way lit by torches staked in the ground and shielded from the wind with heavy glass-and-brass enclosures. Winston turned near the icehouse and headed toward the location where a group had gathered.

Some of the boys sat back there most every night, strumming guitars and banjos, playing harmonicas and an assortment of other instruments they'd acquired over the years. Seth sat there plenty of nights, too, but it wasn't their music filtering through his mind right now, it was an annoying little feeling he hadn't experienced for a very long time. He couldn't be jealous of Winston; the man had simply returned her boots. Yet there was an inkling of envy or perhaps resentment inside Seth. It had appeared as soon as she'd opened the door and smiled at the man.

She had Seth flustered. A crazy thing for him to be, but there was no other way to explain the turmoil swimming through his veins, and that confused him, too. Crazy as it was, he was attracted to her. A fact he'd been trying to deny ever since she'd climbed off the wagon and stomped across the dirt with that adorable uneven gait.

A smile tugged at his lips. Covered in Oklahoma's red dirt, parasol whipping in the wind behind her, with bright red cheeks and windblown hair, she'd been a sight. He'd never seen anything so endearing.

And later, when he'd stepped onto the walkway after Russ had signaled that she'd left the bathing house, his heart had almost stopped in his chest. A puny gust of wind could have blown him over as he'd watched the beautiful woman walk toward him, dressed in a form-fitting blue-and-white dress that had him craving to see what lay beneath it. She still had on that dress, and he'd still like to see what was under it.

He drew in another breath of air, long and hard. The telegraph lines weren't working. A renegade had chopped down several poles recently, and repairs had been ordered, but the troop he'd sent out hadn't returned yet. It was ironic that the last message that had come in had been the one saying his wife was to be picked up in Tulsa.

A short time ago he'd questioned Lieutenant Paisley, but the man couldn't say when the line might be up again. Poles could be down all the way to Tulsa. It had happened before. He'd given Paisley instructions—private ones—that as soon as the lines were working, a message needed to be sent to Richmond. He was determined to confirm his suspicions that it was, in fact, Millie in his cabin.

It had to be Millie. There were too many inconsistencies for her not to be.

Seth pushed off from the post he'd been leaning against. Whether it was Millie or Rosemary, payback was in order. "Lieutenant," he shouted into the barn.

A man appeared instantly. "Yes, sir?"

"Get my saddle and some saddle soap. Bring it to my cabin."

"Now, sir?"

"Yes, now."

"But that soap will stink up your cabin. The Indians make it for us and—"

"I know," Seth said, already heading there.

It took even less time than he'd anticipated. He'd barely opened the tin, had yet to work much of the black slime into the leather when the door to her room opened. Her little nose was curled and her eyes were squinting.

"What are you doing?" she asked.

"Oiling my saddle." He explained the obvious without looking up.

"In here?"

"Why not in here? An army man has to keep his equipment in order."

She crossed the room, opened the door. "Don't you have a barn for that kind of thing?"

He leaned back in his chair, stared at her pointedly. "If you don't like it, you're welcome to leave."

That was a nasty glare, the one she flashed his way, as she stomped across the floor to Russ's old room. Seth allowed himself a moment to gloat.

Only a moment, because in the next instant she was back, pouring something onto the seat of his saddle.

"What the—" He grabbed the bottle, not needing to sniff the container to know she'd just dowsed his saddle with rose oil. "What do you think you're doing?" A stupid question, but it was all he could think to say.

"Disguising the stench," she said with a curl to her lip.

They stood there, across the table from one another. In all his born days, Seth had never backed down from a challenge, and he wasn't about to start now. He even felt the tiniest mingling of guilt. After all, her only weapon was a bottle of rose oil.

Wrong.

Two nights later, Seth conceded her plethora of female things was more than he could take. Like those big bows, all eight of them, tied to the rungs of the ladder leading to his loft. And the bouquet of flowers that had been sitting in his hat this morning, which she'd positioned in the center of the table as if it was some huge, hideous vase.

She had to have done that after he'd gone to bed last night.

He should have heard her. He'd barely slept. Not with the way he was sneezing. The thought of another sleepless, miserable night snapped his last nerve. Two days of trying to out-scent each other hadn't got him anywhere.

Seth barreled through the door of their cabin. "What are you doing here?"

Spinning around from where she stood near the stove, she held up a bundle of weeds. "Drying out wild lavender."

He sneezed.

"Bless you," she said.

He'd been worn down before, but never quite like this. The cabin was overrun with flowers and bows and cushions and curtains. A man couldn't take it.

"No, I mean, why are you here?" He sneezed again. "If it was to make my life as miserable as possible, if the past five years haven't been enough, you've succeeded." They hadn't spoken much over the past forty-eight hours, having been too busy trying to outdo each other. He was ready to talk now. "I did your father a favor—not to mention you—and he promised me a divorce in

return." After one more sneeze, Seth waved a
hand around the cabin. "Instead, I get this."

Her eyes grew wide. "My father promised you
a divorce?"

"Yes, he did." Seth hurried to shut the door
before the entire compound heard him. "What
were you thinking that night? Why'd you climb
into my bed?"

"I—I..."

The way she trembled from head to toe sent a
wave of guilt curdling in his stomach. He took a
step back, but wasn't going to back down on his
questioning. He needed some sleep—in a cabin
that didn't smell like a flower garden.

Another sneezed raked his body.

"Bless you," she repeated. "And I don't know
why I did that." She spun, then walked across
the room so the table separated them. "I thought
I was going to marry another man, but—"

"He was already married," Seth supplied.

"Yes," she answered quietly, "he was."

That despondent little whisper did more to his
insides than it should have. So did the way she
gathered up several pots of flowers and set them
outside the door.

"Why are you here?" he asked as she propped
the door open.

"Because of your letter," she said.

"Which one?"

She frowned slightly. "The one asking for a divorce."

"Which one?" he repeated.

Her frown deepened.

"I've sent you five sets of divorce papers."

"You have?" Shaking her head, she said, "I—I, um, I only saw this last set. The ones that arrived last month."

"How can that be?" he asked. "I know they were delivered." After hearing no response to his first requests he'd insisted upon and received confirmation that the papers had been delivered to the house.

He saw how wide her eyes grew before she turned and headed into his office. "M-my sister, M-Millie, always accepts the correspondence that arrives at the house."

Following, watching her pull dried bundles of flowers from the rope stretched from corner to corner, he sneezed before asking, "And she withholds mail from you?"

"No…" Millie was searching for an explanation. She'd wondered if that had been the first time Seth had sent papers, yet had believed Rosemary when she'd assured her it was. The fact that Papa had promised a divorce was a surprise. He'd never mentioned that, but she had to believe Rosemary knew about it.

The way Seth sneezed several more times had guilt and concern rippling through her.

"Then why didn't you get my other requests?" he asked, somewhat winded.

"There was a lot of mail after Papa died." Millie continued to pull down the flowers. It had been fun, irritating him, but his puffy, bloodshot eyes said this had gone far enough. "Anything to do with the army, anything official looking, was forwarded on. I must assume that's what happened to your previous letters."

He gave a nod that didn't really say if he believed her or not. She, on the other hand, had no doubt that Rosemary had received every set. Squeezing past him, flinching at another of his sneezing bouts, she carried the flowers she'd gathered out the front door.

A fortifying breath helped, as did the memory of comforting Rosemary on her wedding night—after Seth had left for Indian Territory again. "I was distraught the—the night we met. When I crawled into your bed." Mortification had her neck on fire, having him think she'd behave so, but she had to press on. "My father had forbidden me to see the man I thought I loved. I hadn't known Clifton was married, and I thought…" She had no idea what Rosemary had been thinking when she'd acted so. Back in the office, Millie pulled down the rope. "I guess I hoped the action might make him change his mind."

"How was that going to help?"

"I don't know," she growled. The answers weren't coming to her, and him sounding so plugged and miserable didn't help. "I told you, I was distraught and not thinking straight."

He sneezed again and Millie speeded up her gathering. Word had gotten out that Mrs. Ketchum had given her permission to pick a few flowers from the garden in the center of the fort, and the soldiers started bringing her wild ones by the dozens. It had been kind of them, and the flowers had worked to combat the foul-smelling concoctions Seth kept bringing in—including the cigar he'd puffed on until the entire cabin was full of blue smoke. But making him ill was not in Millie's plan. The cabin had shaken with his sneezes last night. She'd grinned then, but this morning guilt had hit her when she saw how wretched he looked. Rosemary or not, it had gone too far.

Millie had known a few things about Seth before arriving, such as how his work was revered from here to Washington. But it was the respect the others had for him that told her more. Even while traveling over the barren land, Mr. Winston and Mr. Cutter had nothing but admiration for the man they assumed was her husband. An individual didn't earn that type of esteem by chance.

"Whatever happened to him?"

Drawing a blank, Millie asked, "Who?"

"The man you thought you loved. The one that was married."

"I don't know." Rosemary had never mentioned Clifton again. "He left town, I guess."

"You guess?"

She nodded and carried the last of the flowers out the door. After the wedding, Rosemary had been forbidden to leave the house. There had been a few months where life had been relatively calm. Then Papa had died and things had changed all over again. Especially when Rosemary had discovered the clout that came with being a major's wife. She used that to open doors regularly. Special events and ceremonies she insisted she needed to attend—escorted by many different men.

"You guess?" Seth repeated.

Sighing heavily, Millie reentered the cabin as a new bout of guilt turned into a hard knot in her stomach. "Yeah, I guess. I guess we all do things from time to time without knowing why we do them." She was speaking about herself, and crossed the room to wet a towel in the basin. "Here, wash your face to get rid of the pollen."

He eyed her warily.

"It'll help. Honest." As he followed her directions, she said, "I'm sorry, too. I'll put everything back the way it was tomorrow, and ask To-She-Wi if she knows how to eliminate the rose oil smell."

Seth folded the towel and hung it on the wash-stand. "I'm sorry, as well, for the saddle soap and stuff."

When the silence grew into a lingering still-ness that had her nerves ticking, Millie inched her skirt up to show the tips of her boots. "I no longer need new boots. I'll cancel the order first thing in the morning."

His gaze stayed on her boots. "No. It's too late. Besides, it won't hurt to have a spare pair."

There'd been a time when she'd had several pairs of boots, when Papa was alive. But like ev-erything else, that too had changed. "All right, but I do have money. I'll pay for them."

"Have you been short of money lately?"

He'd stopped sneezing and was no longer wheezing. That alone allowed her to sigh with relief.

"Have you been short of money lately?" he repeated.

"No," she answered, for Rosemary hadn't been short of money. And that's who she was. Rose-mary. Flowers or not.

Her gaze caught his then, and the way he squinted had her all but choking on the lump that bubbled up the back of her throat. Faltering, inside and out, she gestured toward her room. "I think I'll turn in now. It's been a long day."

He nodded and she hurried toward the door, but was turning the knob when he asked, "Why didn't you just sign the divorce papers? There was no reason for you to travel out here."

A chill flowed over her, but she ignored it as best she could. "This way you won't need to travel to Richmond."

"It's only a short distance to there from Washington."

She turned, gave him a smile that wobbled on her lips. "Now you won't need to go there, either."

"Yes, I will. I have to appear before Congress. Explain in person how important it is to increase the provisions sent to the tribes out here."

Millie felt like a mouse in the corner, trapped, with Lola's whisk broom about to fall on top of her. Rosemary's pregnancy wasn't known outside the family, and before leaving for the fort Millie had taken precautions, told several people that both she and her sister were traveling out of town. But nothing was foolproof, and the news could spread to Washington. Rosemary did have a few enemies who would like nothing more than to be the one to tell Seth about his wife's behavior over the past five years.

"Perhaps you can send someone else," Millie said hopefully.

"No. It's my job, and I'll see to it."

"Oh."

Finally able to breathe without sneezing, Seth gulped in air. His eyes no longer burned and he could actually see how the lamplight reflected in the depths of her eyes and highlighted the flaw-less perfection of her skin, the shine of her hair. She was a beauty, but what he found more en-chanting was her tender presence. There was sweetness in her voice and movements, even during those times when she reminded him of Rosemary. Which only proved she was Millie. Rosemary was about as gentle as a water mocca-sin. She would never have fought him with flow-ers. If they hadn't made him as miserable as a kid with a runny nose, he'd have kept up the game. He'd run out of ammunition, though. His next choice would have been a bucket from the barn, and he wasn't willing to do that.

"Why is it your job?" she asked.

His mind was circling like a wagon train in fear of attack, and before he remembered any-thing beyond their game, she was speaking again.

"Surely they're other army men that could relay the message."

Oh, yes, his trip to Washington.

"I—I was hoping to stay out here until Decem-ber," she said, stammering slightly. "Maybe you could postpone your trip until then."

December? That was impossible. Yet, needing time to think why, he said, "We'll talk about it tomorrow. You look tired."

She bowed her head bashfully. "I'll remove everything in the morning. Including the curtains."

He'd won their game, so why didn't it feel that way? "Good night."

She turned and pushed open the door to her room before saying, "Good night, Seth."

Something, maybe the sadness, or it might have been the softness of her voice and how sweet his name sounded when she said it, pinched him deep inside. Seth turned and, after glancing into his office, climbed the ladder to the loft, careful of the bows. Once there, laid out on his bed, he wondered if the open window let in that much fresh air or if he'd just got used to the smell of the rose oil. It hadn't made him sneeze, not like those crazy weeds. Wild lavender, she'd called it.

The next morning Russ woke him with the news that someone was requesting a meeting. A scout demanding army escorts for a wild-game hunting party coming down from Kansas. While walking across the compound to where the man waited, Russ said Seth smelled like the tents of the soiled doves that camped nearby a couple times a year.

Seth held his tongue and his temper while talking with Otis Field, a scout known for finding buffalo for rich men to shoot. Not only was the man sniffing the air like a wolf picking up a scent, he was demanding three dozen men—which Seth wasn't about to give out.

In the end, he agreed to provide four soldiers, and he dictated the amount of days they could be gone, exactly where the hunting party could travel and what specifically could be hunted. Otis tried haggling, but Seth didn't give an inch, and the scout was the one to accept defeat, or at least he claimed he'd accept the conditions. Long ago Seth had figured out who to trust and who not to, and the scout was not trustworthy.

As Otis and four privates left, Seth made his way back to his cabin, where he planned on retrieving a fresh shirt and coat before riding out to find one of his Indian scouts. White Bird was never too far away, and he'd spread the word of the hunting party, letting all the tribes know to stay clear. For their safety, not the hunters'.

When Seth opened the door, a sound had him walking directly into his office, where his heart did a somersault. Single-handedly she was dragging his desk across the room—or attempting to. The exertion had her face red and her chest heaving, even though the desk had been moved only a few feet.

The room had been cleared out, including the

curtains, cushions and rug, but it was the impish grimace on her face he reacted to.

Without a word, he pulled the desk across the room. She pushed, and he hadn't yet found his tongue, so he didn't tell her not to.

Once the desk was in place, along with his chair, he told her, "I'll be gone all of today and probably most of tomorrow."

She frowned, which on her was cute. "Where are you going?"

"I have to go find someone." He chose not to say more, regretting the way he'd attempted to scare her about the Indians.

"Who?" she asked, following him out of the office.

"Just a man." He climbed the bowless ladder, and pulling down his spare jacket from its hook, figured it probably smelled more like roses than the one he was wearing. That didn't infuriate him. Perhaps because he now knew for certain that the woman downstairs was not his wife. Rosemary must have put her up to it, and the only way he was going to find out why was to gain Millie's trust. She was a worthy opponent, and might have won their skirmish if the wildflowers hadn't gotten to him—he'd seen how bad she felt about that. Fighting on someone else's terms was the best way to lose; he'd learned that years ago. He would set the terms this round, and the battlefield. This time he would win.

She was waiting at the bottom of the ladder and he couldn't help but respond to the worry in her eyes. "Don't fret. No one's going to turn you over to the Indians, whether they attack or not."

A tiny grin formed, then she gave him an impudent stare. "I know that."

"Do you?" he asked, touching the end of her nose with the tip of one finger.

"Yes, I do." She spun, watched him shrug on and button his coat. "And I know there is a fort full of men who could ride out to find someone, so why you?"

"Because I'm in charge." He caught her beneath the chin with the same fingertip. "No harm will come to you while you're here. I'll personally see to that."

The trepidation in her eyes grew. "But who protects you?"

He chuckled, already enjoying the second battle of their war. His finger trailed down her neck before he lifted it to tap her nose yet again. "Never fear, I won't make you a widow before I truly make you a wife."

Chapter Five

"I swear, Seth, the harder I look, the less I see," Millie declared, pulling the horse to a stop to study the land. It was like looking at the sea, except instead of rolling waves of water, there was flat ground covered with brown grass that didn't end until it met the sky at the ridge of the horizon.

His baritone laugh, a sound she'd heard more and more over the past week, had her insides doing somersaults. Fun ones, the kind that made her smile. There hadn't been any more flower or saddle soap incidents, and a unique kind of truce had formed between them. One she could definitely live with. Seth was by far the most charming and attentive husband imaginable.

He was resting one arm across his saddle horn, and his hat shadowed the upper part of his face as he studied her directly. "That, I think, is the best description of Indian Territory I've ever heard."

The grin on his face made hers increase. She turned back to the empty scene that in an odd way was quite magnificent. "There's barely a tree."

"There are trees north of the fort. In the Wichita Mountains."

"Mountains?" This had been her first excursion outside the tall walls since her arrival, but from what she'd seen during the wagon ride, and from what spread out before her, she couldn't imagine the flatness becoming mountainous.

"Well, they're more like foothills," he said. "It's a full day's ride, though, and not a trip I'm willing to let you attempt."

The hammering of her heart told her what she thought about that even before her mind kicked in. His protectiveness was uncanny, and wonderful. "Oh, you let me travel two hundred miles with two men in a wagon with no canopy, for five days, seeing nothing but prairie grass and red dirt, yet you won't let me ride for a day to see mountains?"

Not even the sky overhead was as blue as his eyes when he removed his hat. The smile on his face grew, revealing the dimple in his cheek. He winked, and her insides jolted and fluttered so fast and hard her breath locked in her lungs.

"That," he said, "was before I knew you."

A heated sensation engulfed her chest, and went lower, all the way past her stomach. Bowing her head, for her face was on fire, she pressed her bottom against the saddle. Goodness, but he had an effect on her. His kindness and generosity had her thinking about things she'd never thought of before. Ridiculous things. Like kissing.

Especially at bedtime, when he'd wish her good-night from her bedroom doorway, the desire inside her grew so strong it was troubling. Pretty much like it was right now.

"Come on," he said. "It's time we headed back. I have a surprise for you."

Her head snapped up so fast her hat jostled. "A surprise?"

She turned the horse around, kept it even with his. The happiness she'd experienced the past week was amazing, and it just kept increasing. Every day she awoke with a newfound freedom. Never before had she been able to climb out of bed knowing there was no merchant she had to confront, no "friend" she had to assure had misheard something her sister supposedly said, and no fear she might accidently say the wrong thing and have her sister as furious with her as she was with the rest of the world. Lately all Millie had to wonder about was how bright the sun would shine. There was still the pretense of her being here, but Seth never brought it up, and that was utterly liberating.

Glowing inside and out, she asked, "What kind of surprise?"

He reached over and tipped the brim of her hat lower. It was dark blue with a flat brim, an army-issued one just like his, but smaller, and he'd fastened a string through the felt to tie beneath her chin.

"If I tell you, it won't be a surprise."

"I can keep a secret," she insisted.

His laughter was like a song that made her want to dance with all the joy it inspired.

"Is it a pot of tea?" she asked. That wouldn't necessarily be a surprise. Even when he was busy over at the headquarters in a meeting, or out with a troop, one of Briggs Ryan's maidens would unexpectedly bring a pot to the cabin, saying the major had requested it be delivered to her.

He made a point of showing her how tightly his lips were clasped together, teasingly illustrating he wasn't about to tell her anything. She laughed, but her mind went back to kissing, and she pulled her gaze away. He didn't kiss her. Hadn't, not once. But there were so many times he acted as if he was going to that she was going mad. It didn't even help to pull up images of Rosemary. Matter of fact, it was becoming difficult to think like her sister most times.

A twinge of guilt made Millie take a moment to silently chide herself. Seth Parker wasn't her husband, and kissing him should never, ever enter her thoughts.

Telling herself that was like telling the sun not to shine. It was a good thing he was a gentleman. She liked that about him. His manners and honor, and overall charisma. Truth be told, there wasn't much she didn't like about him. Perhaps that was why there were all these thoughts about kissing. A person should want to kiss someone they liked—shouldn't they? Another type of guilt spilled inside her. She'd never thought about kissing Martin like this. Had never even wondered about it. All these other things had never surfaced when he'd taken her arm or aided her in some way, either. Then again, she'd never thought of Martin as anything more than a friend.

The pressure in her lungs released slowly as she huffed out a long sigh. Millie didn't know what she thought of Seth, as he seemed more than a friend. He was her husband, or at least her pretend husband. The stirring warmth in the depths of her body throbbed when she thought of him, and there was nothing she could do about it. Truth was, she loved being called the major's wife.

Seth turned her way, and she almost gulped at the heat that flared.

"No, it's not tea," he said, "but I'm sure Briggs will have a pot brewing."

"Steeping," she corrected, attempting to re-route her thoughts.

He gave her a somewhat puzzled look. "Steeping?"

"Yes, one brews coffee, but steeps tea."

His chuckle was accompanied by a head shake. "I'll remember that."

"Good, you do that." He had her insides bubbling, but there was also a carefree feeling she'd never experienced. "Want to race to that rock?"

"You'll be careful?" he asked.

"I always am."

He stretched his long legs by standing in the stirrups for a moment as he took a look around the area. When he sat back down, he nodded. "All right, but just to the rock."

Excitement zipped under her skin. "On the count of three?"

He nodded again.

"One," she said, hunching down. Riding always lifted her spirits. It was the one thing she'd always done just for her, and she missed it so much. It had been years since she'd gone riding just for the pleasure of it. Watching Seth out of the corner of her eye, she said, "Two…"

Then, whipping the reins across the horse's

rump, she sent the animal into a full gallop before yelling, "Three!"

He was at her side in no time, and remained there, his horse neck and neck with hers the entire race. The wind, the air, the dirt churning beneath the animals' hooves, it was all so wonderful she was sorry when they passed the rock. But true to her word, she reined the horse in and glanced to her side.

"You cheated," Seth said, grinning.

A giggle tickled her throat. "I thought I'd need a head start."

His laugh had her floating on a cloud, and she still felt that way a short time later, when he lifted her from the saddle as Russ appeared to lead the horses into the stable.

"Thank you, Corporal Kemper," she said, while wrapping a hand around Seth's proffered elbow. The simple action never failed to make her heart swell.

"You're welcome, ma'am. Did you enjoy the ride?"

She smiled at the tall young man, but something tugging at her heart had her turning to Seth as she answered, "Yes, thank you very much."

His smile was like the sun, with the ability to make amazing sensations grow inside her, as high and thick as morning glories on a trellis.

"This way," he said, pivoting about.

"Our cabin is that way." She glanced over her shoulder toward the little rooms that no longer smelled like roses. To-She-Wi had helped her scrub the place with water boiled with a minty-scented plant, while Seth had been gone that day and a half. That's when things had changed between them. Ever since his return, he hadn't questioned who she was. Instead he treated her with the utmost respect, and actually seemed to enjoy her company as much as she did his.

"I know," he said, with a noteworthy twinkle in his eyes. "But your surprise is this way."

Butterflies once again inhabited her insides, too strong to ignore even if she wanted to. "Ah, yes, my tea."

Several steps later, as they walked toward the officers' quarters, she asked, "Are we visiting the Ketchums?"

"No."

He angled their path toward the last house on the left, the big one she'd learned was a storage building. A sad thing for sure. The inside of the Ketchums' home was roomy, not at all like their tiny cabin, and she assumed this one must be, as well. Identical in size and shape, it was made of thick round rocks and mortar, like most of the rest of the fort, including sections of the tall wall.

During the past week, Seth had given her tours of every building on the property except this one.

He'd said there might be mice in there, with all the boxes and crates. Hard to believe, with all the people scurrying in and out of it every day. The activity would surely scare away the varmints.

Perhaps that was her surprise—a tour of what was kept in the building. Not that it mattered. The ride he'd already taken her on had been a wonderful gesture, and just being with him had made the world seem brighter and her steps lighter. He was a busy man and she couldn't expect him to keep her entertained when there was work to be done. Yet she didn't have the wherewithal not to want him near whenever possible.

He escorted her up the short set of stairs, onto a porch where two high-back rocking chairs swayed in the wind. A day didn't go by when the steady gusts weren't stirring up dust, leaving no choice but to accept it. Therefore, in her mind, the breezes were no longer a bother.

The contemplative look on Seth's face as he paused near the doorway made Millie's stomach flip. "What?" The moment that followed had her brows twitching and pulling downward.

With a bow of his head, he opened the door. "After you."

The smell of beeswax reminded her of the hours she'd spent coating the banister, floors and furniture back in Richmond. She'd never minded the work, for afterward the house had shone.

Taking a step forward, she removed her hat to get a better look while glancing around. The house back in Richmond gleamed as brightly as this one did right now.

The left side boasted a large front parlor and the right held an arched doorway that led to a kitchen. Both rooms were fully furnished with pieces as finely crafted as those in her father's home. A staircase straight ahead created a wall that led toward the back of the house, and the sun shining into the hallway proved there were more rooms with their doors open.

She spun all the way around. There wasn't a box, crate or barrel anywhere to be seen. Her gaze stopped on Seth, who wore an endearing, secretive grin. A chill not of fear or apprehension, but of anticipation zipped up her arms.

He took her hat, and removing his, placed them both on a nearby table. When he turned, he held out his hands.

Curious and delighted, she laid her fingertips in his palms, and drew a breath at how tenderly his hands folded around hers.

"Welcome home," he whispered.

She tilted her head, to make sure she'd heard what he said, and to quickly scan the area again. His touch created a unique craving inside her that had her pulse racing and blood pounding in her ears. "Home?"

"Yes, I decided it was time for the major to start living in the major's house."

"Oh." A nervous quiver made her ask, "But what about the cabin? Who'll live...?" She swallowed, stopping the question as she suddenly remembered they weren't married and truly shouldn't be living as such. A shower of sadness rained inside her.

"Russ will move back in there."

"Oh," she repeated, glancing to where her feet had glued themselves to the polished floor. Just this morning he'd compared the quiet nights they'd shared to the ones where Russ had filled the cabin with snores. "I guess I'll get used to his snoring," she mumbled.

Seth had wondered how this moment would go, and now that it was upon him, anticipation had his insides kicking like a lassoed pronghorn. He let loose one of her hands to lift her chin with his knuckle. The forlorn look in her eyes only heightened his excitement. His plan was working, almost too well. He found himself looking forward to spending every waking moment in her company, but he was still in control. Was always in control. "No, you won't get used to Russ's snoring," he assured her, "because you'll be living here. With me."

Her little gasp was accompanied by another

flash of those big doe eyes, and Seth couldn't help but grin at the sight.

"Had you really thought I'd move in here without you?" he asked, keeping her chin up with his knuckle.

The flush that appeared on her cheeks sent a jolt through his system. The desire to kiss her, taste those sweet lips, feel the way they curved, had been building over the past few days to the point where he thought of little else. It was tough at times, remembering just who she was, or rather, who she wasn't. He uncurled his finger, ran the tip of it along the graceful curve of her chin.

"This house," he said, "is for the commander of the fort and his wife."

A tiny smile pulled at the sides of her lips. He knew this wasn't Rosemary, but playing along with the game the two sisters had concocted did have its rewards. No harm could come from a simple kiss. Seth slid his hand along the softness of her neck and held her head in place as he lowered his lips to hers, slowly, giving her time to step back if she chose. His entire body sighed with pleasure when his mouth met hers. Soft and precious, the touch was perfect, just as he'd known it would be.

A tiny gasp escaped her lips when he pulled his away, and a bashful smile covered her face.

Oh, yes, soon she'd be telling him everything he wanted to know.

Folding his other arm around her, he eased her closer, and this time, when their mouths met, he explored every sweet inch of her lips.

Her hands were pressed against his chest, and the collar of his coat tugged downward as her fingers curled, clutching the material.

He kissed her again, and again, long and hard, short and sweet, delighting in the way her lips moved to meet his, until his lungs screamed for a full breath of air. It would be so easy to forget the past, focus on the future. A chill rippled over him at that contradiction. His past held no women, and his future wouldn't, either, once he'd found out what she wanted. He needed to remember that. And that this was a game.

"Aw, Rosemary," he whispered, purposely calling her that. Just as he expected, her entire body went as stiff as a rifle barrel.

She pushed on his chest and spun around before he could glimpse her expression. It didn't matter. He knew this was Millie, and he needed to find out why she was here.

He caught her hand and tugged her back around. The fingers beneath his trembled, and her cheeks were red. When she attempted to step past him, he blocked her path. "Where are you going?"

"I—I…" She took a breath. "I must pack. My clothes. My trunks. They're at the cabin."

The rise and fall of her breasts as she gasped drew his eyes. The low neckline of the yellow-and-brown dress showed just enough skin to taunt his heightened senses. He fought to remind himself that this was all part of a plan. "Your trunks are already here," he said. "Come on, I'll show you around."

Stepping into the closest room, he stated, "This is the kitchen, obviously. It's up to you if you want to prepare our meals, or continue to…"

By the time the tour ended in the last room upstairs, where her four trunks lined the walls, tension no longer snapped inside him and her easy conversation said the kisses downstairs hadn't had any lasting side effects in her. They had in him. The pleasure of the connection had him wanting to do it over and over again. And then some. Which would be overplaying his hand, but he couldn't seem to stop the visions when they started forming.

"I thought this was the storage house," she said, running a hand over the quilt covering the bed.

"It was," he admitted. "Until I ordered it cleaned and made ready."

"When did you do that?"

She was shy and skittish. He had to remember to take it slow. "Several days ago." Leaning against the door frame, he gestured about the room. "What do you think?"

She glanced at the windows, the walls, the furniture, and then quite nonchalantly, but grinning mischievously, said, "It's certainly larger than the cabin. I suppose I could get used to it if I had to."

He chuckled. Her mocking banter never failed to delight him. Hoping she sincerely was pleased, he asked, "So do you like your surprise?"

The way she smiled and kept her gaze locked with his as she walked toward him, led him to believe she did. Charm practically floated in the air around her, a magical essence no one at the fort was immune to. In a sense, Jasper had been right. She was what the place needed. In the short time she'd been here, there'd been changes. The men were showing up at mealtimes with their hair combed and their uniforms brushed, and they'd been watching their language. Their manners had improved, too, as had the overall mood of just about everyone. Seth couldn't attribute it to anything but her.

"Well," she said, ducking around him and heading down the hallway, "I was hoping for a cup of tea."

It had been years since he'd laughed as much as he had over the past few days, and chuckling now, he snagged her arm. The desire to pull her against him and kiss her again was tempting, but he quelled it. Holding her in place, he pivoted and then walked down the hallway beside her.

"I'm sure Briggs stocked tea in the kitchen."

A coy little smirk sat on her lips as she glanced his way. "You specifically requested it, didn't you?"

His ears heated up, but he admitted, "Yes, I did."

Her eyes dimmed and a flash of sadness crossed her face, but then her smile returned and she reached over to rub his hand. "Thank you."

There were times when the sincerity of her appreciation had him questioning his deceit. Pretending not to know who she was. The more he got to know her, the more things he found to like. Seth hadn't expected that. He'd seen how the general had doted on his daughters, and knew full well the man's death had left them very wealthy women. Yet she acted as if no one had ever given her anything, had ever taken an interest in her or truly cared for her.

Something opened within him, as if someone had just pulled aside a shutter to reveal a window glowing with light. Caring for her, about her, was so easy, and gave him a pleasure he'd never quite experienced before. It was a little worrisome, but nothing he couldn't deal with. Letting go of her elbow, he slipped his arm around her shoulders and brushed her hair with his lips. "You're welcome."

Millie wanted to close her eyes, but his comforting touch made the chance of tripping and tumbling down the stairs a real possibility. She chose instead to hold her breath and try not to focus on how he kissed her hair, or how his hand tightened on her upper arm, holding her close to his side. It was so wonderful, yet so painful that the tears behind her eyes grew hotter, sharper.

Being Rosemary had become agonizing. No, that wasn't it. Not being Rosemary was what had become agonizing. His kiss had been all Millie had dreamed it would be and more, but unbearable pain had sliced through her the moment he'd whispered her sister's name.

He'd been kissing Rosemary, not her. The lump that formed inside her was massive and sore, and try as she might, she couldn't think beyond it.

"Hey," he said. "You don't seem very excited about your tea."

She stopped next to him at the bottom of the stairs—had no choice, with his arm around her. And digging deeper than ever, she searched for the ability to pull up yet another smile. The past hour had been grueling, pretending nothing had happened, trying to be excited about the house—

a beautiful home indeed—all the while knowing it was a sham. A farce.

No, she was the farce, and that wasn't new. Her entire life had been a charade, at least as long as she could remember. She'd always had to pretend to be someone she wasn't. Had to pretend she wasn't the reason her mother took her own life—that an innocent baby couldn't be to blame. Yet inside, Millie knew it was true, and knew she was as selfish as Rosemary always claimed.

Maybe that's what hurt so badly this time. All these years she'd wished for a way to prove otherwise, but Rosemary didn't want to have anything to do with Seth. She didn't want his attention—didn't want him to kiss her. But Millie did, and here she was, focusing on that instead of the reason she was here. To save her sister's life, and the baby's.

A sob bubbled in her throat even as she tried to pull up an ounce of fortitude. The baby depended on her and she couldn't forget that. She'd just have to stop thinking about other things, and make sure kissing Seth never happened again. No matter how badly she wanted it.

Resolve came—at least that's what she told herself—but a smile couldn't be found. So instead, she just shook her head. "I'm afraid I'll never be able to steep a pot of tea as well as Mr. Ryan."

The tenderness in Seth's face stabbed her already breaking heart, and when he leaned forward, pressed his forehead against hers, an ache shrouded her entire body.

"Then," he whispered, "I'll go have Briggs steep you a pot and have it delivered."

"Major."

Millie didn't turn at the sound of Russ's voice. Tears were pressing too firmly against the backs of her eyes. Crying wouldn't help, and it wouldn't stop the urge to fall into Seth's arms and tell him the truth. He'd be furious and hate her, and that would be worse than having him believe she was Rosemary.

"Yes, Corporal Kemper?" Seth answered, lifting his head.

"I'm sorry to intrude, sir," Russ said. "But riders are coming in. It's Per-Cum-Ske."

Seth's hands continued to tenderly rub Millie's upper arms, and his affection had her insides twisting into knots.

"I'll be right there," he answered.

She kept her eyes closed for as long as possible, until one of his hands lifted her chin, forcing her to look at him. The breath she was pulling in snagged in her throat at the solemn expression on his face. Concern set her heart throbbing. "Who is Per-Cum-Ske?"

His sober gaze went to the door behind her. "He's the current leader of the Comanche."

All her self-pity and sorrows vanished, while fear gripped her insides like a huge fist at the seriousness of his tone. She latched on to his shoulders, grasping the material of his jacket. "Seth—"

"There's nothing to fear," he said. "I've known Per-Cum-Ske for years."

"Why then do I see worry in your eyes?" The question surprised her, for she hadn't realized that was what she'd say. But his troubled look sent a chill clear to her toes.

He smiled, though it was as false as some of the ones she forced upon her own lips. She'd created so many, they were easy to spot. Yet this was the first one she'd seen him display.

"I," he said, brushing her forehead with his lips, "am worried about your tea." He took one of her hands, led her to the table by the door. "I'll have Briggs send over a pot. You stay here. Acclimate yourself to your new home."

Her mind insisted she didn't need tea, but her voice refused to comply, so she simply nodded.

"Good girl," he said, squeezing her hand before letting go. Then he put his hat on and walked out the door.

The tremors in her knees kept her legs from moving. It was several moments before the ability returned and she followed his footsteps. On the front porch, she grasped one of the porch pillars to hold her up. The Indians on horseback, the ones slowly riding toward Seth as he stood in the center of the courtyard, were not like the ones in Tulsa, nor the ones she'd encountered here at the fort. Dressed in animal skins, with feathers in their hair and on their horses, they rode through the wide gate with guns in their hands and scowls on their faces. These were the ones that lived in Indian Territory. The ones her father had spoken about behind closed doors.

Seth spoke to the man in front, the one with a large amount of feathers sticking out of the hat on his head. Though no words carried all the way to the house on the breeze, Millie could tell by his gestures that Seth was welcoming them to the fort. The Indian nodded while turning his head, scanning his surroundings, and when his gaze stopped on her, it was as if his eyes bore right into her skin, leaving it burning.

"Come, dear, we mustn't stare at them."

"Mrs. Ketchum…" Unaware that anyone had joined her, Millie found a touch of comfort in the older woman's presence. She wanted to ask about the Indians, but the pull to turn back to the gathering in the courtyard was too strong.

Seth's gaze was what held her attention, and though he was a distance away, she clearly understood his request. Still fearing for him, she comprehended he had a job to do, and so did she. Being a major's wife included allowing him to complete his duties without interference. Her father had instilled in her years ago the importance of not interfering in army business.

"Come along, dear," Mrs. Ketchum repeated.

Millie turned, and remembering her manners, waved a hand for the other woman to cross the threshold first.

"I know they're frightening at first, dear, but your husband is an excellent commander. One of the best, and you have nothing to fear." Ilene Ketchum closed the door. "Now, why don't I take this opportunity to show you where everything is? I was so excited when I heard you and Seth were moving into the major's house. I stocked the kitchen for the two of you myself."

"You did?" Millie bit her tongue and quickly added, "Thank you."

"You're welcome. Seth was adamant that you not learn about what we were doing. He said everything had to be in order the first time he showed it to you. He wanted it to be a surprise. It was, wasn't it?"

The other's woman's features were angular and stern upon first glance, but Millie saw beyond that, especially after the meal she and Seth had shared with Jasper and Ilene upon her arrival. The woman's kindness seemed to have no bounds, and Millie found herself looking up to her, wishing she could be more like her. Ilene had such confidence and poise, and Millie couldn't help but wonder if her mother had been like that at one time.

"I was surprised," she answered. "Still am."

"Good." The woman smiled brightly. "I'm glad. Now, as I said, I put the kitchen in order and I'll show you where everything is. Jasper and I usually have our meals brought over by one of Mr. Ryan's maidens, especially in the summer months. Even the smallest fire in the stove heats up the house and there really is no sense in wasting the wood. It's so precious out here."

They'd crossed the room, and stood near the long wall adorned with cupboards. Gesturing toward the back door with one hand, Ilene continued, "You'll see the woodshed out by the facilities. All of the officers' homes share it. I will caution you to watch for snakes."

"Snakes?" Millie tried to keep the quiver out of her voice, but didn't succeed.

"Don't worry. They're just bull snakes. They keep the mice population down and the rattlesnakes away. But they do like to hide in the woodpile, and have startled me a time or two." Ilene gave a carefree giggle. "Now, this is where I put the dishes, plates and bowls. Cups are over here...."

The woman's voice seemed to fade away. Mr. Cutter and Mr. Winston had warned of snakes while traveling, but Millie hadn't thought of them inside the stockade walls. Of course, there were snakes in Virginia, but not in town. She'd never seen one in person and would be happy to keep it that way.

"Rosemary?"

A shiver had Millie glancing up, wondering how many times Ilene had called her by that name and she hadn't answered.

"Someone is knocking on the door. Would you like me to answer it?"

Chapter Six

The tea To-She-Wi delivered was a magical elixir, and after sharing the pot with Ilene, Millie was much more prepared to be shown about her new home—and *see* it this time with a clear mind. The house had all the comforts of her Richmond home, and more, for Seth's clothes hung in the room across the hall from hers.

Back downstairs, in the hall beyond the staircase, Ilene pointed into a windowless room. "I saved this for last. It's the bathing area. It was my idea, as was the bathing house for the men living in the barracks. Men just don't think of such things, yet they use them as regularly as women," she said. "Most of the year, just leaving water on the back porch will heat it enough to use. Of course, Briggs always has a stove going, and will heat water if you don't wish to start your own fire."

A large tub, bench and small dressing table filled the room, and the thought of the private area was welcome. Yet other things were filling Millie's mind. "There's barely a tree out here," she noted. "Where does the wood come from?"

"The Wichita Mountains are fifteen or so miles from here. Troops of soldiers are regularly deployed to gather enough wood to last a couple of months."

"Is that where the Indians live?"

"Sometimes. Most of them still move from place to place every few months or so."

"Why?"

"Let's return to the kitchen," Ilene suggested. "I added more water to the teapot so we can have another cup."

Millie followed, and once seated, sipping the tepid, weak but still refreshing tea, asked again, "Why do they move around?"

"It's their way of life." Ilene shrugged as she held her teacup, but her face and tone held compassion and understanding. "They used to follow the buffalo, and now some follow the cattle drives, gathering chips and whatnot for fuel."

"Chips?"

"After the cattle defecate, the sun dries the piles hard and they burn quite well." Ilene smiled, setting her cup down. "It's not as unpleasant as it sounds. The Indians also cut tall grass and twist it into small bundles to burn in their fires." She sighed then. "They aren't bad people or evil, they're just like you and me, and the rest of the world. Families with babies and children to take care of. But unlike a lot of us, their entire way of life has been unbalanced. For the most part, they're trying very hard to adjust. The buffalo used to provide them with almost everything they needed." She shook her head as if confused or disgusted. "And now the army sends them flour."

"That's bad?" Millie asked.

"Well, yes, they don't know what to do with flour and baking powder. They've never used it before. They don't have ovens, just open fires." Ilene pushed her cup away and folded her hands upon the table. "That's why Seth is going to Washington in person next month. To insist that the provisions sent out here are ones the tribes can use. Things that will feed their families. It used to be the cattlemen would give the Indians a few head of cows to cross their land, but now they bring bottles of whiskey to trade instead. A very sad thing for sure."

Millie pushed her cup aside, as well, no longer thirsty. Seth's trip to Washington was imperative. She understood that and couldn't ask him not to go, but she had to find a way to postpone it.

"Don't frown so," Ilene said. "I know Seth will make progress. He can be quite persuasive." She reached over and laid a hand upon Millie's. "And I'm so glad you're here for him."

Millie had no idea how to respond, so she simply nodded. "Thank you."

"Did your sister go off to school, or marry?"

Her blood turned cold. "My sister?"

"Yes," Ilene said. "Seth said you have a younger sister, that you had to take care of her, raise her. That's why you never came out here before."

"He did?"

Ilene patted her hand. "Last winter Seth was very ill. That's when I discovered he was married. I wrote you a letter. I know I'd have wanted someone to tell me if Jasper was ill."

Millie's heart was pounding as she thought of Seth, so strong and healthy, becoming ill. It seemed almost impossible, and frightening at the same time. "I—I never received a letter."

"That's what Seth assumed once he was better. And that's when he told me about your younger sister. Millie, isn't it?"

The lump was too large to swallow around.

Would the lies never end? Millie nodded and reached for the tepid tea.

Seth was still at the headquarters building along with Jasper Ketchum and several others, including the Indian Per-Cum-Ske, when Millie carried a lamp up to her room and prepared for bed. Ilene had returned and they'd eaten together the meal To-She-Wi had delivered. Millie had worked hard to keep the conversation off herself. Had to. Confusion was overwhelming her mind. She knew she wasn't Rosemary, but she couldn't help but wish she was. Pretending Seth was her husband—speaking of him as if he was—was so easy and enchanting. It was as if she'd landed in the life she'd always imagined having, except she wasn't herself. She was a Millie-Rosemary person who didn't even exist.

Flopping onto the bed, she lay on top of the covers wearing just her nightgown. The weather hadn't cooled off yet this evening, and even with the window open, the room was hot. Or maybe it was just her body. When it wasn't heated by thoughts of Seth, it was boiling with all the things Rosemary hadn't told her.

If Millie had seen Ilene's letter, she'd have come. She'd have taken care of Seth.

The rolling of her stomach said that wasn't true. Rosemary would never have let her, and the chance she'd have come upon Ilene's letter was next to nil. Not only would Millie never have read someone else's private message, she was often away from home when correspondence arrived. Either staying clear, not wanting to know who was visiting her sister, or on an errand for Rose-mary. Returning a garment to the dressmaker that didn't fit quite right, or a hat to the milliner, or...her eyes went across the room, to where her boots sat upon one of her trunks...shoes to the shoemaker.

She pressed a hand to her chest, where it felt as if someone was stitching up her heart and pull-ing the string tight, telling her once again how selfish she was. Focusing on the boots, she tried to think other thoughts. The heel was as good as new. It hadn't given her any problems, and every morning, when she pulled the boots on, she was reminded of her mission. Yet it didn't stop her from wishing things were different.

Sighing, she turned her gaze to the window, wondering again when Seth would return. To-She-Wi had said he'd eaten. All the men in the meeting had, and that was comforting, but not as soothing as the way he wished her a good-night. She'd wait up, as long as it took, to hear those words again tonight, too.

Without much effort, her mind pulled up a picture of him standing in the doorway, leaning against the frame as he had back at the cabin. His grin would be a bit cockeyed—showing his dimple—and sweet, and he'd say the words softly. Not necessarily a whisper, but in a low tone that was like a lullaby. Kissing entered her mind again, and she could almost see him walking across the room, sitting down on the edge of her bed.... A sigh left her chest, and she let her mind wander, creating a most pleasurable dream.

A thud, thump, or some such sound tugged her from slumber. Blinking, she fought to chase away the groggy thickness in her mind and vision. The flame in the lamp still flickered, and she reached for it, wondering when she'd fallen asleep.

Her hand stalled as she sat up. Fine-tuning her hearing, she waited for another sound, something to let her know Seth had returned.

The quiet was interrupted by an odd, faint scratching. Flipping her legs over the edge of the bed, she scanned the room, noting one boot on the floor.

She was halfway across the room when she noticed the other boot, still atop the trunk, wobble. She took another step, but froze as a tiny head popped up over the top. Her heart jolted, throbbed against her rib cage, and then the snake noticed her. Or she realized it was a snake. Either way, it hissed and she screamed.

In a single bound she was back on top of the

bed, screaming the only name her mind knew. "Seth! *Seth...!*"

Shrugging out of his coat, having just walked into the house, Seth left the garment in his wake as he flew up the stairs. The terror-filled screams sent ice pumping through his veins.

He shot down the hall, and rounding the corner into her room, slid to a stop. She stood on the bed, up against the wall near the headboard. The lamp beside her bed flickered in the darkness, turning her thin nightgown gossamer and silhouetting a shape beneath that stole his breath away.

Another scream, his name, pierced the air. One of her trembling arms was held out, pointing toward the far side of the room. He saw it then, the bull snake. A young one from the size of it. They all had bad attitudes, and this one was no different. Reared up, forming an *S* with its body, it lunged forward while backtracking across the top of the trunk. He was thankful such a minor thing was the cause of the commotion. For a moment he'd imagined one of Per-Cum-Ske's braves climbing through a window. The man had been too curious about her, and that had got Seth's goat early on in the meeting.

He crossed the room, snatched up the critter by the back of the neck and tossed it out the open window. A brave would have needed a ladder to enter her window, and none were left lying around. Turning back to assure her all was fine, he felt his heart jolt again. Not only was her gown see-through, her face was colorless.

"Shhh," he whispered. "It's gone."

Still cowering near the wall, she shook her head.

"It's gone," he repeated, walking slowly to the side of the bed and holding out a hand. "Come here."

Her head didn't move, but her eyes did. "Seth?"

"Yes, it's me. Come here, sweetheart." The endearment rolled off his tongue without thought as he took her hand and tugged her toward him.

She crumpled onto her knees and latched her hands around his neck. Catching her with both arms, he pulled her forward, held her trembling body against his chest. "Shhh," he repeated as his insides filled with unfathomable warmth. "It's gone."

"It was huge," she gasped.

"No, he was just a little guy," he teased, hoping to ease her fears. "And he's gone now."

"Where'd it come from?"

He shouldn't be enjoying holding her, for she was scared, but she felt so good pressed against him like this. Just the thin cotton of his shirt and her gown separated his chest from her breasts, and that had his blood pulsing. Running a hand down the length of her hair, stopping to press his palm into the small of her back, he answered, "It must have been left over from one of the crates or barrels."

"What did it want?"

She was calming down a touch. Her breath was no longer coming out in tiny gasps, but he continued to run a hand up and down her back. "A mouse or two, I'd suspect."

"I don't mind mice."

Her voice was so tiny and meek he smiled and brushed a kiss to the top of her hair, which hung between her shoulder blades. He'd watched her brush it out, standing in the doorway back at their cabin last night, and wondered. Five years ago, Millie's hair had hung past her waist. He remembered that because Rosemary had pointed it out, when noting differences between them. She'd said Millie had no style.

People could cut their hair, did all the time. Millie could have, too. He'd contemplated that again in the past few hours, while telling himself he wasn't jealous of Per-Cum-Ske's interest in her. Yet Seth had also started to wonder if he'd judged too quickly. Started questioning if this *could* in fact be Rosemary, his wife; maybe she'd changed. They'd spent only a few hours together back then, and she had been upset—which could bring out the worst in people. If only he had a picture to compare. But he didn't. Other than the one in his mind, which, he had to admit, he'd painted very unflatteringly over the years.

"Will it be back?"

He nestled his chin against the top of her head, curled his arms tighter around her. "No, he won't be back."

She shivered slightly. "Does he have friends?"

Seth chuckled and scooped her off the bed.

They were halfway across the room before she asked, "Where are we going?"

"To my room." It wasn't that he was surprised by his actions, just unsure, and he considered turning around, but didn't.

Once in his room, straight across the hall from hers, he leaned down and threw back the covers before setting her on the bed. "You can sleep right there."

"Are there snakes in here?"

Her arms were still locked around his neck and he gradually eased them off, questioning if he'd lost his mind. "I'll go get the lamp from your room and check."

Back within seconds, he made a show of looking beneath the dresser and in the wardrobe closet, and a touch of apprehension clutched him as he bent to peer under the bed, as if he half expected to find another snake himself. It was doubtful, but he'd have the men sweep the house again tomorrow and make sure there were no others.

"No snakes," he declared, setting the lamp on the table. He pondered sleeping in her room, but only for a moment. Taking a seat on the edge of the bed, he removed his boots, using the toe of the opposite foot against the heel. The pants would stay on, even though they were wool, but the socks and shirt would have to go. It was too hot to remain fully dressed.

"Where will you sleep?"

Once his socks found a place on the floor beside the boots, he twisted and patted the pillow beside hers. "Right here."

She bit her bottom lip and swallowed hard, and a part of him wanted to copy her actions. Instead, he removed his shirt, tossed it on the chair and stretched out, tucking his feet and knees beneath the covers still folded back on his side. "This way, any snake will have to crawl over me to get to you, and I won't let that happen."

Her relieved sigh was probably heard in Texas, but it did little to ease his apprehension.

"Thank you," she whispered.

She needed his protection. That's all this was. He repeated the justification as he reached over and turned down the lamp wick, and then, as if it was the most natural thing on earth, he slid an arm beneath her neck and tugged her close. "Come here."

She stiffened, but only for a moment, and then rolled onto her side to snuggle against him, resting her head on his shoulder and her hand on his chest, right over his thudding heart. This time he did swallow hard, for something deep inside called a warning, while another part of him rejoiced. He slipped his free hand beneath the covers and cupped her hip to hold her in place.

"Better?" he asked.

"Much," she whispered. "Much, much better."

"Good. Go to sleep now, it's late."

"How late is it?"

"After midnight."

"I was trying to stay awake, to wish you goodnight."

Her hand was playing havoc on his already heated body as her fingertips teased and parted the hair on his chest. "You can say it now," he whispered, as hoarse as a frog with a cold.

"Good night, Seth."

"Good night, sweetheart," he answered. This was crazy. He should have heeded the warning. Or he should crawl out of the bed now, while he still could. Her leg had curled up and one knee was resting on his thigh, awfully close to the other part of his body that was growing more eager by the second. He'd never wanted a woman as badly as he wanted her, as thoroughly. Had never reacted to anything this way. Even in the heat of battle his heart hadn't raced like this. Furthermore, patience wasn't his best virtue, and right now he found himself wishing she was Rosemary. Wishing he could be sure. Actually, her name didn't matter. Truth was he'd gotten caught in his own snare. He was no longer pretending. Might never have been. He wanted her, this beautiful woman that the entire fort was talking about. His wife.

Millie couldn't quite grasp what was happening inside her. The fear of the snake—though she'd never been more afraid in her life—was gone, and the way Seth called her sweetheart had her heart singing the sweetest tune imaginable. But beyond all that there was an energy building inside her that wouldn't slow down, and her breasts were on fire. They felt heavy and swollen. An odd thing for sure, and embarrassing to think about, but the sensation of being pressed against Seth heightened their sensitivity and consumed her thoughts. As did her leg. It was folded over his, and her inner thigh could feel the coarse fibers of his wool britches. She'd never experienced anything like this awareness before.

If it was possible, her body wanted to get even closer to him.

She wiggled slightly, pressing tighter against

him. Her heart leaped as if rewarded when his hand, the one resting on her hip, slid upward, rubbing her side, and the stirring in her stomach increased as he kissed the top of her head.

Millie shifted, just to glance up. The room was dark, but she could see his smile. His blue eyes held hers for several quiet moments and then a wave of delight flooded her being as his face came down to meet hers.

His lips were tender and warm, and swept over hers so gently her lips chased after them. It was fun, and created a tiny giggle. He chuckled, too, and then softly bit her bottom lip. She laughed again.

It was unfathomable, but goodness gracious, wonderful. So much so that she copied his action. It was like a game of copycat, or hide-and-seek, that ended when his mouth completely covered hers. His lips were firmer, more precise, and his hand held the back of her head. Astounded, having never experienced anything so magnificent, she arched upward and pressed her mouth fully against his.

With her head spinning and her body flaming with an inner heat, all Millie could comprehend was that his kisses were all she'd ever wanted.

Or so she thought, until his hand glided to the edge of her breast. The sensation had her toes curling, and then his palm covered one, kneading it in a way that provided such bliss she couldn't contain the moan that bubbled in her throat.

His tongue had entered her mouth, and hers had leaped to life, twisted with his, and she didn't want it to stop. Didn't want any of it to end.

The heat and pressure building inside her was agonizing and wonderful at the same time. His body was so firm and hard beneath her fingertips, and a driving inner force had her scooting closer.

He stopped the kiss so abruptly she gasped, or maybe she was just breathless. She pulled air into her lungs as he kissed her forehead and then rested his chin on her head.

"We have to go to sleep. Now. Or we never will," he whispered.

She nodded, not really sure why. There was no way she could sleep. Her very center was on fire, and her breasts were stinging, wanting him to touch them again. His hold was still strong, kept her firmly pressed against him, and she hoped—no, prayed—that he wouldn't let her loose. Not yet, or maybe not ever.

He rubbed the top of her head with his chin and stroked her side with his hand, and the actions were comforting, slowly allowing her to relax. But even as sleep crept in, Millie continued to relive the moment, over and over again. It had been extraordinary.

The next thing she knew was that she was alone in the bed.

Startled, she sat up. Sunlight was streaming in the window. Turning, she stared at the bed, half afraid she'd dreamed it all. There was a clear indentation in the pillow next to her and a smile formed as she recalled the comfort of his shoulder beneath her head.

"Good morning."

Her gaze snapped to the doorway, where Seth was leaning against the frame, as handsome as ever, perhaps more so.

"Good morning." Noting he was freshly shaved and fully dressed, she said, "I must have overslept."

"You had a rough night."

A frown pulled at her brows. It had been the most delightful night of her life.

"I have men coming over in an hour. They'll sweep the house for snakes."

Her heart leaped, and she scanned the room.

A warm and gentle hand folded around her fingers. "Come on," he said. "I'll take you back to your room so you can dress before the men arrive."

Embarrassment at wearing nothing more than her bedclothes stung her cheeks, but she shook her head.

"All right," he said, "just tell me what you need and I'll get it for you."

She did, and he gathered it all, and then stood outside his closed bedroom door as she dressed. Her hands had never shaken so, and it had nothing to do with snakes. The fact that Seth had touched her private garments had her heart threatening to pound its way right out of her body. This should never have happened—him gathering her under-clothes or her sleeping in his bed.

Once fully dressed, she fixed her hair and then straightened the bedcovers. Not sure what to do with her nightgown, Millie draped it over the footboard of the bed before moving to the door. Once the men had checked for snakes, she'd take it into her room, and make sure nothing like this happened again. Rosemary would be furious.

"Ready for breakfast?" Seth asked, holding out his arm as she opened the door.

Her heart did a complete cartwheel when he took her hand, but she managed to nod demurely. She couldn't pull away—she was his wife. But not really, so she shouldn't encourages such advances. Oh, good heavens, nothing made sense.

"Our food was just delivered," he said as they walked down the hallway. "At least that's what I'm assuming. I heard the front door close."

He was so very handsome, she could spend hours just looking at him and never tire of the sight, and when he smiled at her as he was right now, her insides turned all warm and soft, making her want to feel like this forever. That, too, was wrong and selfish, and she had to put a stop to it.

Once they were at the bottom of the stairs, she sought what she hoped was a safe subject. "Would you prefer I cooked our meals?" Cooking wasn't her best talent. Lola had made all the meals back in Richmond, but Mr. Ryan was sincerely kind, and he'd probably assist her if she asked.

Seth tugged her toward the kitchen. "I," he said, leading her toward the table, "prefer that you do whatever you want. If you want to cook, cook. If you don't, don't."

Sitting in the chair he held out, she glanced over her shoulder. "You don't even know whether I can cook or not."

He paused, gazing at her curiously as he pushed her chair in. Her stomach flipped. Rosemary would never have offered to cook, and his look said he knew that.

"I have some things to see to this morning," he said, after sitting down across from her and filling her cup with tea. "But this afternoon, I can take you over to see Jenkins. A cargo wagon pulled in a short time ago. Your boots might be in it."

"Oh, I forgot about them," she admitted. Shopping was something Rosemary would do. She lived for it. "I can go over there this morning. There's no need for you to take me. It's only across the compound." She cut a piece of bread in half, thankful her insides were returning to normal—or as normal as they could be. "It'll give me something to do while the men look for snakes."

"I can send Russ with you if you want."

"That's not necessary," she answered, pulling up Rosemary's tone. It chilled her to the bone, but it was the only thing she could do to still her heart and fulfill her purpose.

Chapter Seven

Damn, he was tired of these eerie feelings. Fighting the urge to devour her all night had left him so full of frustration his skin was too tight. But right now, her tone sliced him deep, as did the set of her chin. Together they caused a peculiar inner instinct to kick in, as if he somehow knew a storm was brewing.

They finished the meal in silence and that irritated Seth even more. The shine was gone from her eyes, the glow from her cheeks. She was like a chameleon, changing her skin color to adapt to her surroundings.

A knock on the door had him pushing away from the table. The movement didn't help the knot in his stomach, the one that coiled itself around his spine until his back ached. That gutwrenching sensation occurred whenever he was reminded of the old Rosemary, and nothing relieved it. Hadn't for years.

Aw, hell. He was putting too much thought into all this, that was the problem. This wasn't an Indian uprising, where he had to strategically consider every move, find a way to think ahead of his opponent. This was about one tiny woman. He had to quit questioning if she was Millie or Rosemary. He knew the answer to that. Carrying Rosemary to his bed would never have happened. Would never happen. Ever. His goal, to get to the bottom of why Millie was here, and send her home, hadn't changed. The fort was no place for her. She was too innocent for this untamed territory, and for him.

"Major? We're here to check for snakes."

Shaking his head, Seth glanced up, half unaware he'd even opened the door. Stepping aside, he waved a hand. "Come in, Private."

"Ma'am," Kent Wickham said, clicking his heels together as he squared his shoulders and pulled the hat off his head.

From the archway between the two rooms, she nodded. "Good morning."

The way her cheeks grew pink again when Seth caught her gaze had him clenching his teeth. Leaving as soon as possible was what would be best for everyone. The men were taking too much notice. Even in the simple dress, green with tiny white stripes, without lace or ruffles or other embellishments, she looked as stunning as a woman decked out in finery for a fancy ball. The form-fitting gown enhanced her slender figure, but it was more than that. Natural beauty hovered around her like a glow an artist painted around images of angels.

He'd discovered that something soft and whimsical swirled around his heart whenever he looked at her lately. A reaction he'd never before experienced, and that worried him. Almost as much as what had happened last night worried him. He had a fort to oversee and couldn't afford to be distracted. He certainly couldn't afford to take Millie's innocence.

Two other privates greeted her as they entered, and Seth quickly explained the situation last night, before he moved to where she stood in the archway as the searchers went upstairs.

He was a military man, had embraced that choice for years. But when it came to spending time with her or carrying out his duties, resentment toward his obligations tended to flare up. That had never happened before and couldn't happen now. Things were precarious out here, and needed his constant attention. Per-Cum-Ske was insistent upon going to Washington, and that was what needed Seth's focus right now. He should have been at it an hour ago.

"I'll walk with you as far as headquarters," he said.

"I'll need my bonnet and wrist bag."

The grimace when she glanced toward the stairs made him grin, even though he didn't want to. "I'll get them," he offered. "Where are they?"

"Thank you," she said. "They're in the wardrobe closet. Hanging on a hook on the left."

He nodded and shot up the stairs. After insisting the men double- and triple-check every nook and cranny, he grabbed her items and found her waiting on the front porch.

"I'm sure there aren't any more snakes," he said, pulling the door closed behind him.

"I hope not." She took the bonnet, slipped it on and tied the long ribbons on the side of her chin before taking the bag. "Thank you. Both for getting my things and for having the men search the house."

There was a shyness about her again, and with it came the desire to kiss her again. It had been there the moment he'd awakened with her still snuggled against his side, and had been with him ever since, other than that fleeting moment in the kitchen when she'd reminded him of the past. Then he'd wanted her out of here as fast as possible. Now, looking into those clear brown eyes, he didn't want her to be anywhere but at his side. Which was impossible.

Seth dwelled on that as they walked, and if she hadn't stopped, he'd have kept going right past headquarters. The big stone building with its wide double doors mocked him this morning. Challenged him to ignore the responsibilities that lay inside it. Inside him.

"Have a good meeting," she said.

Accepting his duties, as he always would, he let loose her arm.

Millie, with her hands trembling and her insides fluttering, turned, knowing he wouldn't go into his meeting while she was standing there. He was too much of a gentleman for that. Putting one foot in front of the other had never been quite this difficult before. The desire to tell him the truth, the entire truth, created a rather intense argument inside her.

By the time she reached the trading post she had resigned herself again to the fact that she couldn't tell Seth anything, but it left her stomach churning. She told herself to ignore it. Not that it helped.

"Aw, Mrs. Parker, your boots are in."

"Good morning, Mr. Jenkins," she said, maneuvering through the space, which was even more crowded than usual. Crates made of thin wooden slats were balanced precariously and stacked head high in most every direction. "My husband thought they might have arrived." A thrill circled her heart. *Husband*. One word had never filled her with such pride.

"Yes, yes, just this morning," the bearded store owner answered. "I'd sent a wagon to Denver the day you ordered them, to make sure I'd get them as soon as possible. No one wants to disappoint the major."

"I'm sure they don't," she answered, turning toward the dusty window, where the faint out-line of the headquarters building could be seen. Seth was a firm leader, but well respected and admired. She'd gathered that from the first day, and every day since.

"Here they are, ma'am."

Mr. Jenkins, the lower half of his face covered in white whiskers, had set a pair of black boots very similar to the ones she was wearing on the counter. "These are perfect," she said. "Thank you."

"Would you like to try them on?"

"I don't believe there is any need." Then, re-membering the soldiers searching for snakes, she realized spending time at the trading post seemed a much better idea than returning home. Espe-cially if another slithering creature was uncov-ered. "On second thought, I believe I will."

Mr. Jenkins pulled a stool around the plank-and-barrel counter and set it down, patting the round top. "Here you go. Sit right here."

In no hurry, she removed a boot and slipped her foot into one of the new ones. It fit perfectly and the inner sole was as soft as a pillow. "These are very nice boots, Mr. Jenkins."

"Only the best," he said with a wide grin. "I have something else for you, ma'am."

"Oh?" she answered absently, while removing the boot. The idea that Seth had picked them out filled her with a unique sense of endearment. She'd save them for special occasions.

"Here you go." The man held out a yellow parasol, complete with cane handle.

Shaking her head, she sought for an explanation. "I don't recall ordering that, Mr. Jenkins, though it is very beautiful."

"You didn't order it, ma'am. It's my gift to you." The top of his head, very close to being hairless, took on a pink glow. "Seeing how your other one was ruined on your journey out here."

His smile was so bright and his tone so sincere, she had a hard time shaking her head again. "I couldn't accept such a gift, Mr. Jenkins. But thank you for the thought."

He extended it farther. "I insist, Mrs. Parker. It's a gift to welcome you to our fort. Please take it."

"Oh, but I couldn't."

Shaking his head, the man said, "Then I'll have to tell the major."

Her stomach flipped. "Tell the major what?"

"That you wouldn't accept my welcoming gift." There was a teasing glint in his eyes. "He'll make you take it. He likes to keep everyone happy. Makes for easier living."

Relieved, because for a split second she'd thought he had discovered her true identity, Millie clicked her tongue. "You, Mr. Jenkins, are a rascal."

His guffaw echoed off the walls, ceiling and unevenly stacked crates. "That I am, ma'am. Now are you gonna take my present or not?"

"I believe I have no choice." She grasped the handle and ran her other hand over the silk and lace folded and tied along the intricate woodwork. It was a beautiful piece, and finely made. "Thank you, Mr. Jenkins. I appreciate your thoughtfulness."

"And we appreciate you. The major's been grinning ever since you stepped off that wagon."

Her heart seemed to double in size. Everyone at the fort was so kind to her. Had been since her arrival. She leaned closer to the man and teasingly whispered, "He's probably still thinking about the comical limp my broken heel gave me."

The storekeeper's rumbling laughter filled the room again. "You were a sight, ma'am."

She couldn't help but giggle. "I know." Happiness like this was so new, sometimes she won-

dered if she should pinch herself. Setting the
parasol on the counter next to her boots, she
asked, "May I leave these here? I'd like to look
around a bit."

"Of course." He picked a can out of the box
next to him and set it on the shelf. "I gotta get
this freight unloaded, but you just holler if you
find something you can't reach."

"I will," she assured him, already scanning the
shelves and tables. There truly wasn't anything
she needed, but it would take the men time to
check the house, so she might as well explore the
merchandise. Besides, with Seth at headquarters,
there was little else to fill her time.

Time. Now that was an amazing thing. A week
ago, she'd thought Mr. Jenkins a scary-looking
character, but now recognized he was an enter-
prising shop owner who was also generous. A
kind-hearted soul. Not even the Indians filing in
and out of the doorway fazed her. She offered a
smile to those who glanced her way. Who'd have
ever imagined she'd adjust so well, so quickly? It
just proved people could get used to new things
if they would only try.

Her hand stalled on the glass chimney of the
oil lamp she'd been admiring. The tiny flowers
on the base no longer drew her attention. She'd
adjusted all right. More than she should have. A
heavy weight settled in her chest.

She'd tried to become Rosemary this morning, but hadn't put forth much effort. It was as if something inside her refused to allow the disguise to manifest, and she'd readily accepted that. How would she ever make it to December? September was barely over, and every day it grew more difficult to remember why she was here. It wasn't that she didn't think of her sister and the baby regularly. But being here wasn't so much of a chore anymore, and that wasn't right. Rosemary wouldn't be enjoying life at the fort, and that's who Seth had to divorce. Rosemary. Not Millie.

The air around her grew suffocating. It was as if she no longer existed, yet at the same time, she had never been happier. And that was the problem. This wasn't about her. It was about her sister and Seth. Millie felt as if her head was spinning. The harder she thought, the more confusing everything became. Of all the skirmishes and incidents she'd had to clean up for Rosemary, this was the most complicated, especially for her.

Millie cleared her lungs with a long sigh, but it didn't help. What kept her head spinning and belly churning the most, what turned her inside out, was that she didn't want Seth to not like her. But he had to dislike her in order to divorce her, didn't he? Divorced people didn't like each other—at least she assumed they didn't. She'd never known a divorced person.

"Do you like the lamp?" Mr. Jenkins asked.

She spun around, and walked to the counter. "Yes, it's very pretty, but I have no need for it." Pointing to the shelf behind him, at items that had caught her eye earlier, she asked, "Could I have one of those tablets, and a pencil holder and lead?"

"Do you like to draw?" he asked, stepping onto a stool to reach the paper.

"Yes, I do." There was no reason to explain that she hadn't spent much time drawing lately. She hadn't done a lot of things she used to do. Lack of money. Lack of time. Lack of desire. The reasons just continued. Right now, she needed to draw. Needed something to occupy her mind.

"I have this new lead holder." The shopkeeper held up a metal tube much larger than her miniature ones at home. "The men swear by it. They say the size is much easier to use. I have smaller ones if you prefer."

"No, actually, I'd like to try the larger one, thank you. I'll need a box of leads, as well."

"Anything else?"

"No, that will do." She pulled open the top of her wrist bag. "How much do I owe you?"

"I'll just put it on the major's account," Mr.

Jenkins said, arranging the boots, paper tablet and pencil set in a small crate.

"I'd rather not. I'll just pay you."

He was shaking his head. "Can't do that, Mrs. Parker. The major would have my scalp, and I ain't got much hair left to lose. If you wanna pay someone, pay your husband." Jenkins turned then and shouted over his shoulder, "Wind, come carry this for the major's wife."

Short of arguing, insisting she'd pay for her supplies and causing undue distress for the shopkeeper, Millie closed her bag and hooked the string over her wrist. "I can carry the crate. There's no need to trouble anyone."

"Wind likes doing it," Mr. Jenkins said as a young boy, no more than ten or so, came running through a blanket-draped doorway next to the long set of shelves behind the counter. "Don't you, boy?"

"Haa." The child nodded. "Yes."

"Here then, follow the major's wife to her place. But come back, and no dillydallying. We've got a lot of freight to put away."

The boy grabbed the crate off the counter, looking at her expectantly with big brown eyes. His black hair hung to his shoulders, which were thin and bare, showing the sharp edges of his collarbones. The only clothing he wore was a pair of brown leather pants that stopped near his knees.

Smiling, Millie said, "Hello, Wind."

"*Maruawe,* hello, Major's wife." Turning to the shopkeeper, Wind tipped his head toward the parasol. "That, too?"

Mr. Jenkins nodded.

"I can carry it." She lifted the parasol off the counter. "Good day, Mr. Jenkins. Thank you for all your assistance."

With a nod and a smile that was hard to see with all his facial hair, he said, "My pleasure."

The day was warm, as most every day since she'd arrived had been, yet winter was around the corner. Popping open the parasol, she shielded both herself and the boy from the bright sunlight. "Do you live here, Wind, at the fort?" she asked, already thinking of the material in Mr. Jenkins's shop, and wondering if the boy would let her sew clothes for him. Not that she knew how, but she could learn.

"*Kee,* no. We came for Per-Cum-Ske to talk to Major."

"Per-Cum-Ske? Is he your father?"

"No. He Comanche leader."

"A chief?

"*Kee,* no. A leader." The boy hoisted the crate higher in his arms. "He go talk to Wash-ing-ton man. Tell him we need buffalo."

"Washington man? Do you mean the president?"

"*Haa.* Yes."

Sadness welled inside her. Congress couldn't know there were children out here, hungry and without clothes. Surely they would have done something more if they did. Wouldn't they? It would be nice to believe they would have, but deep down, she had an inclination they knew. The army had been out here for years. They would have reported such things. Another welling happened, one that filled her with warmth and pride. Seth would make them listen. He'd make things better.

Smiling at the boy, she asked, "Mr. Jenkins hired you to help him?"

The child spoke well, better than some of the older Indians she'd encountered, yet a frown rippled his forehead as he asked, "Hired?"

"Yes, he pays you to help him. Gives you money?"

"*Haa,* yes. Trade. Gives sweet stick."

"Sweet stick?"

A smile took up his entire face. "*Haa.* Good. Much good."

"Candy?" she asked. "He pays you with candy?"

"*Haa.* Much good. My...my, uh, seester, she like."

"You share it with your sister?" Imagining a little girl as adorable as Wind was easy, yet a candy stick wasn't an appropriate payment. Though Millie had come to understand money meant nothing to the tribes. They bartered for everything.

"Haa," he answered, still grinning.

They were approaching the house, where Russ stood near the corner talking with the three men who had been looking for snakes. "Corporal Kemper, may I speak with you?"

"Yes, ma'am," he answered, and after nodding to the men, turned and met her on the short walkway leading to the porch. Standing stiff and straight, with his hands behind his back, he asked, "What can I do for you, Mrs. Parker?"

Already digging in her bag, she pulled out several coins. "Would you please escort Wind back to the trading post and purchase as much candy as this will buy for him?"

Russ's green eyes went from sparkling to dull and filled with unease. "Ma'am, I don't—"

"Corporal Kemper," she interrupted, and though it felt wrong to use her status so, in this instance she would, and be glad of the power being a major's wife allowed. "I wouldn't want to tell my husband you've disappointed me."

"No, ma'am." Blushing red, the corporal took the coins.

"Just put the box right there, Wind." She collapsed the parasol while waiting for the boy to set the crate on the bottom step, and then bent down in front of him. "Thank you very much for helping me. You follow Corporal Kemper back to Mr. Jenkins's store and take what he gives you. It's for you and your sister. It's my trade for your assistance. For carrying the crate for me."

His little shoulders squared with what she assumed to be dignity. *"Haa. Ura."*

"Ura," she repeated, watching the boy walk away. Pins seemed to prickle her skin. Wind had nothing, yet what he did have, he shared with his sister, whereas she and Rosemary, having whatever they'd wanted when they were his age, had rarely shared anything. Well, Millie had, but she'd always felt resentful. Another shameful thing to admit, even to herself. But it was the truth. She'd resented the fact that she owed her sister, and right now she resented what she was doing for payment of that debt.

Millie walked up the steps toward one of the high-back chairs. This trip had her thinking about things she'd never thought of before, seeing a side of herself she'd never admitted to having. Plopping into the chair and sending it rocking back and forth, she thought of the reason she was here. A baby, who someday would be a boy not so unlike Wind, or a girl, like his sister. A child who would need love and care, food and clothing, and a candy stick every now and again. A child who was depending on Millie this very moment.

"This just ain't right," Lola had said in the early morning dawn weeks ago, yet the words echoed in Millie's mind as clearly as if the woman was standing beside her right now. "Your Papa wouldn't like this, not at all."

"I know," Millie whispered, just as she had that morning—the day she'd left.

"That girl ain't never gonna learn if you keep stepping in, righting her wrongs," Lola had added.

A long sigh escaped as Millie continued to rock. Lola didn't understand Rosemary's need for affection. Never had, but Millie did. Not so unlike Rosemary, she'd always longed for their mother, too.

Big tears had cascaded down Lola's coffee-hued cheeks when they'd hugged goodbye, and Millie had cried, too. She hadn't wanted to go, but there had been no choice.

Rosemary had said she didn't want Seth disgraced, which he certainly would be if others learned of her pregnancy, and now that Millie knew Seth, she felt even more strongly about that. He was such an honorable man, and truly didn't deserve the way his wife had carried on with other men.

"I'll wire you as soon as the child's born," Lola

had said. "But once you get those papers signed, don't you bring them back here. You mail them, and then go to Texas, tell that young Martin you'll be the best wife he ever hoped to have."

Lola hadn't given her time to answer before continuing, "I'll take care of everything here. No harm will come to that baby, not before it arrives or after."

Tears pressed on Millie's eyes now, just as they had that morning. Although she believed Lola would see to the baby's safety, she wouldn't be going to Texas. She'd known that then, but hadn't told Lola. During the train and wagon rides, Millie had tried to convince herself she could go to Texas when this was all over, but knew the entire time she wouldn't. That would be as big a sham as this one. She and Martin didn't love each other—not like that. Not as a husband and wife should.

Flinching inside, she rerouted her thoughts.

Weeks before the morning of her departure, she'd told Rosemary she would help, had even offered to claim the child as hers. But her sister would hear nothing of that. She'd announced that as soon as the child was born, and her divorce settled, she and the baby's father would marry. Lola insisted the baby's father was already married, and Millie believed that to be true. Most of the men that "frequented" the house were married. Millie had tried to talk to Rosemary about it over the years, only to have her insist that Millie knew nothing about the needs a woman had. She couldn't argue with that, but she did know right from wrong.

Shortly after Papa had died, Martin had told her about her sister's trysts. He'd been over in Charlottesville and seen Rosemary, who'd pretended not to know him.

Millie's stomach started churning again. Martin had been disgusted by her sister's behavior, and he'd feel the same way about what Millie was doing. Though he'd been her best friend for as long as she could remember, he'd never understood the guilt that churned inside her. She'd never told him about it, either. That she was the reason Rosemary was the way she was. As an infant, Millie had been too young to remember their mother, but Rosemary had been older, and the loss had scarred her—forever.

Quiet, thoughtful, Millie sat for several minutes. She'd have to return to Richmond when this was all over. Rosemary would need her more than ever.

Eventually, she pushed herself out of the chair and walked down the steps, to carry the box onto the porch. Digging out the pad and pencil, she sat back down, and after loading the lead in the holder, flipped open the cover on the tablet.

Despite starting over several times, she found

Seth's features appearing on the paper again and again. It was the only image her fingers wanted to draw. After the seventh or eighth picture, she gave up, though her eyes remained on the tablet. How had the plan suddenly become so complicated? First, she hadn't known how to delay him in demanding a divorce, and now she didn't know how to convince him that she wanted one, after all. No, that Rosemary wanted one. But she was supposed to be Rosemary. Oh, how had it come to this? Millie pressed her fingers to her temples to try to ward off what was building into a fearsome headache. The thought of leaving Seth tugged at her heart as fiercely as if they truly were married.

A heavy lump formed in her throat. She was being selfish again, thinking about herself and not her sister.

Flipping to a new page, she found her pencil strokes flowed easily, quickly. From practice. Rosemary loved to have her likeness sketched, until a few years ago, when out of frustration at her sister's latest antics, Millie had drawn Rosemary a bit chunkier than she was. That, too, had been selfish. Other than in the secrecy of her room, Millie hadn't drawn since then.

Her heartbeat quickened, and she didn't understand why until she lifted her head.

Seth stood at the bottom of the steps, more handsome than when he'd left this morning. But it was the smile on his face that was almost her undoing.

The tip of the lead snapped against the paper.

"Hi," he said, walking forward.

Wiping away the chunk of lead, which left a smear across the bottom of the page, Millie answered, "Hello." Thank goodness her voice wasn't as out of control as the flock of butterflies dancing a cotillion in her stomach. Ignoring them was next to impossible. So was finding where she'd buried her sister inside her.

"What are you doing?"

"Just drawing," she answered, making a few more strokes.

"May I?" He held a hand toward the pad of paper.

Shrugging, she passed it over. He'd already seen the picture, so there was no use attempting to hide it.

His gaze made several trips from the paper to her face, until her cheeks were burning.

"This isn't you."

Gulping inwardly, she searched for an answer that would make him believe it was a self-portrait and not a picture of Rosemary. "My hair is styled differently."

He studied the paper again. "No, that's not it. It's a good likeness, but it's not you."

Why had she been so foolish as to draw Rosemary? It was as if her very spirit wanted the truth out and was scheming against her. "Actually, it's my sister. Millie."

He pointed to the paper. "This is Millie?"

"Yes. That's her."

Seth studied her face for a moment more before gazing back at the pad. "Do you miss her?" he asked, before flipping through the other pages.

Her heart started hammering. He'd have to notice the drawings were all of him. "Doesn't everyone miss those left behind?" she asked, hoping to distract him from looking too closely at the pictures.

"Yes, we do," he answered, without looking up.

Folding her trembling hands in her lap, she asked, "Where's your family?"

"My brother is in Montana, my mother in Boston."

"You never mention them."

He shrugged. "I haven't seen them for years. Sam is in the army, too, and my mother writes to both of us regularly. She's remarried, to Ralph Wadsworth. They have three children together. They're all doing well." He flipped through a few more pages. "These are good. I didn't know you liked to draw."

"I guess there are a lot of things we don't know about each other."

His eyes were back on her, staring thoughtfully. The longing inside her, to kiss him again and have him hold her in his arms as he had last night in bed, stole her ability to think. The swirling in her stomach went lower, to the very spot it had been last night, and stirred up a tremendous heat and ache.

Still watching her, he leaned down, and it was as if a fire had been lit between them. She couldn't breathe, had never felt such intensity inside her. It was chaotic and exciting at the same time.

He took the pencil from her fingers and, barely moving, set both it and the tablet in the crate near his feet.

Millie was still holding her breath. Her lips were now trembling and the heat between them was growing. His eyes were watching hers and she didn't dare so much as blink for fear she'd miss something. She wasn't exactly sure what, but anticipation said it would be wonderful.

A smile lifted the corners of his mouth as his hands folded around hers, gently towing her out of the chair as he stepped back.

"Let's go inside," he whispered.

A thrill shot through her veins and she nodded.

"I'll get the box. You get your new umbrella."

The haze surrounding her thoughts dissipated enough for her to move and pick up the parasol from where it leaned against the porch railing. "Mr. Jenkins gave it to me."

"I know," Seth said, opening the door.

She was about to step inside when a wail like she'd never heard before echoed over the compound. Millie spun about, but couldn't see anything other than Seth, who was pushing her through the doorway.

"Stay here," he said, and then pulled the door shut.

Millie stood there for a matter of seconds, before her heart leaped into her throat and she wrenched the door open. Once on the porch, she saw Seth running across the compound, and she gave chase.

Chapter Eight

Millie hadn't gained any headway in catching up with Seth when someone grabbed her arm. She attempted to break loose, but the hold was too strong and brought her to an abrupt stop.

"It's not for you to become involved in, dear," Ilene Ketchum said. "Come back to the house."

Millie twisted, finding Seth among a swarm of men near the trading post. "What's happening?"

"I don't know for sure," the woman said, forcing her to turn about. "But I believe it's a skirmish between two Indian boys."

Twisting to keep her eyes on the crowd, her heart fluttering, Millie asked, "Was Wind one of them?"

"The men will take care of it."

"But—"

"Su-Ma and Ku-Ma-Quai are here with your

husband's lunch." Ilene pointed out the two women standing on the porch. "That is what you need to be concerned about. As Major Parker's wife, taking care of him should always be your first thought."

Millie stumbled, both physically and mentally, but caught herself and walked back to the house. She knew nothing about being a wife. Her gaze once again went to the crowd taking her husband, which included several Indian men.

Ilene pulled her across the threshold and shut the door. "Just put it in the kitchen, ladies. I'll help Mrs. Parker lay it out," she instructed.

Once again Millie faltered. The maidens had set the table back at the cabin, and she'd never questioned it. Frowning, she followed the others into the house and kitchen.

"We won't need those." Ilene gestured toward the tin plates Su-Ma set on the table. "That will be all now. Thank you."

Millie thanked the maidens as they piled the plates back in one of their crates and took their leave. But her attention was on Ilene, who'd started lifting fine china dishes out of the cupboards.

"Here, take these," she said. "I'll show you how to wrap the food so it stays warm until the major arrives."

Taking the matching plates and serving dishes,

Millie carried them to the table, listening as Ilene started to explain, "Now, in the winter, it's easier to keep food hot with a fire in the stove. During the summer months, I wrap the kettles with these miniature quilts. I made them myself and they work quite well. When the major arrives you just spoon everything into the serving bowls." While wrapping the kettles the maidens had left, Ilene gestured across the room. "You'll find the napkins in the drawer over there. I embroidered them with blue *P*s when I heard you were coming. Seth wasn't sure what your favorite color was, but I knew his was blue."

Millie found the napkins, beautiful cream-colored ones with a fancy *P* stitched in one corner. "Blue is my favorite color, too," she whispered, more to herself than the other woman. The letters were the same deep blue as Seth's eyes. If she'd never had a favorite color before, she did now.

"You know, dear, being a major's wife—an army wife in general—isn't for everyone. It's hard work." Ilene took the napkins and set them beside the plates.

Millie placed the silverware atop them, noting how nice the table looked compared to the tin plates and cups they'd used back at the cabin.

"I believe a proper wife knows how to make

a home presentable wherever that home may be located."

Pride had filled the woman's words and an invisible weight settled on Millie's shoulders.

"It is part of taking care of our husbands," Ilene continued. "Another part of being married to a commander is never questioning his actions. If they want to talk about things, we need to be good listeners, but we should never ask about what they've seen or had to do."

A hard knot formed in Millie's throat. "I don't know very much about being a wife."

"Of course you don't, dear, living apart as you have the past five years. When Jasper and I were first married, we lived apart, too. It's the way it was back then, for army wives. A tragedy for sure. Your mother wasn't the only wife to succumb to the loneliness."

A chill ran so deep Millie's entire body shivered. "You know about my mother?"

Ilene stepped closer, laid a tender hand on Millie's arm. "I knew your mother."

"You did?"

The other woman nodded. "Not well, but I met her a couple of times. Jasper and your father were well acquainted."

There were so many things swimming in her mind, Millie didn't know how to respond, and didn't have time to figure it out before the front door opened.

"That must be the major," Ilene whispered. "I'll let myself out the back door."

Maybe dreaming about kissing her all morning, or worrying about her while dealing with the incident with the children—even though he'd seen Ilene Ketchum take her back to the house—was the reason he was so anxious to see her. Either way, when Seth rounded the corner, saw her standing near the table set for lunch, his heartbeat sped up.

He'd been about to kiss her earlier, and the desire was just as strong now. But the atmosphere had changed. Releasing an inward sigh, knowing the moment was long gone, he wondered what to say, and finally stated, "The men didn't find any more snakes." He held in the groan that tried to escape. Reminding her of the snake had not been a good choice of words.

"That's a relief," she said, offering a wobbly smile. "Lunch is ready."

"It smells good," he answered, then pointed to the table. "This looks nice."

"Thank you." She carried a serving dish from the counter. "Mrs. Ketchum helped me."

He waited until she had the food set on the table, and then held her chair before taking his own. After filling his plate from the assortment of bowls, he ate slowly, watching her pick at the food she'd served herself. "Aren't you hungry?"

She nodded and lifted her fork, but it was obviously a show. He opened his mouth. Wind was fine, but she should never have purchased so much candy for him. Seth took another bite of food instead of voicing his thoughts. This was all new to her. She didn't understand that trading a single item was fine, but multiple items needed to be distributed evenly. That was the tribe's way, but Wind hadn't wanted to share his jackpot. If anyone but her had caused the skirmish, Seth would have already reprimanded the instigator. Things were precarious right now, and even fighting children could be enough to set off some of the tribes.

When his plate was empty—an act of habit, since his mind was ticking away—he laid his fork down and refilled his coffee cup. "I have to go back to headquarters. Will probably be there until evening."

She nodded, but was clearly deep in thought.

The silent treatment wasn't like her. Mealtime usually was full of her questions about everything from the meaning of Briggs's maidens' names to how many horses were in the stables. "Wind is fine," Seth finally said.

Her head snapped up, but she bit her lips together as if afraid to speak.

"Please don't purchase any more candy for him without asking me first."

She frowned. "I didn't charge it. I used my own money."

"That's not the issue. Everything given to the Indians has to be distributed evenly. It causes trouble if it's not."

She gave a slight nod, and after setting her cup on the table, lowered her hands to her lap and looked everywhere but at him. The air in the room seemed to take on a tension it hadn't before, not unlike how it did during deep negotiations with one of the tribal leaders.

"Did something else happen? Something I should know about?" Seth asked.

She barely blinked. Just sat as stiff and straight and stubborn as a mule, and her brown eyes had a dull glaze instead of their usual luster. He bristled. Rosemary was back. Leastwise, Millie was attempting to be her again.

"Nothing happened, and nothing is wrong," she said, lifting her chin slightly.

The way she sat there, had ire inching up his back like a slow-growing vine, twisting and curling along the way. "I'd prefer you not lie to me."

Her neck reddened as she drew an audible breath.

He knew how to handle soldiers, but this woman... He hadn't known what to do with her from the start. Then, as her eyes squinted and her lips pursed, life pitched him backward five years, except he wasn't sitting in her father's office.

Millie was good. Right now she caused an image of Rosemary to shoot across his mind like a bird flying past a window. Seth ran a hand through his hair. "Why are you here?" The back of his throat felt laced with shards of glass, suggesting he might not want to know her answer, yet he said, "The truth this time."

She swallowed hard, then answered, "Because you want a divorce."

He lifted a brow, waiting for more.

"And—and I'm not sure if I do."

That split him in two. He took the route he knew best. "Why? So you can go on seeing other men?" He'd heard things over the years, but chose not to pay attention, for they hadn't bothered him. Then. Now they did. If men at the fort heard of Rosemary's activities, they might assume Millie, in her guise as Rosemary, would behave in the same way.

"I'm not..." She took several deep breaths before pushing the chair away from the table. "I believe I shall pack my things. Corporal Kemper's snoring can't be as—as ghastly as your manners."

He was already on his feet, had been from the moment she'd spit out the word *pack*. Taking her arm, he willed self-control to keep his tone even. "No, you will not pack your bags. This is your house. This is my house. This is where we *both* will live."

She tugged free of his grasp. "I find it impossible to remain here."

He snatched both arms this time, with a hold she couldn't break, while frustration ate at his neck muscles. He should tell her he'd have a wagon ready in an hour to take her to Tulsa, but his tongue didn't want to create the words. He didn't want her to go, and that was a reality he couldn't quite accept. Nor was the idea of her living anywhere but at his side.

Her arms trembled and she closed her eyes. The glistening tear slipping out the corner of one eye melted his heart, or the armor around it, anyway. Without even knowing he'd declared it, she'd won their second battle, too. This time she hadn't even needed flowers and weeds.

He'd always been a sore loser. As evenly as possible, Seth demanded, "Why did you come here? Truthfully."

She covered her mouth with one hand for a moment, before lowering it to say, "To have you sign the divorce papers."

Tension burned his locked jaw. Releasing the muscles, he declared, "There was no need for that. I'd already signed them. All you had to do was sign on the line and return them to the law-yer in Richmond."

Shaking her head, she lowered her hand to the base of her throat. "Not those ones. Another set was drawn up."

"Why?"

She blinked several times. "B-because there are stipulations that needed to be addressed."

Anger was mounting inside him, but the tears she fought so hard to hide kept it simmering below the surface, which was worse. "Like what?"

Sniffling, she wiped a finger under her nose before answering, "I—I need to ensure my fu-ture is set…financially."

When she said certain things, he found him-self questioning how sure he was that this was Millie and not Rosemary, and that had his stomach churning. "I don't want your money," he snapped. "I told your father that the day we married."

Panic flashed across her face, so quickly he wondered if he'd imagined it, because the next moment she callously replied, "Perhaps it's not my money I'm talking about."

His blood turned colder than the Boston winters he clearly remembered. He'd never laid a hand on a woman, and wouldn't start now, but she could fear him. Should fear him. He wasn't going to be taken twice. Not by her sister and not by her. Ten-sion ate at his neck muscles, left them burning, and he used the sensation to fill his gaze with loathing. "My family's wealth is none of your concern." He'd made that perfectly clear before the wedding, as well. His seething mind told him to get rid of her now, but his damnable heart wouldn't let him.

There had to be a way to put a stop to her acting. For that's what this was again—the rational part of his brain had finally kicked in, and assured him that was so. It was just Millie trying to be Rosemary. His last attempt hadn't worked, not as he'd planned. Perhaps it was time to be himself. An army major.

"I won't stand for temper tantrums like your father did, and you'll do well to remember that." Pointing around the room, Seth continued slowly, clearly, so there'd be no mistaking his order. "Until we can safely travel to Tulsa, to Washington, this is where you live, so don't think you can throw a fit and move into one of the cabins. I will not—*will not*—" he repeated for emphasis "—have men I lead into battle believing my wife and I can't get along. In private you can do whatever you want, but in public you will behave as a major's wife. Is that understood?"

She gave a slight nod, which gave him absolutely no satisfaction.

"Good," he growled, spinning around. It wouldn't hurt for her to have one more thing to think about. "You also need to remember that only army personnel and wives of army men are allowed to live inside the barracks." He stopped shy of saying "not sisters."

Seth left then, grabbing his hat along the way and not caring how hard the door slammed behind him.

A coherent thought hadn't had time to enter his mind when someone said his name. Planting the hat on his head, and attempting to hide all that was going on inside him, he met the man at the end of the walkway. "Yes, Lieutenant?"

Paisley, with his eyes magnified behind thick glasses, held a piece of paper in his ink-stained fingers. "The lines are up. I sent the wire this morning and this reply just arrived."

Seth almost ripped the note out of the other man's hold. Unfolding it, he read the simple sentence. "NEITHER SISTER IS IN ATTENDANCE. STOP."

An invisible pull had him turning, glancing over his shoulder to his house. Handing the note back to the man, he said, "Burn this and find out where they both are."

"Yes, sir."

"And Paisley, no one knows about this except you and me. Make sure of that."

"Yes, sir."

Millie barely made it upstairs before sobs racked her so hard she could no longer move.

Not only had her muscles melted, her bones had dissolved, and pain encrusted her entire being. Pulling up Rosemary had been her only defense, but the hurt in Seth's eyes, the disbelief and loathing, had dissolved all thoughts of her sister and now had tears pumping out of her eyes like water from an artesian well.

Sometime later a noise below had Millie scurrying into her bedroom. There, drained, she crawled onto the bed and curled into a ball against the pain.

Tears still blurred her vision, but her gaze went to where her trunks sat. The divorce decree was in one, the papers Rosemary had drawn up— ones that said Seth had to give her a small fortune. Papa's money was all gone, and her sister insisted they'd need the money to care for the baby. Ultimately, that was the reason Millie was here.

Rosemary wouldn't care that her demands were hurting Seth, but she did, and she couldn't do it. Couldn't hurt him. It left her feeling disgraced beyond all she'd ever experienced.

The noise below had long since ended—the maidens gathering the dishes, no doubt. Millie rolled onto her back. Seth had explained how some Indian names translated into English, whereas others didn't—not into anything comparable, anyway. To-She-Wi meant Silver Brooch.

He'd said she'd given herself that name a few years ago when Briggs had given her a brooch. Su-Ma meant Number One, and Ku-Ma-Quai was Woman Who Eats Buffalo Meat. If Millie were a Comanche her name would mean One That Lies and Lies and Lies.

She hadn't lied about the divorce papers, but there was little solace to be found for one truth in a stack of deceit.

Pushing herself off the bed, Millie walked across the room, and looked out the window without really seeing anything, as she was too busy gazing inward. The thick, dreadful gloom inside her was massive, and grew when her eyes snagged on the other houses and buildings. Her deceit embraced so much.

Spinning around, she found the trunks lining the walls seemed to jeer at her, and the room threatened to close in, suffocating her. She had to get away from everything, everyone, at least for a few minutes.

Once she was downstairs, Seth's demand of how she appear in public had her repairing her hair and washing her face, while ghosts of their argument screamed at her from the kitchen, increasing her need to escape. Grabbing her sketchbook and pencil, she left the house and didn't stop walking until she'd exited the wide gates of the fort.

A short distance from the stone-and-wooden walls a cluster of tepees had a large number of people mingling around them. The sight of Indians no longer startled her; instead she found interest in their clothing and way of life. That was due to Seth. He held such respect when he spoke of them and their ways.

Moving closer, she found a rock to rest against, and sat down. The sound of a child crying reached her ears and she lifted her gaze, watched a woman pick up a toddler and cuddle it close.

The ache in her heart increased. Millie drew a breath, trying to control it, yet at the same time she couldn't pull her focus off the scene before her—how children need love and protection.

The child was soon consoled and waddled off again, but Millie continued watching the Indians, mainly the women and children.

Her mind played havoc on her emotions, recalling specific events that left her eyes burning with more unshed tears. She'd never met anyone who'd known her mother. Not even Lola had. Father had moved them to Richmond shortly afterward. He never spoke of what had happened.

Yet Ilene had said she'd known her. Millie shook her shoulders, repressing a quiver.

Your mother wasn't the only wife to succumb to the loneliness.

Loneliness? Millie understood loneliness, had

for years. Truth was, the only time she hadn't felt it had been since arriving at the fort. Not once in the past few days, even while Seth had been out with troops or over at headquarters, had she been lonely. She'd missed him, but knew he'd be home soon, and people stopped in to see her continuously. Moments of the past few days, times of laughter and joy, flashed through her mind, and then came the poignant moment of the argument with Seth.

The air in her lungs grew stale, and she let it out slowly. If he told her to leave...

Millie pressed a hand to her aching forehead. Her mind was exhausted, couldn't comprehend that event right now.

Flipping open her tablet, she picked up the pencil to let whatever wanted to be drawn appear on the paper.

The first few pictures included Seth, but eventually her fingers copied what lay before her, the Indian village. Page after page, she drew images. Some of single people—a woman building a fire—and some of groups: three children chasing each other; young boys caring for a herd of horses grazing on the stiff brown grass; women dumping ingredients into large wooden bowls and then mixing everything together with their hands.

The sun was low in the sky when Millie felt

her heartbeat speed up. Only one person did that to her. She closed her eyes when an elongated shadow fell over her paper.

He sat down next to her, and though Millie opened her eyes, she didn't glance his way, merely absorbed his nearness. Keeping her gaze on the paper, she continued drawing a scene of three women she assumed were tanning a deer hide.

As badly as she knew what had to be done, the energy it would take was currently beyond her. Perhaps if she ignored him he'd go away. A smile almost touched her lips at the absurdity of that. Seth was not a man who could be ignored, nor one who would leave a woman sitting in the middle of the prairie by herself, no matter who she was and how much he despised her.

She flinched and the pencil shot across the page.

"I didn't mean to disturb you," he said.

"You didn't." She set the pencil on top of the paper resting on her lap, and shifted slightly to make sure her skirt covered her ankles, just for something to do. "This one wasn't turning out like I wanted."

"I think it's very good."

Unable to accept praise of any kind right now, she frowned. Mrs. Ketchum had said a good wife didn't ask questions, but Millie was as far from being a good wife as could be.

Gesturing toward the tepees, she asked, "Why'd they set up their homes here? They weren't here yesterday." She stopped shy of adding, "when you took me riding." Reminding herself of that joy right now would spoil the memory, and someday she'd want it to be pure, so she could smile when it came to mind.

"Per-Cum-Ske wants to go to Washington with me," Seth answered, plucking a blade of grass to twirl between his fingers.

She still hadn't looked his way, couldn't, but hearing his voice, and seeing his hands out the corner of her eye, had her heart thudding again. "Why?"

"To make sure the needs of his people are heard."

"I thought that was why you're going."

He tossed aside the grass. "It is, but others have gone before me, and things haven't improved. He has no reason to believe they will this time, either."

The distress in Seth's voice had compassion swirling inside her. No matter what her issues were, they didn't change him. He was a good person who cared deeply about the Indians and his duties to oversee their welfare.

"Will you let him go?" she asked.

"I haven't decided yet."

"Are you still planning on going soon?"

"Yes. Before the end of the month."

Knowing she couldn't ask him to wait until December again, since she'd seen for herself how important the trip was, Millie searched for another topic. "Where do they get the poles for their tepees?"

"They bring them with them," he said. "When they leave there won't be a single sign left behind that they've been here, except some trampled grass."

"What are they made of, the walls of the tepees?"

"Hides they tan and sew together. Then they decorate them with die made from berries and such."

"They're very resourceful people," she said.

"Yes, they are. There was a time when the land gave them everything they needed."

Millie nodded. Seth had explained the way things used to be for the Indians one night while eating supper. During the silence that settled between them now, she picked up the pencil and filled in the deer hide on the drawing.

The clothes of the women—one wearing a leather tunic-type shift, and two others wearing cotton dresses they'd cut off near their knees—had been filled in, as well, when he let out a sigh.

Unable not to, Millie glanced his way, and the

sincerity in his eyes had her dropping her gaze instantly.

"I didn't come out here to talk about them," he said.

Sorrow tightened the skin on her cheeks and a heaviness invaded her stomach, yet she nodded.

"I came to apologize to you. I'm sor—"

"Don't," she insisted, swallowing the sob burning her throat. He held no fault in any of this, and she couldn't bear to hear him apologize. "Please don't say you're sorry."

"I am. I shouldn't have—"

"Please, Seth." The tears were back, pressing hard and making her blink. Taking a breath, she said, "I'm sorry, too, but that's not… I can't…" An explanation wouldn't come out. How could it when she didn't know what she was trying to say? What she could say.

"What do you want me to say?" he asked.

Millie thought for a moment, wondered what Rosemary would say, and if she had the wherewithal to pull her sister up right now. The uncertainty in Seth's voice—a man who was so full of confidence—was like a knife slicing her heart in two. Knowing her sister would never say what Millie was about to didn't stop her. Right now she had to be herself, and be honest with him.

"I don't know what I want," she whispered.

He was quiet for a few minutes, and she tried

to put her emotions back into the little imaginary box she'd enclosed them in earlier. Saving them for a day when she could cherish every moment.

"Can I put my arm around you?" he asked.

Her little box wasn't very strong, for it exploded as if hit by the force of a locomotive. Not trusting her voice, she nodded.

The arm that stretched over her back to cup her shoulder was not only familiar, its touch sent calming relief spreading through her system. It was so comforting that even her spirit felt soothed. Drawn to him, she leaned his way and tilted her head to rest it against his shoulder.

His jaw gently bumped her forehead, and a sweet blanket of solace covered her from top to bottom and inside out. She loved her body when it touched his. The sensations were unique and precious, and so utterly amazing. This was for her imaginary box, something she'd remember forever, and she closed her eyes, embedding the moment deep inside.

Not so long ago she'd wondered how a person knew when he or she had fallen in love. Well, now she knew. And the thread of pain flowing through these wonderful, life-changing feelings was enough to make her wish she didn't. Loving Seth altered everything. Inside her, that was. But it didn't alter the fact there was nothing she could do.

When she opened her eyes, the brilliance before her had her blinking. The sun had met the earth at the far-off horizon, and the way it splayed a rainbow of colors—reds, yellows, oranges, pinks, blues and purples—over the great flat land made it impossible to tell where the ground ended and the sky began. The irony of the scene made a heartrending smile tug on her lips. The sunset was exactly like the feelings overwhelming her. There was no way to tell where the love began or ended, nor the pain.

"Beautiful, isn't it?" Seth asked, knowing she was staring at the sunset. He'd never been in this state before, this gray area of being neither right nor wrong. It was not only frustrating, it left him lacking, searching for answers that wouldn't come.

"Yes, it is," she whispered.

Even though he was holding her, he wanted more, and it wasn't just physical. This went deeper than that. He'd known that right after walking out of the house this afternoon. When it came to her, he didn't want to be an army major. He just wanted to be man. A plain and simple man.

Russ had came to headquarters an hour or so after lunch, said she'd walked out the gate. The corporal offered to go after her, but Seth said he'd go himself. He had, and for the past several hours he'd sat a short distance away, watching her.

A dozen scenarios had played in his mind during that time, but the one that stood out was that he had to face the truth. He could put himself in dangerous situations, lead a charge of men into a heated battle, and defy death head-on, because there was no one he had to worry about leaving behind. No widow or children to mourn him.

Somehow, in some unimaginable way, he'd fallen in love. The one thing he'd sworn never to do. With a woman who didn't exist. She was flesh and blood, but beyond that it all became a little hazy. The very fact that he felt the way he did proved she was Millie and not Rosemary, and that, too, only complicated things.

The fort was no place for her. She was too gentle for such harshness. But he couldn't come clean, either, tell her he knew who she was, because then he'd have to send her away. Army regulations stated she couldn't live here, not without being married. He'd pointed that out himself, which meant the sham had to continue.

Sitting there watching her, he'd thought of many things, including his mother. How she'd cried after his father had died, but only when she thought no one was near.

Amanda Parker-Wadsworth was a strong woman. He'd heard that his entire life, still did, and knew it to be true. Though she hadn't wallowed in her grief, it had changed her. He'd seen that, too. His father's death had changed Seth, too. His dreams, his plans. And that had led to something else he couldn't abide. His death—that of a husband, or someday, maybe a father—would affect other people. People he loved. Namely, one very pretty woman currently nestled against his side.

Seth had also wondered, while thinking of his mother, what her dreams had been. He'd bet they hadn't been to run a shipbuilding company, yet she had. When her husband and brothers were called to fight in the war, she'd taken over the helm, overseen the building of ships that were still carrying supplies up and down the eastern seaboard and making the entire family very wealthy.

Some thought marrying Ralph Wadsworth had been a business move for her. The man had worked for a competitor before their marriage, but Seth now wondered if his mother had remarried so that he and his brother could move on. Go to West Point as they'd always dreamed. He hoped not, but while entertaining the fact that he'd fallen in love, he'd started to wonder just how far people might go to make someone they loved happy. Perhaps even as far as pretending to be someone they weren't.

The sun was slowly fading and early stars were

popping out in a purple-hued sky when Per-Cum-Ske walked toward them.

"Major." The Indian leader stepped closer as they rose to their feet. "Your wife?"

Seth hooked a hand on Millie's hip and tugged her a bit closer to his side. "Yes, this is my wife. Mrs. Parker."

Per-Cum-Ske, standing tall with shoulders squared, gestured toward the three women behind him. "My wives."

Tightening his hold when she wobbled slightly against him, Seth nodded toward the women. "*Maruawe.* Hello."

Once they'd responded in kind, Per-Cum-Ske said, "You, your wife, eat with my family."

Seth looked down at the woman beside him, letting her know it was her choice. Her eyes were thoughtful, glimmering in the fading light, yet a little smile formed as she nodded.

"Yes," he told Per-Cum-Ske. "We'll join you." As the others started walking toward their tepees, he held her back. "Are you sure?"

She glanced from the camp to him before nodding. "Yes, I'm sure." Seconds later, as they started to follow, she whispered, "What does Per-Cum-Ske mean?"

"The Hairy One."

"Oh." Glancing up with a mystified expression, she asked, "And all three of those women are his wives?"

Smiling, for some of her expressions were too adorable not to grin at, Seth answered, "Yes, all three of them."

Eyes wide, she gazed at the women.

His mind, the one small section he still had control over, wondered how she was going to react to the meal. There would be no table, no chairs, no silverware or pot of tea. His nerves started ticking, and he glanced over his shoulder, checking the sentry seated in his lookout post. If the Rosemary he'd met five years ago suddenly appeared and sat down on the ground with Per-Cum-Ske and his wives, there just might be an Indian uprising before the meal ended.

An hour later, Seth was eating his thoughts, while his wife had the entire tribe eating out of her hand. The charm and grace she'd portrayed most of the time since arriving at the fort had captured the band as easily as it had won him over, especially when she allowed them to pass her sketchbook around. Laughter had abounded as members pointed to themselves on the pages.

Per-Cum-Ske now rested the book across his folded legs, carefully examining each page, and frowning so deeply Seth's spine quivered.

"How you draw," Per-Cum-Ske asked, gesturing across the fire, "Major Parker so—" the leader squared his shoulders and lifted his thick, square jaw "—perfect, and draw you—" he was now gesturing toward Millie as he pulled his face into a fierce grimace "—so ugly?"

Fire shot up Seth's back, but his wife's laughter launched the entire tribe into hoots and guffawing.

Still laughing, she reached over and folded her fingers around his hand. The firelight shone in her eyes and made her cheeks glow as she glanced up at him. "Because," she said, "I can look at him." Turning to Per-Cum-Ske, she pointed to her eyes and then patted her chest. "I can't look at myself. I have to draw from memory." She pointed to her temple. "I have to think what I look like."

The leader shook his head and, making a show of turning the page, said, "Think better. Harder."

Her giggle floated on the air and swirled all the way around Seth as she leaned her head against his shoulder.

Gently bumping her, he teased, "I told you it wasn't a good likeness."

"Yes, you did," she said, still giggling.

It was amazing all the things she manifested inside him, the way she had him looking at the world in a different way.

"You draw me and my wives?" Per-Cum-Ske

asked, handing her the tablet. "So I take to Washington, show Great Chief."

"Yes, I will draw you and your wives," she said, setting the paper on the ground beside her. "But not now." Pointing to the sky, she explained, "I need the sunlight."

"Tomorrow?" the leader asked.

Chapter Nine

Millie dipped her head beneath the warm bath-water and rubbed her scalp with both hands, rinsing away the bubbles. Goodness, drawing was exhausting. Sitting up and wringing the excess water out her long hair, she rebuked herself. Not exhausting. Exhilarating. Never had anything consumed her as her art had the past several days. The hours between when Seth left her near the rock in the morning until he came to fetch her each afternoon were spent drawing, and drawing, and drawing.

From braves carrying deer carcasses across the backs of their horses, to babies tied in cradle boards leaning against rocks as their mothers foraged for things Millie would never have imagined were edible, and everything in between. It was amazing to have a job to do, something people wanted from her. But the most thrilling aspect was the pride in Seth's eyes every night when he looked through the tablets. She'd never experienced anything like it, was amazed at how it made her feel so significant, so useful and important.

She did try to convince herself she should be uncomfortable with all his praise. Tried, but failed, because his attention was far from unpleasant. Frustrating maybe, but that was her fault. Since the day—ten excruciating days ago—when she'd seen the snake, he hadn't tried to kiss her.

Sometimes, especially during lunchtime, when he'd carry a basket out and they'd share the meal on her blanket beneath the open sky, she sensed he wanted to. Something in his eyes said so, but she pretended not to notice.

It's what needed to happen, but not kissing him felt worse than kissing him. Desire had compounded inside her until she was so fraught with need she was sure that if she sat on a pin she'd explode.

After they'd left the Indian camp the night Per-Cum-Ske had asked her to draw him, they'd come home and prepared for bed, and Seth had asked if she was fearful of sleeping in her room. She'd had to say she wasn't. He'd still offered his room, said they could trade, but she assured him she'd be fine, and had been every night since.

Fine was hardly the word. She was miserable.

There hadn't been any more snakes, and she rarely thought of them, but that had little to do with it. A serious change had happened between her and Seth. He was still attentive and charming, and they'd formed a unique companionship—something akin to friendship that went deeper, filled her with such warmth there was no place for fear or worry.

"Where are you?"

Just the sound of his voice filtering into the room had her heart racing and put a smile on her lips.

"Come out, come out, wherever you are."

Millie stifled a giggle. "I'm taking a bath," she yelled, and then held her breath as footfalls stopped outside the door. Just knowing he was in the hall had her skin tingling.

"Need any help?" he asked through the wood.

He'd started teasing her lately, in a way no one had ever done before, and the delight lingered long after the moment. In an ironic way, it satisfied some of her longing, while increasing it at the same time. It had all been baffling until she'd come to understand it. Mrs. Ketchum had explained it while sitting with her as she drew one day. The woman said a wife's role was to relieve her husband of the worries he constantly carried, and how teasing brought out the child within and made a person feel carefree. Millie enjoyed knowing she did that for Seth, and welcomed his bouts of playfulness.

"No," she said, while wondering what he'd do if she said yes. "What do you need?" She slid the bar of soap up and down her arms, hurrying to complete her bath and join him in the parlor, where they'd sit and talk of little things. Afterward he'd walk her up the stairs and wish her good-night, at which point her longing to cross the hall and lie next to him would keep her awake for hours.

The doorknob rattled. "If I tell you what I really want, will you give it to me?"

The bar of soap shot out of her hand, landed on the floor with a thud.

"Is that a yes?" he asked.

Splashing to quickly rinse the last of the suds from her arms before her heart exploded, she searched for an answer to keep him on the other side of the door. He was using the tone that made her stomach simmer like a pot about to boil, and when he sounded like that the glow in his eyes made her toes curls. Leaping out of the tub, she answered, "I'll save my bathwater for you."

"You always save me your water."

She lifted a towel off the stool. "There's no sense wasting it."

"Wasting it? You only save it because you don't want to carry it out back."

With the towel tucked beneath her armpits, covering her front to her thighs, and her hair still dripping water, she opened the door a crack. "There might be snakes out there."

His blue eyes were sparkling and her toes curled against the floor.

"There might be. So don't empty the tub. I'll do it when I get back." He touched the tip of her nose with one finger.

Excitement zipped under her skin at the simple connection, yet disappointment pulled her lips downward. "You have to go back to headquarters? It's been dark for hours."

His grin widened. "Yes, Jasper and Per-Cum-Ske and I are going through the pictures to send to Washington, but we can't find a specific one." Reaching through the narrow opening, he brushed a clump of hair off her forehead. "It's one of three women tanning a deer hide. Do you remember it?"

Breathing was difficult, and thinking hard, yet she managed a nod.

"You drew it that first day," he said, tucking the hair behind her ear. "Do you know where that sketchbook is?"

Her fingers wrapped more firmly around the door handle, clutching it with all her might in order to keep her trembling body from melting onto the floor and joining the water dripping into a pool between her feet. The notion of stretching onto the tips of her toes and kissing him was so strong she had to shake her head in order to clear her mind enough to answer. "It's in my trunk. The one next to the door. There's a pouch inside the lid."

"Mind if I get it?" he asked, now smoothing the hair behind her ear all the way to her shoulder.

She wondered what he'd do if she pulled the door open and let the towel slip to the floor. Heavens, but that was a wanton thought if ever she had one. But an enticing one, too. Swallowing against the growing urge to do just that, she answered, "No, I don't mind, go ahead."

"Thanks." Pinching her cheek, he winked. "I'll be home as soon as I can. Leave the water."

He was long gone, thudding up the stairs, when she whispered, "I will." After shutting the door, she plopped onto the bench and let the air out of her lungs slowly. Goodness, he continued to grow more handsome, and more endearing, and more lovable every day, and she grew more desperate.

Martin had been right. Women did grow amorous when alone for long period of times. Like an hour. Pressing a hand to the heat beneath her belly, she sighed heavily. Yes, she now fully understood what Martin had meant. She even had a touch of understanding for Rosemary's behavior. Millie had thought it outrageous then, but now she could grasp what her sister meant.

Another sigh built and she had to let it out. She'd even spoken to Mrs. Ketchum about it. Not that she'd broached the topic; Ilene had brought it up on one of her visits. The woman's companionship had become very special to Millie. They'd even spoken of her mother, and loving Seth as she did—all these reactions boiling around inside her body were confirmation of the love she had for him —she grew to understand how much her parents must have loved each other. How badly it had pained them to be separated.

She wished her mother—and Rosemary— could have had the friends she now did. Other women to help them understand all the complexities of men. One of Per-Cum-Ske's wives had become a dear friend, too, which was another part of the reason everything made sense now.

Leah-Widd-I-Kah—One Who Stirs Up Water— had explained it, as well as many other things. The Indian leader was very amorous. All he had to do was look at one of his wives and they'd followed him into his tepee. No matter what they were doing or what time of day it was.

A few days ago, extremely curious as to what took place, Millie had asked her newfound friend. Without a hint of embarrassment, Leah-Widd-I-Kah had explained everything. Everything. Even in broken English, Millie had completely understood. Perhaps because now, unlike when Martin had told her a few things, she could relate, knew exactly what the other woman described. And it not only had increased a hundred times over the desire she had to lie with Seth, it prevented her from thinking of just about anything else. Leah-Widd-I-Kah didn't understand how a married couple hadn't already shared their love, and assured her that when they did, it would make them both very, very happy.

The one thing Millie couldn't understand was how Leah-Widd-I-Kah could allow her husband to do that with other women. Millie could never share Seth.

A knock on the door had her jumping to her feet.

"I got it. I'll be back soon," Seth said, before she gathered the towel off the floor. "Don't float away in there."

Giggling, for even with all the frustration eating at her, he made her smile, she said, "I won't." Hearing his footfalls, she eased the door open an inch, just enough to watch him walk out the front door.

It was more than an hour later when he finally walked through it again.

Over her nightgown she wore a blue flannel housecoat that had three large pearl buttons she absolutely adored. It was very pretty and Mrs. Ketchum had told her how important it was to always look pretty for her husband, so she was sitting on the divan in the parlor, where she'd brushed her hair until it was completely dry. Millie smiled, watching him remove his hat and jacket. She cherished this time, when all was calm and quiet, and it was just the two of them.

"Hi," she murmured.

"Hi." He walked into the room. "I'm glad to see you didn't float away."

"There was no chance of that," she said, setting the brush aside. "And I saved you my water."

He nodded, but the grin on his face wasn't quite as bright as normal.

A shiver rippled her back, settled deep between her shoulder blades. Concerned, she asked, "Didn't you find the picture you needed?"

"Yes." He held the sketch pad in one hand, and as he lifted the cover she noticed an envelope.

Her stomach rolled. It was Rosemary's divorce papers. If Millie had been thinking straight she'd have remembered they were in the same pouch as the sketchbook.

Tapping a corner of the envelope against the

pouch, he said, "It was inside the tablet. I didn't notice it until I was back at my office."

A chill had her skin quivering. "Did you sign it?"

Frowning, he stared at her for a moment before he shook his head. "No, I didn't even open it."

Relief had her wanting to close her eyes, but she didn't. Just nodded, accepting his answer.

He set the envelope and her sketchbook on one of the two tapestry chairs in front of the fireplace, and then moved to the window, where he held the curtain aside and stared out into the darkness. His broad back was stiff and the air in the room grew dreary and heavy.

"Will you answer a question for me?" He moved back to the chair, leaned both hands on the back. "Tell me the truth?"

"Yes," she said, even with anxiety welling in her chest.

"Do you want a divorce?"

A bone-chilling fear raced through her, so fast it felt as if flames leaped to life under her skin. An impossibility, so cold it was hot, yet it was fitting. Telling him the truth was just as impossible. Unable to face him, she studied her hands, ran a thumb over the slickness of her fingernails. But when they started trembling too hard, she laced her fingers together, all the while searching for an answer. There was no sense trying to pull up Rosemary. That wouldn't help. Besides, Millie was done playing that game. She'd given it up the day of their last argument.

"Do you?" he asked quietly.

She had to close her eyes in order to find the fortitude to answer. Blinking at the moisture on her lashes, she said, "If our marriage was…" Shaking her head, she tried again. "If you and I had said the words spoken five years ago, and meant them, then no, I wouldn't want a divorce." Hurrying, before he could grasp exactly what she'd said, what she'd just told him, she continued, "However, as it is, with the way things are, resulting from that day, then yes, the divorce is still needed."

He turned, walked back to the window, and she bowed her head, biting her lip so hard she tasted blood. Here, too, things were convoluted. She'd never want to divorce him, but she wasn't married to him. Rosemary was.

It was several minutes before he moved, turned around and then walked all the way across the room without glancing her way. "I'm going to empty your bathwater. I'll see you in the morning."

Her mouth had a mind of its own. Before she realized it had opened, she heard herself saying, "It doesn't have to happen until December."

With one hand on the banister as he turned

the corner toward the hallway, he stiffened and twisted to look at her.

She pressed the hand she'd slapped over her mouth harder against her lips. His frown was fierce, but it was the squint of his eyes that sent her heart into her throat.

Shaking his head again, he turned, and a moment later the bathing room door shut so hard she flinched.

A powerful anger rose, so fast and severe that Millie wanted to scream, hurl things across the room or pummel both fists against something until it hurt as bad as she did. Never in her entire life had she thrown a fit, but right now, she wanted to throw one that would leave all of Rosemary's in the dust.

Instead, Millie grabbed the brush and yanked it through her hair until her scalp burned. Then she marched up the steps. This wasn't right. It wasn't fair. It wasn't how things should be. Seth didn't deserve to be treated this way, and neither did she.

In her room, Millie moved to the window, stared into the darkness. Not even thinking about the baby helped, an innocent life that held no blame. She was beyond that. Past living her life for what others needed. It was unseemly to think only about herself, her desires, but ultimately, she only had until December to love Seth. Then

she'd have to leave. Return to Richmond and—
A growl filled her throat.

This whole thing was erroneous. Her entire
life had been.

The freedom she'd experienced lately, and the
hours she'd spent drawing, where her mind had
time to quiet down and reveal things she'd never
had time to focus on before, had given her a new
perspective on so many things. As had the friend-
ships she'd made. The foremost one being with
the man downstairs. The only husband she'd ever
want.

A single star appeared in the cloudy night
sky on the other side of the glass. October was
well upon them, bringing cooler days and colder
nights. Six weeks at most and this would all be
over, and no one would ever know how painful it
had been for her. As Millie found the star again,
a somewhat shocking, but appealing thought occurred to her. No one would ever know what took
place out here, except for her and Seth.

She pressed a hand over her lips as the thought
expanded. She spun toward the bed as a thrill
had her sucking in her stomach. That would be
so improper. So inappropriate.

Spinning around, she paced the floor. Pretending to be his wife—really his wife, in every
way—would only increase the deception. Furthermore, it would be entirely selfish on her part.

The thought of kissing him, of doing all the things Leah-Widd-I-Kah had told her about, had her insides swirling. Steaming. Millie closed her eyes against the temptation pounding inside her.

It would be wrong. Wrong. And trickery. Worse than what she was already doing.

Stopping at the window, she searched the darkness for an answer that couldn't be found. There wasn't a solution, leastwise not one she could fathom justifiable. Even while the longing to give herself to Seth, to have what other married couples had, if only for a short time, grew stronger, more intense.

Her skin became clammy and she lifted the window sash, hoping for a cooling breeze. A faint drumming sound entered with the night air, and the steady beats resounded in her soul, matching the thuds of her heart. Leah-Widd-I-Kah had said the Comanche would call to the Great Spirit tonight, asking for guidance in Per-Cum-Ske's journey to speak with the men in Washington.

The beats continued to resonate, all the way to her befuddled mind. "Oh, dear Lord," she whispered, her words matching the steady thumps of the drums. "I need your help. A sign. Something that will tell me what to do."

The drumming stopped. She opened her eyes and stared into the darkness. Even the tiny star was gone, and no matter how hard she searched, its flickering light couldn't be found. A long and hollow sigh left her slumped against the window-sill. What had she hoped? That all of a sudden the stars would spell out Seth's name? Tell her it was all right to love him? To be with him? That was a foolish thought if ever she had one.

Noises echoed from below, hoofbeats and shouts, but such sounds no longer startled her, for the fort was seldom silent. The knock that came at the front door, though, had her rushing across the room.

She was halfway down the stairs when she froze.

Seth stood in the doorway. His hair was wet, still held the comb marks, and he wore nothing but his britches, with both suspenders hanging from the waistband, the loops resting near his knees.

His arms were bare and bulged with muscles, as was his back, and she wrapped her fingers around the banister at the sight of his glistening skin.

"Ma'am."

Millie tugged her gaze away and nodded at the corporal tipping his hat.

"What is it?" Seth asked.

"Sorry to interrupt, Major, sir, but two mule skinners just rode in. Said they'd been chased by Indians the entire way. Their animals looked it, too."

"Have the M troop mount up," Seth instructed, spinning to hurry back down the hallway.

Millie didn't even nod when Corporal Kemper bade her farewell and pulled the door closed. The only thing keeping her where she stood was Mrs. Ketchum's advice. A major's wife doesn't question her husband's actions. But Millie wasn't his wife. Not really, and even if she was, she doubted she'd ever be a good one.

Seth came out of the bathing room, snapping his suspenders over his white shirt, and she lost the ability to keep her mouth shut. "When will you be back?" she asked, in place of begging him not to go.

"I don't know." He lifted his coat off the back of the chair near the door, where he always hung it. "Don't leave the house."

"I won't." She moved down the steps, somewhat amazed at how calm she could pretend to be when fear had her heart racing. The way he watched her made her try harder, to force even her fingers not to tremble. Brushing his hands aside, she buttoned the jacket, holding her breath at the way his eyes followed her movements.

"You'll be fine," he said, reaching for his hat.

"Yes, I will," she said. "And so will you."

The smile that appeared on his lips played with

her heart, filling it with sweetness, while panic squeezed the life from it at the same time. She pulled the ends of the yellow scarf held on his jacket by the shoulder bars, and tied it in a loose knot.

One of his fingers settled beneath her chin, forcing her face up. She closed her eyes for a moment, contemplating. Right or wrong, she loved this man, and knowing she might very well be sending him into battle made that love even more precious.

Lifting her lids, she met the gentle caress of his gaze, and in that moment she honestly didn't care whose husband he was. He'd become a hero in her eyes, some magnificent knight in armor that had swept into her life and saved her from fire-breathing dragons, highwaymen and all the other evil-doers of the world, all the while remaining a flesh-and-blood man who had stolen her heart.

He stared directly into her eyes for what seemed an eternity before he said, "Yes, I'll be fine."

"I'll wait up for you."

"No, you go to bed," he said. "It may be several hours."

The desire to beg him not to go grew, and there was only one thing she could think to do. Rising on the tips of her toes, she pressed her lips to his.

He hesitated, a brief poignant moment in

which Millie was too afraid to breathe. Then his hands grasped her waist and lifted her into his arms. She caught his shoulders, and held on as their lips met and parted and met again in an almost desperate fashion.

He pulled back, but then, cupping her cheek, kissed her again, before whispering, "I have to go."

"I know," she answered. "I'll be here when you get back."

His lips quirked in the confident grin she loved as he cupped her other cheek. "You'd better be."

This time his kiss was long and tender, and when she wobbled, he held on tighter. As soon as the kiss ended, he turned and left. Which was for the best. That way he didn't see the tears flowing down her cheeks.

Chapter Ten

Seth rode front and center, flanked by the M troop on both sides and followed by a dozen more soldiers. It was where he always rode. That was about the only thing that hadn't changed. He hadn't really thought about it before, where he rode. It hadn't mattered, because if something were to happen to him, the men beside him would continue on. On the field or at the fort. Jasper would take over. Nothing would change.

Nothing.

But inside him, everything had changed, making this the first time he'd ever ridden though the gates desperately praying he'd return in one piece. For her and for him. For them.

A man could take only so much before he snapped. Seth had used that fact against his opponents regularly, but this was the first time he'd felt it himself. When he'd left the house earlier this evening, the image of Millie peeking around the washroom door with dripping, tangled hair falling across wet, glowing shoulders, and grinning like a mystical imp, had danced in his head, and that picture returned now. Actually, it had never really left him, not even when he'd found the envelope tucked between the pages of the tablet.

His question had been a fact finding mission, he'd thought. Whereas really, there was no right or wrong answer. He'd realized that sitting in the bathtub full of chilly water still carrying her scent. The papers had thrown him for a loop— had him thinking it was her he'd be divorcing. It wouldn't be. It would be her sister. He'd remembered that, too, in the bathtub. Millie was the woman he'd fallen in love with, and Millie was the one waiting for him back at their house. Yet he wasn't married to Millie.

Was this some kind of demonic curse? He'd never wanted to fall in love, and when he had, it was to a woman he couldn't marry, one he couldn't proclaim his love to because she couldn't know he knew who she was.

Even with his mind twisted, his sight was clear, and he reined in his horse, holding up an arm for the soldiers to follow suit, near the edge of Per-Cum-Ske's village.

The leader stood there, flanked by braves. The

two of them, Seth and the chief, had known each other for years as allies and enemies, and at times that had made dealings more difficult.

"No one in Washington will talk to either of us about better provisions if an attack happens right now," Seth said, without dismounting. "Even an attack on one man."

Per-Cum-Ske waved an arm. "We are here."

Seth showed no emotion, which in the past hadn't been this difficult. Knowing Millie, with sweet, petal-soft lips and smelling like a bouquet of sun-kissed flowers, was depending on him to return, made his desire for peace stronger than ever. "Are you saying those weren't Comanches chasing those men?"

The leader made no sign of a response.

Riding off in the dark of night, chasing down braves who'd had the time to find strategic hiding places and set up their attack, was dangerous, crazy even, but Seth would do it. They wouldn't expect that, which was what had made him the commander he was today. Doing whatever it took to gain the upper hand and keep it. He'd been able to because he'd had no worries. No one to leave behind if his plan failed. That wasn't so now, but he couldn't let it change him.

"I know they're Comanche," he said, displaying none of the companionship he'd shown to the leader the past several days. "No other tribe would come this close to your village." His horse shifted and he let it take a full step closer to Per-Cum-Ske. "You round them up or else I will. But know that if I go after them, I will make no concessions, show no mercy, and when I return neither of us will be going to Washington."

The air grew heavy, tense, as they faced off, neither man blinking an eye. Seth knew staredowns. There'd been a time he'd thrived on reading what was playing inside his opponent's mind. Right now he was impatient for it to end. As the realization clicked, so did something else. He'd never had anyone to protect before, either, and thinking of Millie, her safety, had a mountain of determination growing inside him.

"I warned you," he said, wrenching on his horse's reins.

"Wait," Per-Cum-Ske said. "I go to Washington."

Seth issued a silent curse. He hadn't yet agreed to let the Indian go, and this had been Per-Cum-Ske's way of pushing him into a decision. If Seth had been paying closer attention, he'd have seen it coming. His mind may have been elsewhere before, but it was focused now. He had more to lose than ever before.

"I haven't decided that yet," he said. "Behavior like this makes my decision more difficult. I won't travel with men I can't trust."

The movement was slight, but Seth saw it—the slight bow of disgrace Per-Cum-Ske displayed. "I find them. I stop them."

"I'll go with you."

The leader surveyed the soldiers with a cold gaze.

"Just me," Seth said.

Per-Cum-Ske lifted his square jaw.

"I don't ride with men I don't trust," Seth said again.

This time the Indian let his action be seen by everyone. He bowed his head in acceptance and waved for his horse to be brought forward. "Just you and me."

"Just me and you," Seth repeated, hoping he wasn't making the second biggest mistake in his life. As an army commander, he knew when to send others to do a chore and when he had to do it himself. This was one of those times where he had to be the one to go, and that had his stomach churning.

It was several hours later, deep in the night, when even the locusts were sleeping, that he finally rode back through the gates of the fort. The four braves, who he'd seen at Per-Cum-Ske's village mere days ago, had been apprehended, and he did believe the leader when he'd vowed there were no more.

Seth relayed the outcome of the event to

Jasper, who met him in the stables, and then hurried toward his house, where he found Corporal Kemper sitting guard on his front porch.

"She's asleep in the parlor," Russ said. "I checked on her a few minutes ago."

"Thank you," Seth said, with a throat full of gravel. He'd been gone only a few hours, but he missed her. Missed her like he hadn't ever missed anything before, and in all honesty, he didn't want it any other way.

She wasn't his wife—that bit of reality had worn down the more he'd rolled it around in his mind, became less of an issue. He was the only one who knew, besides her and her sister. Rosemary wasn't a concern to him. Their marriage wasn't real. Never had been. To him it was even more nonexistent than it had been before. What he'd focused on the last few hours was the fact that Millie didn't want a divorce—had said so herself. Any number of things could have happened out there tonight and she would have never known how he really felt.

He wasn't going to take that chance again.

Seth entered quietly and removed his coat and hat, and after one step, when his boot heels echoed in the silence, he removed his footwear, as well. Then he crossed the room and knelt down next to the sofa, where she was curled on her side, both hands folded beneath one cheek.

Beautiful didn't start to describe her. Her glorious hair, her fine and delicate features, were exquisite, but her loveliness went beneath that. He'd seen inside her the past weeks, and that's where her true beauty emerged from.

"Sweetheart," he whispered, brushing his fingers over the silky skin of her forehead.

Her eyes opened slowly and a smile formed as she blinked. "I like it when you call me that," she answered sleepily, and her lids closed again.

"Then that's all I will call you," he said, nuzzling her hair with the tip of his nose. "Sweetheart." It was the perfect name. He couldn't call her by her given name, wouldn't call her by her sister's name. Someday he'd have to admit to knowing who she was, get to the reason she was here, but right now, it didn't matter.

He leaned over and blew out the light. "It's time for bed," he whispered, easing his hands beneath her.

She stiffened and her eyes popped open. "You're home."

"Yes, I'm home." He lifted her into his arms.

Hers wrapped around his neck and she snuggled against him. "I missed you."

"I missed you, too."

"I knew you'd be back."

"And I knew you'd be here."

"Always," she said, tightening her hold.

His hold tightened, too, as he started up the stairs. He'd never held anything more precious. More perfect. "Always," he repeated.

No part of him suggested he take her to her room, yet once they'd entered his, and he arrived at the bed, a flash of uncertainty had him wondering what to do next. The way her hands roamed his neck, shoulders, chest and back said she was now fully conscious, and there wasn't a single thing about him that wasn't wide-awake.

"You're all right?" she asked.

Wondering about his answer, he said, "Yes."

"You weren't hurt, were you?"

He eased his arm from beneath her knees, lowered her feet to the floor, so they ended up standing with their arms around each other and their gazes locked. "Not so much as a scratch," he answered.

"I knew you would be fine." She lifted her face, and he accepted the invitation, thrilled beyond coherent thoughts. The kiss went from soft and sweet to hot and needy within seconds. When their lips parted and they'd both inhaled, she whispered, "I want to be a wife you can be proud of."

His heart doubled in size. "I am proud of you," he said, running a single fingertip down the side of her face.

"You are?"

"Very."

"I'm very proud of you, too," she whispered.

Their next kiss lasted twice as long and had him losing control of how much longer he could wait. He'd never wanted a woman the way he wanted her. Fully. Completely. "I think it's time we take this thing off." Digging beneath the ruffles of lace on her housecoat, he added, "If I can find the buttons."

She giggled, that sweet lifting laugh that made the world a bright and amazing place.

"They're too big to miss," she insisted, pushing his hands aside. "Here, let me." She folded back the lace and slipped three huge buttons through their holes. Then slowly, one after the other, she shrugged her arms out, and let the gown fall to the floor. "How's that?"

He raised a brow while running his fingertip along the neckline of a thinner, but just as concealing gown. "Better, but I don't believe we need this one, either."

Watching his fingers tug on the pink ribbon tied just above her breasts, she asked demurely, "But what will I sleep in?"

He let loose the ties and used one knuckle to lift her chin. "From this night forward, you'll have me to keep you warm."

Blinking those dense lashes shyly, adorably,

she met his gaze, and a flash of excitement sent his blood humming, his soul ablaze.

"I'll like that," she said.

"Me, too."

He kissed her again, deeply and intensely, for he couldn't get enough of her lips. Then he gathered handfuls of the gown near her thighs and gently eased the material upward. It was as if he was opening the greatest gift of his life, a treasure he'd guard forever.

She lifted her arms, raised them above her head as he slid the gown up and over. Tossing it aside, he caught her hands, kept them raised while turning her in a slow pirouette. Twice. Once hadn't been enough for him to grasp her absolute perfection. From her shoulders to her ankles, the mysterious elegance of every curve, her graceful poise, was flawless in every way, and divine.

After watching him over a shoulder, she twisted her head around to face him as the second twirl ended. "You'll make me dizzy," she said, her hair swirling to catch up.

"Then we're even," he said, lowering her arms enough to kiss the backs of both hands. "Your beauty makes me dizzy."

It was true, her body was the epitome of perfection, and glimmering in the lamplight, her skin looked as fine and delicate as the thin china cup she sipped tea from. An unexpected, unsettling thought snagged his mind. Compared to her, he was as big as an ox, and nothing he'd experienced before had prepared him for taking a wife to bed.

A woman he loved. *The* woman.

He ran the back of one hand up her arm, from her wrist to her shoulder. Her skin was like velvet, and her hair, cascading over her shoulders, down her back, as well as her front, where it had settled after her twirls, was like silk. Using both hands, he gathered it into two long tails and pulled them over her shoulders. As he smoothed the tresses down her front, the backs of his hands encountered her breasts, and she let out a tiny gasp.

The long, thick mane created an iridescent curtain, hiding her breasts until he was ready to push aside the hair like one would pull open drapes to expose the brightness of the sun. "I want to promise you something," he said, trailing his hands back up her arms, to settle on her shoulders.

Tilting her head, as if listening intently, she nodded.

He wanted to tell her he knew who she was, but that would only complicate things more, and he truly couldn't go any longer without loving her. "I'll never hurt you, not intentionally, and if by some irresponsible act I do, I want you to tell me, so I can make amends and make certain it never happens again." It was a vow he took seriously, as was the silent one in which he willed himself to find the patience and skill and tenderness this woman deserved.

"All right," she whispered. Then, hooking her fingers inside his waistband, she tugged him forward. "Will you do me a favor?"

Momentarily stunned, perhaps because her fingers were testing the very control he sought, Seth paused a second or two before nodding.

"Will you kiss me? The pain I'm feeling at wanting you is quite devastating."

He wanted to throw his head back with laughter. She was an imp. An adorable, charming pixie that was his. All his. Settling for a grin, he framed her face with both hands. "I'd love to."

The kiss started out slow, but quickly escalated into a forceful act of passion that birthed an all-consuming fever. The delirium grew, sent his hands roaming, to explore the swells and curves and sleekness that seemed to form flawlessly beneath his fingers and palms. When at last he gathered the wits and strength to pull back, end the kiss, he lifted her into his arms and, cradling her as he had before, carried her the few feet to the bed.

With one hand, he threw back the covers, to lay her down on the crisp sheets. Her arms were around his neck and she didn't let go, pulling him onto the bed beside her.

They kissed again, by mutual consent, but she was the one to finally break it. Taking short, fast breaths, she cupped the sides of his neck. "Don't you have to take off your britches?"

Already on the brink of desperation to be inside her, Seth groaned. "Eventually I will," he said when able.

"Eventually?"

There was such yearning in her voice, as well as a touch of disappointment, that Seth concluded it was time to start his full exploration of her body. Teach her the sweet nuances of strategic maneuvers. "Eventually," he repeated, while parting the veil of chestnut-shaded tresses to reveal her breasts. Fanning the hair out, he spread it over both pillows before running one fingertip down her neck and then lower, tracing her breastbone.

She let out a pleasure-filled whimper when he used his lips to follow the trail of his finger, and again when he allowed himself to feast leisurely on one delectable nipple.

"Seth," she whispered with a touch of urgency.

"Hush, sweetheart," he said, brushing his lips over hers. "Just relax."

"Relax?" Her brows slanted downward as if she was perplexed, while those big brown eyes held a dreamy quality.

"Yes," he said, kissing each brow. "Just relax."

She let out a ragged sigh as a beautiful smile curled her lips. "I'll try."

He took his time, stroking and kissing places he knew would provide her great pleasure. Some he'd tasted before—her lips, her neck, her eyelids. But others, such as the inside of her elbows, the hollow of her hips, the silken skin near her belly button, were new. He held her hands over her head and kissed along her arms, not stopping until he found her breasts again and she was moaning his name with such desire the blood was beating in his veins as if it wanted out.

Still he held back, pleasured her with tender kisses and caresses that now focused on her legs and the moist cavern where they connected. Offering herself, she arched her back, meeting and aiding his searching fingers. His discipline was waning, but like battling an enemy—the sweetest, most desirable adversary ever—he kept forging onward.

"Seth?" she gasped. "Seth?"

Running a string of kisses from hip to hip, while keeping his hand below, he mumbled, "Yes?"

"I—I...I think you need to take your pants off now."

Unquestionably charmed beyond measure, he grinned. "Oh, I will," he assured her, at the same time sliding a hand beneath one knee and lifting her leg, giving his mouth access to where his finger explored.

Millie gasped at the heat and moisture and all-out pleasure of Seth kissing her in the most private place imaginable. The fever, the need, was like nothing she'd ever known. The past weeks, when she'd thought her desire was at its utmost, had been like a mere candle flame compared to the wildfire blazing inside her now. Her throat was raw, yet she couldn't stop whimpering and moaning, couldn't keep her body from twitching and thrashing while something wild and passionate built inside her.

It was a sweet, heavenly energy that had her calling Seth's name out loud as he held her to him, kissed her as deeply there as he had her mouth. The excitement grew and grew and grew until she was damp with sweat, and a frantic spasm overtook her muscles. She could bear no more and shouted his name, only to have him lift her, hold her hips up and continue to make the frenzy inside her leap to another level. It was like climbing a ladder, higher and higher, and then, when she knew for certain she couldn't go any higher, an explosion happened, sending her in a million directions at once.

Her body was quivering, responding to the sweet tension so suddenly released, and then Millie felt as if she were floating like a feather, gently falling from the sky. The calmness was beautiful, brilliant, and had her sinking deep into the mattress.

"Sweetheart?"

She lifted her eyelids, smiled as Seth's face appeared. "Oh, that was...unbelievable."

"Yes, it was," he said, kissing her forehead. "And there's more."

"More?" She laughed, shaking her head. "There couldn't possibly be."

He was poised over her, and his eyes held a significant glimmer. Her hands, roaming his lower back, encountered nothing but bare skin, and an entirely new flame leaped to life inside her. He'd removed his britches.

Smiling, seeing the perceptive glint in his eyes, she whispered, "Oh, there is more, isn't there?"

"Yes," he said, "there is."

"Now?" she asked, her excitement growing again.

He nodded. "If you're ready."

"I'm ready," she assured him. "I'm ready."

He entered her in one swift movement that took her breath and had her grabbing his shoulders at a quick slice of pain. His body went stiff, and he held her tight for a moment, kissed her softly.

She hadn't expected pain, but it had already faded, and utterly novel and dazzling sensations were once again building, promising to lead her to that ladder again, or beyond.

"Oh, sweetheart," he whispered, kissing her cheeks. "I'm sorry. I should have been slower, gentler."

She shook her head. "I don't think so." Her hands on his back followed the slow rise and fall of his hips, and the friction, the way he glided inside her, coaxed her body into a splendid rhythm.

The journey was long and spectacular, taking her to plateaus and new levels that made her believe in an eternity no one else knew about. Just her and Seth. They stayed there, somehow suspended in time as the whirlwind frenzy spiraled onward. Wrapped around his hips, her legs were locked at the ankles to keep her moving with him as they climbed together, and this time when the sudden eruption happened, it was to both of them.

She shouted his name as a moan rumbled from his chest, and he held her hips, kept them linked with his while wave after wave of limitless fulfillment fanned over her body.

The soothing quiet that came next had her releasing the sheets balled in her hands, and her legs, as weak as the rest of her, released the hold she'd had on him. Kissing her sweetly, tenderly, he rolled off her, and then wrapped both arms around her as he pulled her to his side, cradling her with such affection that moisture slipped from the corner of her eye.

It wasn't a tear, couldn't be, for she'd never felt so amazing. Perhaps it was a tear of joy. She'd heard of such things, and she'd never, ever, known the bliss filling her right now. After rubbing her cheek against his shoulder, she tilted her head to gaze upon him.

He kissed her forehead. "I'm sorry, darling. I promise there won't be any pain next time."

"Pain?" she said, still basking in the tremendous aftermath of all that had occurred. "There was no pain." She closed her eyes. "None whatsoever."

His hold tightened, and she spread one arm across his chest, one leg over his thigh, to snuggle as close as possible.

"I love you," he whispered.

A real tear fell then. "I love you, too," she answered. At least she thought the words came out. Her mind was so consumed with his statement, repeating it over and over, that she wasn't exactly sure if she'd spoken or not. A tiny part of her tried to bring to the surface the deceit she'd just made worse, but Millie refused to allow that to happen. Not now. Content and spent, she drifted into a profound slumber.

It was still dark when something drew her awareness. Stretching, luxuriating in the way

Seth was once again kissing her breasts, Millie moaned and dug her hands into his hair, keeping him there until a fresh, fantastic storm of sorts had her begging him to enter her, join her in yet another journey to the world he'd created just for her.

Afterward, while mini aftershocks still rocked them, she caught Seth's shoulders before he could roll off her. "Don't!" She had to catch her breath before more words could be said.

Breathing almost as hard as she, he rose, balancing on his forearms and knees so as not to crush her. She cupped his face with her hands, kissed his lips soundly. Not knowing how to explain all she felt, she whispered, "I like who I am when I'm with you."

Seth returned her kiss, couldn't stop himself even if he wanted to. Which he didn't. Rolling off, he folded her to his side again. "I like who you are, too." Guilt rose inside him then, and he whispered, "Go to sleep. It'll soon be morning."

Her giggle caught his heart, filled him with elation, while his mind, tangled in a bizarre cobweb, tried to tell him how wrong this was. He had other secrets. Army secrets he'd go to his grave with, but this wasn't one a man could live with. Pretending she was his wife when he knew full well she wasn't. And he'd taken her. Until the moment it had happened, he hadn't thought of the outcome of that.

"I guess sleep is a part of sleeping, isn't it?" she asked, plastering her body against his like a second skin.

He liked that, too, her skin meshing with his. They'd declared their love to one another. Shared that love as intimately as two people could. It had been the greatest, most fulfilling thing he'd ever encountered. Yet in a dark cavern of his mind, a single thought kept leaping forward. She wasn't his wife. Whether he loved her or not. Whether he wanted to be or not, he was married to someone else.

Chapter Eleven

Millie stared with tremendous longing at the bed she'd left less than an hour ago. Not because she was still tired; she awoke every morning more refreshed than the day before. But because she wondered if she'd ever see this bed again. Their bed. She sighed and closed the clasp on her traveling bag before moving to the door. Glancing over her shoulder, she found tears stinging her eyes. It had been ten days since the night he'd ridden into the darkness and she'd vowed to do whatever it took to become his wife in every way upon his return.

And she had. Except for the one way she really wanted. The truth.

The heaviness in her heart grew as she made her way down the stairs. The entire house was full of remarkable places she and Seth had created memories—the parlor sofa, the bath-tub, the kitchen—and it was about to end. She was leaving, going to Washington, where she'd have to fess up to who she was, and he was going to hate her.

"Ma'am?"

Pinpricks of embarrassment stung her cheeks. Russ couldn't know her thoughts, yet her deceit was so close to the surface, she felt as if it was written across her skin.

"Yes, Corporal Kemper?" she responded, step-ping off the last stair.

"The major says it's time to go."

Millie took a deep breath. Needed to. She'd told Seth she'd stay here, wait for him, even dreamed he'd just go to Washington and return, having never learned of the deceit. He wouldn't hear of it. Said he couldn't be separated from her for that long. She'd cherished the statement, for she didn't want to be parted from him, either, but a deep intuition said the trip would change everything.

Corporal Kemper crossed the room and held out one hand. "I'll carry that."

"Thank you." She handed over the bag and pulled down the hem of her once-pale-green trav-eling suit jacket. The color was an odd mixture now, a not overly flattering gray-orange, but it had washed up better than she'd imagined. The white underblouse with a large ruffled collar was tinted orange, as well. At least the shades matched, and there really was no sense in ruining another gown. The trip was bound to be long.

Seth met her on the porch, which had her heart drumming and a smile bouncing onto her lips. He was so handsome, dressed in his full uniform, yellow scarf and all, and she loved him so much it hurt.

"You look as beautiful as ever," he said, bending to brush a kiss to her cheek.

Compliments from him always made her blush. Taking his arm, she said, "I missed you when I awoke this morning."

"I had things to see to, but I'd rather have been there with you." He turned then, escorting her down the steps. "We want to make it as far as possible today. Hopefully, we can cut the trip to Tulsa down to four days."

That wasn't what Millie hoped for. She wanted it to take forever. Yet knowing he was attempting to shorten the trip on account of her made her love him all the more. "We'll be together," she said, "so whether it's four, five or fifteen days, it doesn't matter to me."

His lips brushed her temple before he nodded toward the courtyard. "There are a few folks who'd like to say goodbye."

So engrossed in Seth, she hadn't noticed the

line of people flanking a pathway that ended at two loaded wagons and several saddled horses. "Goodness."

"I think you're going to be missed while we're gone," he whispered in her ear.

Tears pricked her eyes, but humor sparkled in his. So did pride, so she tried to smile.

"I've left a dozen times over and never had this happen before." He waved a hand for her to precede him along the pathway.

It was early, so she'd imagined half the fort would still be sleeping, but they weren't. Besides army men, and the three other wives she'd come to know well, Briggs Ryan and all four of his maidens, as well as Mr. Jenkins and Wind wished her safe travels and a speedy return. Mr. Ryan, right after a bear hug that left her cheeks stinging, and may have broken a rib, handed her a small pouch.

"Tea leaves," the big man said in his gusty voice. "Drop a few in boiling water and let steep for five minutes. No longer, though, or it'll get bitter. No?"

"Yes, yes," she answered. "Five minutes, thank you."

Wind, with his tiny shoulders protected from the cold by a red-and-blue-plaid shirt, handed her a peppermint stick that was no longer white. "For Major's wife."

Taking the candy, which had obviously been hidden, saved for a special moment, Millie felt her heart tumble in her chest. If only she'd known, she'd have saved a coin to give in exchange, but her money—what she'd chosen to take with her—was in her wrist bag inside her traveling satchel, and Russ had already put that in one of the wagons.

"I believe you dropped this, dear."

She turned to Seth, and seeing the coin in his palm, met his gaze with all the love bubbling in her chest. Squaring her shoulders, trying to act as poised as a major's wife should be, she nodded. "Thank you, Major." Taking the coin, she handed it to the boy. "Thank you for the sweet stick, Wind. May I give you this in exchange?"

The boy bowed his head respectfully. "*Haa.* Yes."

After he took the coin, she leaned down and kissed his cheek.

"I'd have given you a peppermint stick if I'd known that was the exchange," Mr. Jenkins said, rousing a chuckle from many of the people standing nearby.

At her side, with a hand on her back, Seth replied, "I may have something to say about that, Jenkins." His retort brought more laughter from the crowd.

Jubilance tussled with a hint of embarrassment

as Millie glanced up, saw the mirth in his eyes. Rubbing her back, he nodded, directing her to continue along the pathway.

Ilene Ketchum stepped forward from where she stood next to the wagon as they made their way to the end of the line. After giving her a solid hug, the woman said, "I'm assuming you have my list."

"Yes, it's safely packed away," Millie answered.

"Feel free to substitute if you need." Ilene had been to Washington several times and had created a list of very specific items, with substitute options, to be purchased at just as specific stores.

"I'll do my best," Millie promised.

The woman gave her one more hug. "I'm going to miss you," she said. "But I'm glad you're going. You've become the perfect major's wife, and I'm very proud of you."

Millie had to squeeze her eyelids tight to keep the moisture in.

Mrs. Ketchum turned then and gave Seth a long hug. "Godspeed, Major. I'd tell you to take care of your wife, but I know you will. We'll all be joyous to celebrate your return."

"Thank you," he said. "I leave knowing the fort is in most capable hands, both your husband's and yours."

The woman nodded, and Seth took Millie's

elbow, leading her around the first wagon. "Would you prefer to ride in the wagon or on horseback?"

Stunned, she looked down at her traveling suit and then up at him. "I didn't know I had an option."

"My apologies," he said, with a solemn expression. "I should have told you. Are you able to ride in that outfit? We have time if you want to change."

"No, I can ride in this," she assured him, noting the wide width of the skirt. "And I'd like to, for a ways at least." Bouncing for miles upon miles in the wagon hadn't been something she'd been looking forward to, but she would have done it without a word of complaint.

"I'd assumed that," he said, gesturing toward a small buckskin mare. "Allow me to assist you in mounting."

"You are so very thoughtful," she said, placing a foot in his clasped hands and a hand on his shoulder. "I fear I've become spoiled since I arrived here."

Once she was settled in the saddle, with her skirt flared to cover her ankles, he handed her the reins. His thumb caught her chin then and tugged slightly, encouraging her to bend toward him.

"And what," he asked, "is wrong with that?"

He kissed her briefly, and she was still recovering, knowing the entire crowd had witnessed the action, when he walked around her animal and mounted his.

Moments later they led the procession out the wide gates, side by side. The pride Millie felt for Seth had her spine straight and her shoulders squared. As if he knew she was thinking of him, he turned and gave her one of his sweet, heart-teasing winks.

A short time later Seth held up a hand, his elbow squared, to stop the men and wagons behind them as they approached Per-Cum-Ske and four of his braves, who were ready to mount their horses.

Stepping out of the crowd nearby, Leah-Widd-I-Kah smiled at Millie, but walked straight to Seth and spoke in a hushed tone.

Nodding, he dismounted and then walked around the head of the buckskin to arrive at Millie's side, where he grasped her waist. "Leah-Widd-I-Kah has a gift for you."

"Goodness, I certainly didn't expect all this," Millie whispered, resting her hands on his shoulders as he lifted her to the ground.

Others, including the leader's additional wives, followed as Leah-Widd-I-Kah walked forward, holding out a necklace that had Millie pressing a hand to her chest. It was a bride's necklace, the Indians' equivalent of a wedding band. The woman had shown her hers.

Seth took the necklace and placed it around her neck, lifting the braid she'd styled her hair in— given what the wind did to combs and coiffures—and letting it fall down her back again once the thin leather strap was around her neck.

"In every way it matters, you are my wife," he whispered softly in her ear. "And I'm very proud of that."

Her eyes closed as his lips brushed her cheek, and she had to swallow at the welling of emotions blocking her throat before she could look up at him. "I'm proud to be your wife," she whispered just as softly.

An intricate design of beads and delicate feathers had been sewn on the leather pendent that settled between her breasts. Lifting her gaze to Leah-Widd-I-Kah, and knowing this time a coin from her husband wouldn't be sufficient, Millie unpinned the dragonfly brooch from the front of her suit jacket. Stepping forward, she kissed her friend's cheek and then handed her the brooch. "Thank you. *Ura*." she said, placing a hand over the necklace. "This means more to me than you'll ever know."

Pinning the dragonfly to her dress, Leah-Widd-I-Kah nodded. *"Ura."*

Seth assisted Millie onto her horse again, and soon not even the tall stockade could be seen when she glanced over her shoulder. She missed it already, but when she caught her husband's gaze, she smiled, even though her heart had never felt so heavy.

That night, Millie was overly surprised to see a tent come out of one of the wagons, because when she'd traveled to the fort they'd simply draped a canvas over the wagon and she'd slept beneath it. Now she crawled under the top blanket of several that created a soft pallet for her and Seth to share, wearing nothing but her new necklace.

Being in a saddle most of the day had left her inner thighs sore and her behind achy, but not so badly their nightly routine should be interrupted. At least those were her hopes, for it was then, when they were alone together, that she forgot the rest of the world existed. If the look on her husband's face a few minutes ago was anything to go by, her hopes would be fulfilled.

They'd stopped shortly before dark, in a spot two men had ridden ahead to find and prepare. The soldiers had set up a total of four tents, while others cooked a meal that thankfully didn't consist of beans—that had been a true fear of Millie's. One of the men had set a kettle to boil on the fire, and she'd added some of the leaves Mr. Ryan had given her. While she'd seen to that, Seth had assisted in erecting their tent, and carried her travel satchel in after asking what she'd need out of the wagon.

The bag now sat near her feet, for the shelters were small, with barely enough room for the blankets creating their bed. She'd undressed while on her knees, but the accommodations were more than adequate.

The makings of a tepee had also been carried in one of the wagons, smaller than those outside the fort. She wondered how all five Comanche would sleep in it.

A breeze had picked up and was making the sides of the tent billow as it seeped in below the canvas, and she snuggled deeper beneath the cover, wondering how long it would be before Seth and the others turned in.

He didn't make her wait much longer before crawling through the split-flap opening. "Hello, my sweet."

The endearments he called her were never ending, and she loved each and every one. "Hello." Voices could still be heard outside, so she kept hers extra quiet. "I was hoping you'd be in soon."

Removing his boots, he answered, "I wanted to give you time to get undressed."

When it came to this man, and her love for him, her boldness seemed to grow daily. Sometimes it even surprised her. Lifting the edge of the blanket, showing him her state of dress, she whispered, "That didn't take long."

He let out a low growl, and shrugged and

scooted out of the rest of his clothes with additional speed. She was still giggling when he slipped beneath the covers and caught her hip, pulling her against him.

"You never cease to amaze me," he said.

She stretched and arched, aligning her body with his while digging her fingers into the silkiness of his thick hair. "That's what I think of you," she said, making a point of moving her hips against his in a now familiar rhythm. "That you're amazing."

His kiss was long and tantalizing, one that had her desire quickening. When his lips left hers, roamed down her neck in a way that made her want to groan, she pressed her lips together. Her body was already responding to him, yet she whispered, "Do you think the men out there know what we're doing in here?"

"Yes," he said, rolling her onto her back. "They know."

His hand molded one breast, and her response, "Oh," was half moan, half reply.

"Do you want me to stop?" he asked, licking the tip of the other breast.

"No," she all but whimpered.

"Forget about them, sweetheart. It's just you and me."

Millie nodded, but was already so far gone, she wasn't sure what she was nodding about. His

hands were like a piano player's and she was the
ivory keys he masterfully turned into a song so
sweet she became lost in the music. A lullaby created by and for them. He took his time, and needing to smother her uncontrollable moans, she bit
his shoulders, or the edge of the blanket, or her
own hand, whatever was near. Then, when her
time came, the moment his name wildly rumbled
from her throat, he smothered her shout with a
long and consuming kiss that left her both winded
and fulfilled.

Seth eased off her, smiling at how adorable
she'd been trying to refrain from being too
loud. He'd tried, too, for even though the men
surely knew—good men who wouldn't make a
comment—he didn't want to do anything that
would cause her undo embarrassment. As she
nestled in the crook of his arm, he fingered the
delicate feathers of her necklace with this other
hand.

Guilt was a hell of a thing for a man to feel. It
weighed him down worse than boulders tied to
his ankles could have. Yet being with her, now
and whenever she was near, Seth found other
emotions covered the shame, made him forget
that what he was doing was wrong. For it certainly felt right to love her. More right than anything he'd ever done.

He never called her Rosemary, nor did he

ever admit he knew she was Millie, and that was wrong. There was no future in it. His plan was to come clean. Confess, and give her the opening to admit her true identity. He no longer cared why she was here.

Before they got to Washington, he would tell her, and once there, he'd see that his ties to Rosemary were cleanly severed, giving him and Millie the opportunity to wed. He'd been as strategic in this plan as any other he'd ever created. There had been times when he could have told her, even right now, snuggled together in the darkness, but he hadn't, and he wouldn't. An indescribable knot in his stomach wouldn't let him. His men couldn't know he was living a lie, and he hadn't yet figured out how to correct that part.

He released the necklace and found her hand, lifted it to kiss the knuckles. "Are you sore from riding all day?"

"Not anymore," she said, somewhere between a giggle and a whisper. "You have a way of making me forget everything." Planting a kiss on his chest, she added, "Everything."

He drew air in through his nose, held it. She opened up such deep, incredible things inside him, and he had to wonder if that wasn't a part of it—why he couldn't say anything. Why that knot in his stomach was coated with dread. In his heart, he didn't want things to change. He could live his entire life letting everyone believe she was his wife, letting her think he didn't know who she was. And that wasn't like him. He'd never taken the immoral path, even when it was clearly the easier one, and that, too, made the pit of his stomach burn.

Furthermore, he still had a job to do, and needed all his faculties in order to convince the government the Indians weren't fairing well with what was being provided to them. Having Per-Cum-Ske with him on this trip made it more vital that his thoughts—every last one of them—were in order.

The Indian wasn't a chief, but he was *leading* the band right now. Eight years ago, when Per-Cum-Ske was just nineteen, he'd gone on the warpath against the white man. He'd made a fierce adversary, with followers throughout the Indian nation, and other tribes banding together to copy his actions. Thankfully, for the army, anyway, a year or so later he realized his actions were fruitless. White men were gaining ground and the Comanche barely maintaining, so he'd cut off his braids and enlisted in the Indian Scout Detachment. In that he'd succeeded, had been one of the best scouts ever, and soon became head of the detachment participating in the Kiowa-Comanche-Cheyenne campaign initiated at Fort Sill.

Seth remembered the crusade as if it had been yesterday. Indians had filled the Wichita Mountains, knew every nook, cranny and tree, and the soldiers, including himself, would have been at their mercy if not for Per-Cum-Ske. He'd not only reported where every last brave was located, he'd shown the troops where to camp, giving themselves the best protection for when the battle started.

Start it had, with a volley of gunfire like nothing any of the soldiers had expected. There had been more troops than Indians, and when the gunfire ceased Per-Cum-Ske had rushed forward, turning over the bodies of the fallen to look in their faces.

Seth had recognized a few of them—Per-Cum-Ske's father-in-law, Ter-Ak-A-Nee-Cut. Pah-Po-Ter-A-Pet, his uncle, and the leader of the band, Pe-Ah-Ter-Who-Noovy. But the scout had recognized the face of almost every fallen body he'd came upon. Friends and relatives, comrades that had followed him on his warpath against the white man just a few years prior, before he'd cut off his braids and joined the army.

To this day, Seth wondered how Per-Cum-Ske had accepted the deaths of so many. His eyes had been hollow, his face showing no emotion as he'd stood on the ground stained by blood. Spine straight, with his square chin thrust forward, he'd said, "We cannot help it. I did my duty."

Seth knew duty—had lived it his entire life—yet in that instance he hadn't understood it. He'd signed Per-Cum-Ske's discharge papers a short time later, one of the first times he'd used "Major" in his signature line. And he'd known then that he'd face the man as an adversary again. It couldn't be helped.

That time was now. The man had become leader of the Comanche, or Komantcia—Anyone Who Wants to Fight All the Time—as other tribes referred to them. A man who knew the life of the Indians, but also the ways of the army, creating a precarious balance that had nerves on end from Indian Territory to Washington, including Seth's. Another reason his mind had to be alert and his instincts intact, and why he couldn't allow issues in his private life to overshadow his duties.

The sound of deep and even breaths had him looking down, and the area around his heart warming as he saw her sleeping. He ran a hand over Millie's hair, pulled the long braid over her shoulder and across his chest.

Once his meeting in Washington was complete and a settlement agreed upon, he could focus on cleaning up the situation between him and Millie. He tilted his head to kiss the top of hers. Something this precious, this beautiful and wonderful, had to be handled gently.

She let out a tiny moan, and the powerful need he had for her, though well-sated a short time ago, sparked low in his belly like the strike of a flintlock. It wasn't unusual; it happened every time he glanced her way. Insatiable, that's what he was when it came to her. Fact was, he didn't even have to look at her; a simple thought caused that reaction inside him. And all day, while riding next to her, he'd practically counted the minutes until sunset.

Running a hand down her arm, he paused when his palm encountered chilled skin, and probing the covers, he found the reason: the wind sneaking under the tent. He bunched up the blankets beneath them, plugging the space as best he could.

"What's wrong?" she murmured.

"Nothing, sweetheart, just the wind sneaking in below the tent."

"Yes," she said groggily, while shifting to burrow against him. "It's cold."

Her entire side was chilled, felt like frost when it met his heated skin. He pulled the top blanket up to her shoulders and then reached below, grasping her waist. "Here, I'll switch sides with you."

When he lifted her, intent on rolling beneath,

she grasped his shoulders, nestled her entire length on top of him. "Mmm," she said. "You're always so warm."

Passion flared, readying him in every way to once again sample all her wares. Rubbing his palms along her silky, chilly skin, he asked, "Would you like me to warm you?"

"Um-hmm," she mumbled, her knees parting his legs.

"Is that a yes?" he asked, pressing her hips to his, with both hands on the round, plump curves of her very delectable hind end.

She giggled, and then suckled his neck before asking, "What do you think, Major?"

Chapter Twelve

Had he known how wonderful the trip would be with her at his side, Seth wouldn't have strived to shorten it. But as it was, four days and three nights after setting out, they were on the outskirts of Tulsa. Then again, as he looked over his shoulder to a sky turning blacker by the moment, he was glad the town was only a few miles ahead. The storm that was brewing was sure to be a doozy.

The wind had picked up throughout the day, and by the looks of those clouds, rain would soon be striking the red dirt with all the gusto of an inland hurricane. His instincts were kicking in, as well as an internal conflict. He'd never left his men before, but he'd never had a wife to protect, either.

Riding the buckskin next to him, she had on

her army-issue hat, a fashion clash with her dress if there ever was one. But the smile she flashed him said her attire was no concern. It also resolved the issues he'd been mulling over.

"I'll be right back," he said over the whistle of the wind.

"Is something wrong?"

"No, I just want to talk to the drivers, see how the wagons are faring in the wind."

She nodded, and he spun his mount around, trotted back and steered the animal to ride next to the first wagon.

"Storm's brewing, aye, Major?" Sergeant Moore said in greeting.

"Yes, I'm afraid it's going to hit soon," Seth admitted, unable to keep his eyes from going back to the head of the line, where his wife rode.

"Roberts and I have the wagons under control. Nothing's going to happen between here and Tulsa. I know the trail. It's clear sailing from here on in." Rex Moore then gestured with his chin. "I'd be obliged, though, if you and your wife were to ride ahead, have warm, dry beds waiting on us."

Seth had to laugh and shake his head. "You would, huh?"

"Yep, bet the entire lot of us would," the man said, grinning. "I reckon we'll look close to drowned rats by the time we get these mules to town. Those horses of yours, though, they might make it before the rain hits too hard."

"Well, then, Sergeant," Seth said, once again thankful for the capable men in his unit, "I'm leaving you in charge while I find shelter for my wife. Rooms are waiting for everyone at Brewster's. I'll see you there."

"Aye, aye, Major, you'll see us there."

Seth rode back then to the other wagon, where the conversation was relatively the same. Jack Roberts made the same suggestion Rex had before Seth could open his mouth, and the four lieutenants riding flank had the same sentiments.

Farther back, Per-Cum-Ske gestured before Seth made it far enough to turn his horse around. "Go. Take woman. Storm coming."

Seth waved, then kneed his mount, galloping back to the front. Reining in next to her, he asked, "Feel like a race?"

She frowned, but there was a flash of excitement in her eyes. "A race?"

"Yup, to town. It's about five miles."

Lifting a trim eyebrow, and the corners of her mouth into a smirk, she asked, "What do I get if I win?"

"Anything you want," he said.

Her smoldering gaze roaming him from boots to hat lit a fire in him not even the rain would be able to dowse. "Anything?" she asked in a sultry tone.

"Anything," he repeated, with a glance that somehow landed on her breasts before her face.

"Ready, set, go," she shouted in a single breath, already slapping her reins against the buckskin's rump.

Seth set his horse into a plunge and then a full gallop, catching her within no time. The animals couldn't run the entire way to town, but they could put some distance between them and the storm. Glancing over, seeing the determined way she lay low over the animal's neck, he settled himself more firmly in the saddle.

Side by side, they soared over the land, and even with the storm fusing the air, he felt the connection of their hearts as they rode in tandem.

Millie was filled with glee, a bright, brilliant joy that not even the rain, plastering her hair to her head and her dress to her skin, could dampen. "I won," she insisted as Seth pulled her out of the saddle.

"Only because you shot in front of that wagon," he said, rushing her under the awning of the hotel. Once there he took her face between his hands. "You scared the life out of me! Don't ever do that again."

His growl didn't scare her. There was too much love in his eyes for that. "I had plenty of room."

"That wagon almost crashed, careening out of your way."

"Oh, it did not," she insisted, wiping at the water dripping into her eyes. Her hat had flipped off her head and now hung between her shoulder blades by the strap. "Did it?" She attempted to turn, glance through the pouring rain to see if there was a wreck down the road they'd just traversed.

"Come on," he said, "I gotta get you inside before you float away."

"You're always saying that," she said.

"I was raised in Boston. My mother always thought we'd float away if we swam in the bay," he said, leading Millie to the door.

At night, while snuggled together inside the tent or back home in their bed at the fort, he'd told her about his childhood, his mother and brother, father and uncles. She loved every tale, but always sensed he wanted her to tell him more than the few clipped answers she'd shared about her own childhood. She was walking a more dangerous path than ever, for he really did make her forget she was living a lie.

Digging her heels in the wood beneath them, she spun around. "The horses."

"Someone inside will see to them," he said, tugging her forward.

In no time, he was leading her up a flight of stairs and down a hall to a door that the key in his hand unlocked. Then he scooped her into his arms, and she laughed out loud as he carried her into the room.

"Put me down, silly. I'm dripping wet." However, she held on tighter, hoping he wouldn't, as he kicked the door shut.

He didn't, but instead captured her mouth. The kiss was the kind she loved, deep and penetrating, warming her from tip to toe. His mouth continued to hold her attention as he slowly let her legs loose. With her arms locked around his neck, she didn't know when her feet touched the floor until she wobbled on them.

A knock on the door had him lifting his face, separating his lips from hers. Millie swayed as his hands slipped away, and they were instantly back, stabilizing her, while silently asking if she was able to stand on her own. Smiling, for his concern was so endearing, she nodded.

Watching her closely, he eased his hands away, and only when she proved she was stable did he move to the door and pull it open.

"Here, Major." A gray-haired woman with a broad smile said, while handing him a wicker basket. "Towels and dry clothes for each of you until your men arrive." She turned then, still smiling. "The bathing room is at the end of the hall, Mrs. Parker. Just put your wet clothes in the basket and leave it outside the door. I'll have them laundered and ready for you first thing in the morning." Once again addressing Seth, the woman continued, "Yours, too, Major. And the meal you ordered will be up promptly."

"Thank you, Mrs. Brewster," he said, setting the basket on the foot of the bed. "We appreciate your efficiency."

"The army keeps us in business, Major. I'm happy to see to whatever needs you have. And your wife." The women then held out a hand. "It's such a pleasure to meet you, ma'am. A real treat."

"Thank you, Mrs. Brewster," Millie said, shaking the older woman's hand. "We do appreciate your kindness, and I'm honored to make your acquaintance."

The woman's smile grew yet again as she turned to Seth. "The heater's been lit, so the water will be hot in no time. I'm sure you'll show your wife how it all works."

"I will. Thank you again, Mrs. Brewster."

Millie waited until the woman had walked out and Seth pushed the door closed before she stepped forward and wrapped her arms around his waist from behind him. "Heater?" she asked, nuzzling his back with her cheek. "As in hot water?"

His hands settled atop hers as her fingers found the brass buttons on his jacket. "Yes," he replied. "As much as you need."

She undid the buttons and then lifted the lapels, helping him shrug his arms out of the sleeves. "Enough for two?" She held the coat as he slipped it off, loving being able to assist him so intimately. Being a major's wife had so many wonderful benefits.

He turned, took the jacket, tossed it on the bed and spanned his hands around her waist. "Yes, enough for two."

Excitement blazed inside her. "I believe," she said, starting on his shirt buttons, "I know what I want my prize to be."

"Prize?"

She nodded. "For winning the race."

"Aw, yes, the race."

Tugging his shirttail from his britches, she reminded him, "You said I could have anything I want."

"Yes, I did."

She slid both hands into the opening of his shirt. His skin was always so warm and captivating, and though she'd been somewhat unsure the first time he'd asked her to wash his back, now she adored the chore. As much as she loved having him wash hers. "I want you to wash my hair."

"Just your hair?" he asked, finding the buttons on her suit jacket.

"We'll see," she answered, no longer chilled by her wet clothing. Then again, she never really was chilled when he was around.

Except at times when, like hours later—after they'd shared a steamy bath, a delicious meal, and had warmed up the sheets of the bed—a re-occurring dream ripped her from a deep sleep, leaving her trembling and ice-cold.

Gasping, beseeching her racing heart to slow, Millie squeezed her eyes shut and burrowed her face into the pillow, letting it absorb the moisture of her tears.

"Sweetheart?" Seth was curled against her back, and his arms, one around her waist, the other below her neck, tightened to pull her closer. "What's wrong?"

"Nothing," she whispered, grasping his arms, silently begging him to save her from the torment still raging inside.

"Did you have another bad dream?" His lips were against the skin on her neck.

She nodded.

"Aw, sweetie, you're safe with me," he whispered. "Besides, we aren't in the tent."

"I know," she mumbled. "It was just a dream. A silly dream."

"Want to tell me about it?"

A new chill hit her, all the way to the center of her bones. "No," she whispered. "I just want to go back to sleep."

"All right," he whispered, kissing her neck and cuddling her close. "I'm here. You're safe."

She nodded again and pressed as much of her face as possible into the pillow, trying to wipe away the tears before they rolled down her cheeks, onto his arm. The nightmare had come the first night they'd slept in the tent, and had appeared every night since, stronger each time. It was her conscience, telling her that what she was doing was wrong. So very wrong. She knew that, but in the light of day, looking upon his handsome, loving face, her heart took over again, pushed the deceit so far away it only had a chance to come forward in her sleep. Where it tormented her.

The dream was the same each time, and she awoke at the same point. They were in Washington, or a place she assumed was Washington, since she'd never been there, and Seth was talking to a faceless man. Yet she knew the man, and knew he was telling Seth the truth. She was running in the dream, screaming at Seth not to listen, but she was too late. The way he looked

at her, the hate and hurt in his eyes... Rosemary
was there, too, in her dream.

Another tremble assaulted Millie's body.

"Hey," he whispered. "It was just a dream."
He shifted then, rolled her onto her back as he
leaned over her. "Honey." He wiped at the tears
on her cheeks. "Don't cry."

The tenderness in his voice and touch had a
piercing pain ripping at her heart. She had to find
a way to tell him, thought of it day after day. But
one look into those eyes that held such love, that
showered her with a devotion she'd never known
existed, and words refused to form. Truth was, it
was no longer her deceit that filled her with fear.
It was living without him. She not only loved
him, she liked herself when she was with him.
That was new. In the past, she'd often loathed herself. Loathed her life. A life she had to go back to.

"I think," he said, rubbing his nose against
hers, "I know a way to make you forget." His
hand roamed down, settled on her breast. "Forget all about a silly old dream."

The ache inside her increased. She'd tried over
and over to come up with a way to tell him everything. Her own selfishness was what stopped
her time and time again. She'd discovered a love
so strong she just might die without it, and ultimately, she didn't want to give it up. Would spend

the rest of her life pretending to be her sister if that was what it took.

Shame, growing stronger, lurched inside her. He was so honorable, so righteous and admirable, he'd never understand why she'd done what she had. Neither would her sister.

"Honey?" He tenderly cupped her face, his eyes searching hers. "Oh, sweetheart. It really was a bad dream, wasn't it?"

She nodded.

Combing her hair away from her face, he settled down beside her. "Come here, I'll just hold you until you go back to sleep."

A desperation sprang forth inside her, and she rolled on top of him, grabbed his shoulders. "No. No, Seth, please, please love me."

She took his mouth fiercely, almost violently, as a raw panic gripped her heart.

Their union was a hot, wild exchange that tore the bedding from the mattress and left her gasping, her lungs burning. Satisfaction was there, too, but this time, for the first time, disgrace came with it.

Unable to face him, she rolled on her side, dug her hands beneath the pillow. He covered her, first with the sheet and then the blanket, and then stationed himself behind her, holding her.

"I love you," he whispered tenderly.

Drawing a breath that had the air wheezing

into her burdened chest, she answered, "I love you, too."

She was afraid to close her eyes, and the sky outside the window was turning gray when sleep finally overcame her.

Seth folded the covers back and, fighting the urge to kiss her cheek, eased off the bed. She was finally sleeping, had rolled over and snuggled close to his side just a short time ago. He crossed the room and pulled the curtain, blocking the rising sun from disturbing her, and then, assuming the thud outside the door was the basket containing their clothes, he donned the pants Mrs. Brewster had loaned him last night and sneaked out of the room as quietly as one of Per-Cum-Ske's braves.

In the washroom, pulling on his stiffly starched uniform, he couldn't help but wonder if he was the cause of Millie's fear. The way it had contorted each of her lovely features last night, from her doe eyes to her petal mouth, had torn at his heart, and left it sore and bruised this morning. She hadn't wanted to come with him to Washington. Had said she'd stay at the fort, wait for him there. He'd refused, said he wanted her with him. He did. Always would, and her pain was his. In an unparalleled way, it hurt worse than any injury he'd ever acquired.

It wasn't until after Seth quietly returned the

basket to their room, resisted yet another urge to kiss her, and made his way downstairs, that another possibility entered his mind. He was penning a brief message Mrs. Brewster promised to slide under the door for his wife when the thought hit.

His wife. That had to be it. Millie was fearful of facing Rosemary. He thanked the hotel owner and left, mulling things over more deeply. Lately, he'd forgotten about Rosemary's part in all this. If she'd behaved the way she had toward him, how had she treated her sister over the years? Millie had such a kind and gentle soul, and he'd bet his best horse that Rosemary had taken advantage of that.

Anger twisted inside him. He'd wanted to wait until after the meeting in Washington to tell Millie the truth, but he couldn't let her fear grow. He'd have to tell her, let her know he was there to protect her. That she hadn't done anything wrong.

He had, though. This was all his fault. Whether his marriage to Rosemary was real or not, he had said the vows and should never have pursued another woman. The fact that he'd fallen in love, had been willing to do whatever it took for her to return his affection, didn't make it right.

Pressing a hand to his aching forehead, Seth made his way to the stables.

From there he went to the train station to oversee the unloading of the items they needed from the wagons, and to ensure that the private sleeping car he'd requested was part of the long, eastbound train.

Normally, he'd have traveled with the rest of his unit and Per-Cum-Ske and his braves, in one of the cars that sported built-in berths. But a major's wife needed more privacy than that. If one of Pullman's hotel railroad cars had been available, he'd have rented that. Men with enough money shot buffalo out windows of those cars, while singing along to an organ, dining on delicacies and drinking wine. A true tale Seth had witnessed and a remembrance that never failed to irk him.

As it was, a smaller, not as lavish private car—with a bed large enough for two, he noted, while touring the accommodations—would suit their purposes. After approving the loading of supplies and the car, he started back for the hotel, but along the way a window display caught his eye.

It was still early and the door securely latched, but he noticed movement beyond the merchandise, and knocked on the glass.

When a woman opened the door, he asked, "That dress in the window, is it for sale?"

"Well, of course—" she pointedly noticed the emblems on his sleeves "—Major." Stepping aside, gesturing for him to enter, she added, "But it's not a dress, it's a traveling suit."

"All the better," he said, moving forward to examine the ensemble. "I'd like to purchase it for my wife."

"Oh, would she be available to try it on? I could make any alterations needed," the woman said.

He hadn't thought about size. Stepping closer, he placed his hands around the waistline and the tailor's form beneath it, and then noted the length, compared to his height. "We're leaving on the morning train, and I believe this size will be about perfect."

"I do have an adjustment string sewn inside the skirt," the woman explained. She unbuttoned the jacket, to expose a white blouse tucked inside a wide waistband made of contrasting black velvet, with a large diamond shape in front, and she pointed out the drawstring.

He nodded, and fingering the soft velvet of the skirt, said, "This color is almost the shade of my wife's eyes." Her hair, as well, and the style would highlight her flawless figure.

"They must be beautiful."

"They are," he answered. "She is."

"She's a lucky woman, Major."

"No. I'm a lucky man." Turning to the woman, he said, "I'd like to take it with me now, please."

He'd tell Millie everything as soon as the train started to roll. They'd have plenty of time to talk it through. Have things settled before they arrived in Washington.

"Yes, sir. Will there be anything else? A new slip, petticoat or underskirt?"

He grinned, thinking of his return to the hotel. "Yes, all the under things needed to make a complete new outfit."

Ten minutes later, as the woman piled package upon package in his arms, she said, "I can help you carry this to the hotel, Major."

"No, I've got it," he insisted, as she set the last packet on top of the pile and he held it in place with his chin. "But could you get the door for me?"

"Certainly," the shopkeeper replied.

Mr. Brewster came running to open the hotel door as he spied Seth walking past the front window. The man also opened the door to the room upstairs, and shut it as Seth cautiously tiptoed to the bed.

Careful to keep the crinkling paper from waking her, he set everything down and then moved to other side of the bed, where he eased his weight onto the mattress. A part of him hated to wake her, yet there wasn't much time before they'd have to board the train.

He smoothed the hair away from her face,

tucking it behind one ear as she lay on her side, and then he kissed the cheek he'd just uncovered. Her sleepy, sweet moan had him kissing it again.

She rolled then, onto her back, and blinked several times.

"Good morning," he whispered.

Stretching one arm overhead, she answered, "Good morning," as a wistful smile appeared on her lips.

He captured her wrist, kept the arm up to run his tongue down its length, stopping when encountering the edge of the blanket laid across her breastbone. "We have to leave soon," he said, though the desire to crawl under the covers beside her had his blood ticking in his veins.

"Oh," she said, popping open her eyes. She grasped the blanket with the hand he let loose and then scooted to sit up. "You should have—" The crackle of paper had her gaze going to the other side of the bed. "What's all that?"

"That," he said, touching the end of her nose with a fingertip, "is a present I bought you."

The tenderness of her sweet sigh floated around his heart. Smiling as she shook her head, she asked, "All that is one present?"

He nodded.

"Why? It's not my birthday or Christmas."

"When is your birthday?" he asked, sincerely

wanting to know, so he could nail it into his memory.

"Janu—J-June." Her cheeks were flushed as she shook her head. "You make me fuddle-headed," she said. "When's yours?"

"August 18," he said. "When is yours? January or June?"

"June 12." She glanced his way briefly, before turning back to the packages, but he'd caught the unease in her eyes.

He took her chin, pulled her face toward his and he leaned down to kiss her, until they were both unable to think of anything else. Which didn't work, because he *was* thinking—about things they didn't have time for right now.

Reaching across the blanket, he grabbed a package, having no idea what it held. "Here, start opening."

She glanced at the parcel, ran a hand over the paper gently.

"Sweetheart." He leaned forward and pressed his forehead to hers. "If you don't start opening, we're going to be late. I have some pull, but I can't hold a train for you."

The first package—containing a white undergarment of some kind—was opened slowly, but by the time she got to the fourth, or maybe it was the fifth, paper was flying. He really had to learn the names of all these ladies' undergarments. They seemed to delight her to no end. as did the dress, or traveling suit, as he was again informed.

After a quick dash down the hall in the dress Mrs. Brewster had loaned her last night, Millie was back in the room, and as he helped her into each garment, Seth was told its names. Not one of which he remembered. As soon as she was dressed, he longed to undress her again, layer by layer. He couldn't wait to get to the privacy of their railway car. She was beautiful. Stunning.

"Perfect," he said, watching as she twirled before him, flaring the luminous brown skirt. "A perfect fit."

Keeping her eyes locked with his, she sashayed toward him. "How did you know my size?"

"By doing this," he said, spanning her waist with both hands. "You fit perfectly into my hands."

A whimsical smile, coupled with the way she slowly blinked those long lashes, had him tightening his hold, pulling her closer.

"You," she said quietly as their faces grew nearer, "fit perfectly into my heart."

Air snagged in his throat, like that of a man falling out of a tree, catching on each branch, and that made their kiss begin as a mere mingling of breath. It grew into several small kisses, open-mouthed so he could catch one of her lips for a second, and then it turned into a passionate exploration that had him wondering how late they could be before the train left without them.

It was the fact they had to talk—today—that made him finally pull the door open.

Chapter Thirteen

Perhaps because an inner part of her was tight with tension that had the rest of her wanting to delay their arrival—forever— time decided to speed past, as if to prove a point, or break her heart, or both.

The sky was starless, a never ending black void that could have overwhelmed her, feeling the way she did. Then again, in order for the sky to overwhelm her, nothing else could be, and something certainly was. Millie pressed her head against the window of the train, which had blown its whistle moments before to signal they were on the outskirts of Washington. Her thoughts were so jumbled nothing made sense.

She folded her hands across her stomach, hugging herself against the dull pain that now throbbed in every part of her being. Even hurting as she was, the soft velvet beneath her fingers made her smile. The traveling suit Seth had bought for her was the most beautiful outfit she'd ever owned. Ever seen. Made of thick velvet, it kept her warm as the climate outside the train dropped lower, and the gorgeous shade of brown—a color she'd never have imagined using for a gown—was perfect for traveling. It seemed to repel even the coal dust that somehow found its way inside the private sleeping car.

They'd left it for meals, gone to the dining car, and a couple of times she'd joined Seth in short visits with the men. Usually, though, she stayed behind. Stepping between cars frightened her, even with him at her side. He was never gone long, yet she missed him terribly every moment.

The whistle sounded again, reverberating up her spine and over her skin until her insides were quaking. The dream had continued, and Seth, dear sweet Seth, was constant in his attempts to calm her, chase away her fears. He kept trying to draw her into conversation, tell him what was wrong, but it wouldn't come out. Instead she did the only thing she could: beg him to love her. And though he did—he loved her thoroughly—the worry she now saw in his eyes increased her cowardice. Not only was she unable to tell him the truth, she was terrified of sleeping. Had barely closed her eyes for days, yet had pretended to be asleep whenever he wanted to talk.

A clang followed by a jolt had her reaching for something to grasp. If only she'd stayed behind! At the fort she might have been able to build up the gumption to tell him the truth upon his return.

The starch left her knees and she sank into a red folding chair. She wouldn't have found the courage there, either. Someone this spineless didn't have the ability to all of a sudden become brave. If so, she'd have done so years ago. Told Rosemary to handle her own problems. Stood up for herself, as Lola and Martin, and even at times, her father, had told her to do.

Now she was in so deep, nothing could save her.

With a screech she'd come to know, the door opened and Seth walked in. Her heart knocked, as if excitedly announcing "he's back!" and the butterflies his smile always awoke started batting their wings against the walls of her stomach.

Returning his grin, she realized that though she was a coward, she was also glad there had been one time in her life she'd been brave. Back at the fort, when she'd told him she loved him for the first time. For she did, and the past weeks had been the most wonderful time of her life. Seth loved her in return. She saw it in his eyes, felt it in his touch, and what cut her to the quick was understanding the severe pain of being betrayed by someone you love.

He was standing in front of her, holding out his hands. She laid hers in them and stood, willingly met his lips for an elevating little kiss.

"I'm hoping you'll sleep better at the hotel," he said, caressing her cheek with the pads of his fingers. "I don't like seeing you so tired."

"It's not your fault."

"Yes, it is," he said.

Millie pressed two fingers to his lips, sensing he was about to say more. As far as hardships, this trip had been a simple undertaking compared to the journey west, where she'd slept sitting up on one of the hard seats in the passenger car, and had had layovers of up to eight hours at different stations, not to mention the wagon ride, which had been something else entirely.

"No," she said, "you have no fault in any of this." Realizing how much she'd just said, she pressed her lips to his, afraid he might understand more than she wanted him to, and right now, that might be enough to make her keel over.

A week later, Millie did keel over, right there at the counter in the little bookstore where she was filling the last items on Ilene Ketchum's list.

When she opened her eyes, lying on some little sofa, the man crouched next to her shoulder

made her wish she could faint again. Though she
loved him for who he was—her oldest and dear-
est friend—he was the last person she wanted to
see: the faceless man in her dream.

"Millie?" he said as she closed her eyes.
"Millie, it's me, Martin."

"I know who you are."

"And you're so shocked to see me you fainted?"

She opened her eyes again, glanced around
long enough to realize they must be in the living
quarters attached to the bookstore. "What are
you doing here? You're supposed to be in Texas."

"That's a mighty fine welcome."

Flipping her legs over the edge of the sofa, she
pulled herself up, taking a deep breath and wishing she was dreaming. But she wasn't. "Hello,
Martin."

"What are you doing here?" he asked. "In
Washington."

Pressing a hand to the pain in her forehead,
she said, "I asked you first."

He took her face between his hands. His hold
wasn't hard or distressing, just so different from
Seth's, so different from how he made her feel,
that she wanted to cry.

"What kind of mission does Rosemary have
you on now?" Martin asked in a firm and somewhat disgusted tone. "You look terrible. I've
never seen you with bags under your eyes."

It was another voice that turned her spine to ice. The one filtering through the curtain hanging behind Martin. "Hide," she insisted, pushing at her friend. "Hide now!"

"Millie—"

"Now!" She leaped to her feet so fast her head spun. Fighting the dizziness, she hurried to the curtain, arriving as it parted. Seeing his face, she felt her heart exploding with a mixture of grief and joy. "Seth."

He grabbed her, held her close. "I was told you fainted."

"I thought you were in a meeting," she said, her heart pounding so hard she couldn't think.

"I was." He leaned back to examine her with scrutinizing eyes. "But we're meeting for lunch, just half a block from here. We decided that this morning. Don't you remember?"

It had been all she'd thought of until a few minutes ago. They'd barely seen each other the past few days, with the way he'd been in meetings from morning to night, and when they were together, neither wasted time talking. "Yes, yes, I do." She tried to push him backward, away from the curtain.

He studied her thoroughly before his gaze lifted. "You there, are you the man who assisted my wife?"

At the sound of Martin's voice saying, "Yes, sir," Millie's world went black again.

Seth's heart—still inhabiting his throat from when he'd seen commotion outside the bookstore, passersby stopping to gawk through the open doorway—threatened to strangle him as he lifted her into his arms. Her body was limp, and reminded him too much of the remains of fallen soldiers he'd carried off battlefields.

"Sergeant," he yelled, noting the stripes on the sleeves of the man standing on the other side of the curtain. "Get me a carriage and a doctor. Room 218 at the Wormley Hotel."

Shifting her weight, so her head rested against his shoulder and her arms no longer hung at her sides, Seth had one thing to compare to the fear and pain charging through him. His throat was on fire and he knew why, even as a hundred scenarios, a thousand why-didn't-I's, and a million if-onlys plagued his mind while he carried her out of the bookstore and into the buggy rolling to a stop. All his proclamations of not wanting to marry because he hadn't wanted to leave anyone behind when he perished were a lie. The truth was *this* was what he didn't want. To again lose someone he loved. Not knowing how to deal with his father's death, how to grieve, Seth had hidden all the pain, focused on others'. His mother's pain. The needs of his family. Eventually, he'd convinced himself that was what he didn't want again.

And that was also why he hadn't told this woman the truth. That he knew she was Millie. He was afraid she'd leave him. He'd wronged her in so many ways, she was sure never to believe him again, or trust him. He wouldn't ride with men he didn't trust, and he couldn't expect her to, either.

Whether it was Millie's body shifting as she regained consciousness or her tiny moan that sent his heart leaping, Seth didn't know or care. He tightened his hold, cradling her on his lap, and kissed her forehead several times before whispering, "Shh, darling, just rest. Just rest."

He was lowering her onto their bed, kissing her closed eyelids, when the doctor entered the hotel room and told him to leave so he could examine her.

Seth refused.

After an exam, in which she responded to all the medical questions, often with sorrow-filled eyes, the doctor pulled Seth to the door. "I can't find anything wrong, Major, other than exhaustion."

Unable to drag his eyes off her, Seth watched as she rolled over, faced the wall and curled into a ball upon the bed.

"Did the two of you have an argument?" the physician asked.

"No," Seth answered, his stomach curdling.

"Something's troubling her." The man opened the door. "Find out what that is, let her get some rest, and she'll be fine."

Seth closed the door after the doctor left. There'd been a hundred times he could have talked to her on the train, told her everything, yet when it came to her, he was as spineless as a dandelion. It had taken little more than one of her soft kisses and he'd given in, told himself they could talk later. And now worry had her physically ill.

At a loss, for he truly had no idea what to do, he crossed the room to lie down on the bed beside her. She started crying when he slid an arm under her, and his feeling of incompetency increased. Rolling her over, he pulled her close. "Shh. It's all right. You're all right."

Shaking her head, rubbing her cheek against his shoulder, she whimpered, "I'm sorry, so sorry."

"Shh," he repeated.

She lay still for several moments, and then quietly said, "I left Mrs. Ketchum's books at the bookstore."

A smile tugged at his lips, and he kissed the top of her head. "No, the owner said she'd have them sent to the hotel." He recalled the woman's words as he'd left the shop with his wife cradled in his arms. An amazing feat, for his mind hadn't been his own right then. "You've spent the entire last week searching for things on that list."

Sniffling, she nodded.

"Well, no more. Today you're not allowed to leave this room. I want you to rest." Holding her as close as possible, he repeated, "Just rest."

She'd relaxed, was no longer trembling, and the hand that had been resting on his chest was now beneath his collar, rubbing the side of his neck in a way that always released the tension that settled there.

"I need to tell you something," she said softly.

His spine could have snapped, it stiffened so hard and fast. "I have to tell you something, too," he said. "But not now. You're exhausted and I…" A lump plugged his throat.

"Need to go back to your meeting."

"Yes." He hated to admit it. "I do." Silently, he cursed. The meetings were not going well. Per-Cum-Ske was getting more agitated every day. As was Seth, listening to the accusations the men in Washington, who rarely left their offices and had no idea what really took place out on the plains, seemed to conjure up out of nowhere. His temper had almost got the best of him more than once, and in reality, it was knowing Millie waited for him back at the hotel every evening that had Seth holding it in. He wasn't about to spend a night in a holding cell, being penalized for actions that might happen if he let his frustration loose, when he could be with her. Which could also happen if he didn't head back to the meeting hall soon.

Perhaps he should just let it all go. Walk away. Let someone else be in charge of Fort Sill and all the troubles that came along with it. But that wouldn't solve this problem. The one he'd created all on his own. They did need to talk, but she was overwrought right now.

"You're going to be late," she whispered.

"Yeah," he answered, his shoulders heavy.

"Then you'd better go."

That, too, tore at him. How she understood his duties, and didn't begrudge them or him for completing them. She was the perfect army wife. He gave her a long hug before pulling away, sitting up on the edge of the bed. Twisting to rub a hand along her arm, he asked, "You'll stay right here? Take a nap, get some rest?"

She scooted around to sit beside him. "Yes."

He nodded toward the bedside table. "The doctor left some medicine. Said it will help you sleep."

"I know."

"I'll be back as soon as I can," he said.

Her smile was about the saddest one he'd ever seen.

Cupping her cheek, he kissed the tip of her nose. "I love you." The first time he'd said those words they'd just tumbled out, but now when he said them, emotions filled the statement, and him.

Tears glistened in her eyes and she pinched her lips together as she nodded again.

"I'll be back," he said, too choked up to say more.

Millie watched him leave through a blinding haze of tears. She couldn't find the strength to say goodbye, or raise a hand. Instead, she sat there, as lifeless as the pillow behind her. She should have told him.

It could have been hours or minutes, she had no way of knowing, but she was still sitting there, not really thinking, not really seeing, when the door opened again. Too raw, too spent to react, she simply asked, "What are you doing here?"

Martin shut the door with the back of one heel before he carried a tray across the room and set it down on the table near the wardrobe closet. He crossed his arms then, stared at her somberly. "You're going to tell me everything, Millie. Everything."

Shrugging, she shook her head. "What's there to tell?"

"Why are you pretending to be married to

Rosemary's husband?" He started to pace. "Of all the things you've done for your sister, this is the most outlandish. The craziest. What the hell were you thinking?"

Never, not once in all the years she'd known him, had Martin ever shown anger toward her, but right now he was furious.

The once numb emptiness inside her erupted with enough force that the contents of her stomach hit the back of her throat. She slapped a hand against her lips, but it didn't help. Thankfully, Martin had pulled out the chamber pot from beneath the bed and held it in front of her.

When she was done, with nothing left inside her, he handed her a glass of water. "Rinse and spit," he said.

She did and then he took the water and the chamber pot, hid them from her view and sat down beside her. "You're so upset you've made yourself sick, Millie."

Closing her eyes against the tears, she nodded.

"I'm not leaving this room until you tell me everything," he said. "And we both know Seth Parker will be back soon."

Injustice erupted inside her, but she was so spent it couldn't go anywhere, except to burst forth in a new set of tears. It all had to end, she knew that, but she didn't know where to start.

"Aw, Millie," Martin said, folding an arm around her.

"I had to do it, Martin," she sobbed. "I had to pretend to be Rosemary. She said she'd kill herself if I didn't."

"Oh, Millie, not that again," he groaned.

"She meant it," Millie insisted. "I know she did."

He sighed heavily. "Start at the beginning and tell me everything. I'll need every detail if I'm going to help you. If that's even possible this time."

Martin had helped her in the past, more than once, when she'd found herself in too deep, and though she doubted there was anything he could do this time, she told him every last detail.

Afterward, while she was shaking her head at the fiasco she'd created, he bolted off the mattress. "Are you loco?" He took off his hat and ran a hand through his straight brown hair. "Do you have any idea who Seth Parker is?"

"Of course I know—"

"No," he said, with eyes wide and his arms flapping at his sides. "I'm talking about Major Seth Parker." Pacing the floor, he continued, "The man half the Indian Nation is afraid of—if not all of it. He's not in charge of Fort Sill by accident. Have you ever noticed how big he is? He was building ships at the age of ten. Carrying beams twice as long and heavy as he was, and running his own crew by the time he was fourteen. Criminy, Millie, Major Parker can hold a man off the ground by the neck with one hand while punching him in the gut with the other."

She sighed at Martin's overinflated antics. "Seth would never—"

"There are men who say they saw it."

"Martin—"

"He's been in wars, Millie."

Martin's eyes were somber, serious, and that had her nerve endings coming to life.

"Battles where people died, yet he came out unscratched." Kneeling in front of her, holding her hands, Martin said, "How do you think the army went from fighting the Indians to befriending them? Men like Seth Parker, that's how. He's a good man, Millie, don't get me wrong. I respect him, as does most every man he encounters. But along with that respect comes a touch of fear."

She shook her head. The thought of people fearing Seth was ludicrous.

"That's why I'm in Washington, Millie. When my commanding officer heard Major Parker was traveling out here..." Her friend shook his head. "Hell, every fort sent representation to be here. They knew he'd get something done. He fights for what he believes in, and Millie...I saw how he feels about you."

An inkling of hope sprang up inside her. Seth did love her, and she had to find a way to make him understand why she'd done what she had.

Martin shook his head. "No, Millie," he said. "It's no good. He loves you, I saw that, but when he learns what you and Rosemary did…"

Millie lifted a hand, ran a finger along the scar on Martin's cheek. It went from the edge of his nose to his ear. Used to it, she hadn't noticed it for years. Until right now, recalling he'd gotten it from a branch when he'd jumped in the river to save Rosemary from drowning herself. "Martin," she whispered. "I did it for the baby."

His eyes narrowed. "Rosemary's threats again." He grabbed her shoulders then. "Millie, when are you going to realize she will never hurt herself? Others, yes. Herself, no."

"I do know that, Martin," she said. "Now. And it's more frightening than ever. I'm doing all this for the baby." Shaking her head, she whispered, "If I don't protect it, who will?"

"Aw, hell," Martin growled. "I'd rather be an Indian right now."

Seth was about as close to losing his patience as he'd ever been. Pigheaded men had kept empty negotiations going deep into the evening, and that built his worries about Millie, ill and alone at the hotel, into mammoth proportions. Spinning at the sound of his name while entering the hotel lobby, he frowned at one of the men he'd just sat across the room from.

"Senator," he said, once again moving forward.

"May I talk to you for a moment, Major?"

His patience was stretched, threatening to snap, but Seth held rein on it and gave a nod.

"Thank you," the portly man said, gesturing toward a more secluded area.

The lobby was empty, yet Seth followed Louis McPhalen to stand next to the wall, and waited. He wasn't a close acquaintance of the man, but knew who he was because he'd been receiving congratulations the last few days. It seemed the man's son had just been born a week or so ago, and hearing it had Seth once again wondering about a family. Children.

"I'm glad a partial agreement was reached this evening," the senator said, wiping at the sweat gathering over brows as red as the hair on his head.

"I just hope you and the rest of Congress will come to a full agreement soon," Seth replied, glancing toward the stairs.

"We will," the man said. "I'll go above and beyond to see it happens."

An odd chill gripped Seth's spine and he couldn't help but glower at the man.

Senator McPhalen's Adam's apple bobbed, but he didn't look away. "I considered not saying anything, Major, but I need you to know I won't forsake my responsibility. Ever."

Seth fought to keep his expression from changing, even though confusion swarmed his mind. Eventually he nodded, just to let the man know he'd heard.

"My son will be raised properly and respected, as any son of mine should be."

Still not letting his bewilderment show, Seth nodded. "I'm glad to know that, Senator."

The man lifted his chin. "I've heard of you, Major, of your...abilities. And though I don't expect us to be friends, I don't want to be enemies, either."

A chill had the hair on Seth's arms standing on end. Thinking of Millie no doubt, because she was on his mind. What he had to tell her. He really didn't have time to listen to this man any longer.

"I'm willing to discuss any type of agreement you wish to suggest, Major," McPhalen said.

Seth's gaze was on the staircase, and his mind on the woman in the room on the second floor. Growing more frustrated, he said, "I expect a full agreement to be reached soon and fulfilled."

"It will, Major," the man answered. "I give you my solemn promise."

Seth had little hope that bucket could hold water. "I hope so, Senator," he said. "Now if you'll excuse me." He didn't bother waiting for an answer, just marched toward the stairs, straight-backed and stiff, as taught all those years ago by his father in their yard, hearing tales of how he'd go to West Point one day. Seth had thought more and more about his father lately, mainly on the train the past few days, while imagining having a son of his own someday.

"Evening, Major."

Seth came to a stop outside his hotel room door, where he'd stationed Rex Moore, to ensure Millie didn't attempt to complete Ilene Ketchum's list instead of resting.

"Mrs. Parker hasn't left all day," the sergeant said.

"Did you see that she ate?"

Rex frowned, shook his head. "Well, I didn't look to see if the plate was empty when Sergeant Clark carried it out."

Seth's hand squeezed the doorknob so hard his knuckles stung. "Who?"

Surprise, worry, maybe fear flashed in the man's eyes. "Martin Clark. He has a scar across his right cheek." Rex gestured to his own face.

"When was he here?" Seth asked, suddenly grasping why the army man at the bookstore had looked vaguely familiar.

Rex Moore swallowed, but Seth made no attempt to hold back the glare he'd settled on the man.

"The second time—"

"Second time?"

"I—I assumed you'd sent him, Major, knowing he and your wife were friends and all."

Something dark and looming grew inside Seth. "How do you know they're friends?"

"Well, 'cause…" The Sergeant cleared his throat. "Just assuming, sir."

"Tell me what you saw," he all but growled.

Wide-eyed, Moore responded, "Nothing, sir."

The desire to grab the man by his shirt had the doorknob digging into Seth's hand. He released it, made sure the man, who'd been on more than one battlefield with him, noticed just how close to being throttled he was. "Tell me now, Sergeant. What did you see?"

Shifting from foot to foot, Rex Moore stuttered, "Well, uh, um, I heard a noise." He pointed toward the door, and then shoved both hands in his pocket. "When I peeked in to check, they were hugging, sir." Snapping his head up, he added, "But just a hug like friends do."

Martin Clark. The man Millie was engaged to. No wonder she'd fainted. "Where's Clark now?"

"I don't know, sir," Rex said. "It was several hours ago."

"Find him," Seth demanded, glancing at the door. It was time to put this sham to rest. All of it. But he wanted all the ammunition he could get before confronting her. Needed it, with the way his insides were turning inside out. How could he ever have imagined the two sisters were different? Teeth clenched, he turned away from the door and snapped, "Have him meet me downstairs in the restaurant."

"Now, sir?"

"Yes, now."

"Don't you want me guarding the door?"

Seth started for the stairs. "Figure it out, Sergeant."

Having no doubt his order would be followed, Seth went straight to a table in the back of the hotel dining room, where he downed two shots of whiskey, something he rarely did. It didn't help. The fire from the liquid only intensified the burning in his throat and stomach.

Within minutes the same soldier from the bookstore walked across the room. Stopped at his table. "Major."

Seth stood, taking in the man's stiff stance. "Sergeant Clark, thank you for answering my summons."

"I was in the lobby. Figured you'd be looking for me."

Waving a hand for the other man to be seated,

Seth returned to his chair, and eyed his opponent as he sat. Average height, common brown hair. The only thing that stood out about Martin Clark was the jagged scar on his cheek. "Why would you expect me to be looking for you?" He knew the answer, just wanted the other man's opinion.

The waitress arrived and when Clark shook his head, Seth waved her away.

"Well, sir," Clark said. "I'm assuming you heard I was in your hotel room, and you already know I caught M-Mrs. Parker when she fainted at the bookstore."

Mrs. Parker. The name could have been a knife, it cut so deep, but Seth nodded and spun his empty glass in a circle on the table. "You mean the woman you're engaged to, don't you, Sergeant?"

The man coughed and patted his chest a couple times while shaking his head before he squeaked, "Engaged?"

"You and Millie."

Clark, wide-eyed, took a deep breath and held it for a minute. "Aw, hell, Major," he said, with all the remorse of an undertaker. "I wish you'd just shoot me now."

"I might," he admitted honestly.

"And I wouldn't blame you, Major."

A chill settled inside Seth, so fast and strong

he probably had frost on his fingertips, the way they'd frozen to the glass he'd been twirling.

"As much as I hate to say this, sir," Clark said, "I can't give you any answers."

Stung, Seth felt the muscles in his neck start to throb, and not trusting his mouth, he simply glared at the man.

Clark touched the scar on his cheek. "I got this when I jumped in a river to save my best friend's sister from drowning. Ironic thing was, she wasn't drowning, just pretending to be."

Seth was listening, but the bile churning in his stomach was burning the back of his throat, and every muscle in his body had gone tight. "Why should I care about that, Sergeant?"

Clark shrugged. "I guess I just wanted you to know."

"Why?" he pressed.

"Because Millie's my best friend." Clark swallowed. "And I love her."

Seth bottled his reaction, refused to let it show, but it was like a steam cooker, spitting bouts of boiling hot mist throughout his system.

"Ultimately, sir," Clark continued, "that's all I can say. It's Millie's story, and she wants to be the one to tell you the truth."

Seth's anger was so thick, thoughts couldn't form. Just actions. His hand came down on the table hard enough to make the empty glass bounce and tumble to the floor.

Clark flinched, but held his gaze. "I told her I'd take her away. Desert the army. Hide. But she refused." The man stood then. "She's in your room. Waiting for you."

Seth didn't move a muscle, just sat there, knowing the man had something else he wanted to say. Seth didn't want to listen to anything more. He didn't like being ambushed. Not by anyone. And Millie, the woman he loved, had ambushed him.

"I know your reputation, sir," Clark said, "and I hope I'm correct in my belief that you won't harm her."

Once again Seth remained still, quiet.

"I'd appreciate it if you'd let her know I'll be in the lobby if she needs me."

That was more than he could take. Snapped the last thread of his patience. "She won't need you tonight, Sergeant."

The man left, and Seth remained sitting in the corner of the dining room until the rest of the hotel was sound asleep, and the black man who operated the Wormley Hotel finally approached the table, asking about his accommodations.

Seth assured him the *accommodations* were fine, it was the rest of the world that wasn't. He could have sat there for a year and still not known what to do about any of it. The emotions filling him as he climbed the stairs were unfamiliar and unidentifiable. Some at least. Others he knew. Anger. Rage. Resentment. Humiliation. Dishonor. Shame.

Separating them was impossible; all he knew was he'd been duped again.

Martin Clark hadn't given him any answers, but Seth now knew more than he wanted to. The man did love Millie. He'd not only said it, it had shone in his eyes as he spoke of her, and by that Seth knew Clark would still marry her, even knowing she'd pretended to be another man's wife. Seth's. Tempted him with that body, whispering words of love. She'd played him well, and in all actuality, she was more dangerous than her sister.

Seth waved the sentry away from the door before he entered, pulling in a deep breath in order to gain the ability to even turn the knob.

She rose as he entered, from the chair near the table on the far side of the room. Her chestnut hair had been recently brushed. It glistened in the glow of the lamp and splayed over her shoulders, except for a few strands that had caught on the three big buttons on her housecoat when she stood up. His throat swelled and he begged for the ability to keep all the anger from seeping away.

He'd need it tonight, tomorrow, the next day, the day after....

It had been years, but the sting and pain was as strong as he remembered—that gut wrenching rip at losing someone you loved. No, it wasn't the same. It was worse this time, because she was still alive. Standing right before him.

Seth took off his hat, mainly to give himself something to do, and kept his back to her well after he'd laid the headwear on the chair by the door. She'd set it there, so he'd have a place for his hat and coat, just like at home. That's what she'd said, anyway, when he'd come in after a meeting the first night they'd been here.

"Seth?"

Quivers shot down his spine. "Say what you have to say," he said, fidgeting with his coat buttons, already knowing he wouldn't be taking it off. Not in this room.

She was crying. He hadn't turned, couldn't see the tears, but heard them, felt them. He closed his eyes. Waited.

"I'm not Rosemary," she said, sounding stronger than he felt. "I'm her sister, Millie."

For an unknown reason, he noted how she said that. Tagging herself as Rosemary's sister before saying her name, almost as if the sister part was more important. It wasn't, and it shouldn't goad him the way it did.

"I know," he finally said.

"You know?"

He turned, which was a mistake. She wasn't sobbing, but the tears glistening on her long lashes hurt worse than if she had been. He couldn't focus on that. Wouldn't. "Did you really think you had me fooled? I told you when you first arrived at the fort that I knew you were Millie."

Her chin quivered as she nodded. "Yes, you did." She closed her eyes, shook her head. "There were so many times I wanted to tell you everything. Explain…"

She was struggling against her tears, and his hands were balling into fists, wanting to comfort her.

"I never meant to hurt you. I'm so sorry, so very sorry." Her sigh sounded laborious. "I know Rosemary is, too. She was lonely and she's always needed more attention than others. I was just supposed to…" Millie shook her head and sniffled. "Papa's money is all gone and—"

"That's what this is all about?" His blood turned cold. "Money?" He should have known. Rosemary was the one who'd brought it up in the "marriage negotiations" all those years ago.

"No."

Her eyes were begging him to listen, and damn if he didn't want to.

"No," Millie repeated, pointing toward the table, where several papers lay. "I scratched out the part about the money. I'll find another way to get it." She took a step forward. "You have to understand, our mother—"

"Your mother?" He took a step back, not able to be any closer. "This has nothing to do with your mother. She's been dead for years."

"Yes, she has been, and Rosemary's baby…"

His hearing failed as the pieces slammed together in his head. Even McPhalen made sense now. "Rosemary's baby," Seth growled. His insides grew uglier by the moment. He'd nursed a futile hope that Millie hadn't been involved in whatever games Rosemary had been playing. That she'd been an innocent bystander. In reality, he'd been duped by not one, but two sisters. One cuckolding him and the other seducing him so he'd never learn about it. "Has already arrived, Millie," he finished, with all the bitterness inside him. "She gave birth to Senator McPhalen's baby well over a week ago."

Millie's face turned ghostly and she wobbled, and he cursed his feet. Told them he'd cut them off if they took a step toward her.

Millie stared at him blankly for several long moments with a hand pressed to her chest, as if it hurt to breathe. "But his wife, Nadine, is Rosemary's best friend."

"And you're her sister," he said.

Chapter Fourteen

Spinning, before he lost his courage, Seth picked up his hat. He'd never walked away from a battle before, never even shied away from marching head-on into whatever came his way, but this time he didn't have the fight in him. Retreat was all he could manage.

Seth was still running the next morning, from himself, anyway.

After he'd seen to errands, which included telling the council members they could court-martial him for desertion, he truly didn't care—in the end they chose to cancel meetings for the day—he made his way back to the hotel, set on completing the plan he'd put in place.

One look at her, wearing the dress he'd bought her, almost made him change his mind. But that couldn't happen.

Rising from her chair, she smoothed the material over her stomach. "Sergeant Moore said you asked me to be ready by ten."

The habit of kissing her every time they met had him clenching his hands into fists. Not trusting his voice, he gestured toward the door, and didn't offer his arm. Couldn't. Her touch would open a vulnerable spot in him, one he couldn't afford to have exposed right now. He'd never known how empty a bed could be until he'd lain in the one across the hall, and the longing it had left in him had him wanting to ask her why. That would be useless. Talking at all would be useless. Besides, he knew. Knew everything now.

Her somber silence helped. Gave him time to let his anger renew itself. In reality what waited at their destination did all that. He led her to the train station and noted her surprise when he boarded beside her and settled in for the ride.

Later, when the train whistle blew, announcing they'd arrived in Richmond, Seth held strong. An army major was used to being ruthless and unsympathetic. Meeting her gaze with one as cold as he felt, he said, "Welcome home, Millie."

One attempt was all she made, asked if she could explain things again. Seth told her there was nothing she could say that he wanted to hear.

Her stiff stance and cold silence when he knocked on the door of her father's house had him keeping his hand balled into a fist, and he forced his mind to remain set on facing her sister. Rosemary. His wife. The thought was enough to make his anger simmer.

The woman who pulled the door open had him wondering how he'd ever, for even a moment, confused the two sisters. Rosemary was just as he remembered. There was a touch of beauty there, but it was hidden beneath an aura of self-importance so sinister and thick it couldn't be cut with a sword. She frowned, pulling dark brows over her frigid eyes as she glanced from him to Millie.

"It's about time you got home," she snapped, before turning to him with eyelashes batting and a slight curtsy. "Thank you, sir, for seeing my sister home."

Millie let out a groan like he'd never heard as she stepped across the threshold. "You must have forgotten what he looks like, Rosemary," she said. "This is your husband, Major Seth Parker."

"My hus—" The glare Rosemary cast Millie hadn't completely left her face when she turned back to him, but she soon concealed it. "Of course I remember. Seth, do come in. I'm assuming you discovered how Millie ran off. Pretending to be me." She pulled her hand from where she'd flattened it near her throat and fluttered it toward her sister. "Millie, get us a drink. Some bourbon perhaps?" she asked him with an expectant gaze.

"Get it yourself," Millie answered, walking toward a black woman who'd appeared on the far side of the entranceway.

"Why, you little…" Rosemary seethed, spinning around as if to chase her sister.

Seth grabbed her arm. He had nothing to say to her, yet had to speak in order to complete the mission. "I have papers for you to sign."

Chin up, nose in the air, Rosemary said, "Oh, yes, our divorce. I've been reconsidering that."

She looked nothing like her sister. Not even their voices sounded alike. "I haven't." Still holding her arm with one hand, he used the other to reach beneath his jacket and pull the envelope out of his shirt pocket. "Matter of fact, I had a new set of papers drawn up this morning."

Batting her lashes again, as if that was supposed to make her look more attractive, which it didn't, she let out a long sigh. "Do come in, Seth," she said. "So we can talk."

"No." He pulled her onto the porch. "There's a table right here you can use to pen your name."

"I'm not sign—"

"Yes, you are," he said. "Or I'll take you to court. Pull in every man you've been with since you were thirteen."

"Thirteen!"

"Yes, behind the carriage house. I believe his name—"

"Shut up," she seethed. "How dare you…"

"Oh, I dare," he insisted.

"I'll have you know I have money. I could take you to court and—"

"And what? Explain you had another man's baby while married to me?"

Her features contorted. "Why, that little snit. How dare she tell you my private business."

"Who? Millie? She didn't tell me." Gritting his teeth, Seth added, "She didn't tell me anything." He pulled the papers out of the envelope and flattened them on the table next to a rocking chair.

"Oh, you just magically know everything about my life?"

"You're a general's daughter. The army knows everything about you," he said, not wanting to implicate Martin Clark, for a reason Seth had yet to discern. Maybe because the man had told him everything he wanted to know about Rosemary when he'd found him sitting in the foyer of the hotel last night—though Clark had refused to utter a word about Millie.

Pulling out a pen, Seth handed it to Rosemary. "Sign."

She glared at him, lips pouted and arms folded across her chest. "No."

The disgust, ire and revulsion he'd acquired

upon their first meeting was just as strong now, making him wonder how he'd ever buried them. "Trust me, Rosemary," he growled. "You don't want to spar with me on this." Leaning close so she could feel the loathing he felt, he glowered directly into her eyes. "If you do, I won't stop until you're ruined from here to England. I have the means, and the ways, and would be more than happy to see you groveling." For added assurance, he said, "I'm sure Senator McPhalen, or his wife, won't take kindly to being dragged through the mud beside you."

Huffing, with steam practically coming out her nose, she glared at him as if she could win the standoff. In the end, she grabbed the pen from his hand. "Fine."

Just as she was about to touch the pen to the paper, he clutched her wrist and nodded toward the open doorway. "What's the Negro woman's name?"

"Lola Burnett, why? She's just the maid."

"Miss Burnett," he called into the house. "Could you step out here, please?" The woman appeared seconds later, and he nodded a greeting. "I need someone to witness Rosemary signing this document. Would you mind?"

"No…yes, sir. I'll watch."

He let loose Rosemary's hand, and after she'd

scrawled her name, he took the pen and handed it to the maid. "Could you sign it, as well, please?"

"Yes, sir."

Once the paper was back in the envelope, and the maid had returned inside, Seth smiled, feeling an ounce of victory. "By the way, Rosemary, those weren't divorce papers."

A spark glistened in her eye, one that galled him to no end. "They weren't?"

"No, they were annulment papers. You and I were never married." He turned then, walked down the steps, while her growling scream echoed in the air and the slam of the door ricocheted against the porch roof.

From the upstairs window, Millie watched Seth climb into the buggy that had brought them from the rail station. Numb beyond feeling, she remained standing at the window until the road was empty and there was nothing left to prove he'd ever been there. Nothing to prove he'd ever been a part of her life.

It was over. Something she'd wished for not so long ago. Well, now she had it. None of it came as a surprise. Her dream had forewarned her, yet the ache, the pain, felt as if something treasured had just been unexpectedly stolen from her.

In some ways, it had been.

The one thing that didn't surprise her was that he'd known she wasn't Rosemary. She'd tried to analyze that, both last night and this morning, but her pain was too strong for rational thought. Somewhere deep inside she just knew. Had always known.

Eventually she moved across the room, climbed onto the bed and, exhausted inside and out, simply lay there. Not thinking. Not seeing. Not living.

Lola came in sometime later, with tea. Millie sat up, took the cup handed to her. Feeling returned to her body, like stinging needles, and she set the cup down. "Where's the baby?"

Lola patted her knee gently. "With his father. He's just fine, so don't worry about that."

Senator McPhalen. That had shocked her. It shouldn't have. Rosemary never cared who she hurt. "A boy," Millie said, with longing tugging at her heart.

"Yes. Good size and healthy."

"He came earlier than I expected."

"Does that surprise you?" Lola asked, her brown eyes full of sympathy.

"No," Millie had to admit.

The housekeeper sighed heavily. "She wants to see you downstairs."

"What for?"

"I could guess, but I won't." Lola patted Millie's knee again. "I'll tell her you're tired."

"No," she said, standing up. "What good will that do?"

"I'm glad you're home, Millie," the woman said sadly. "I'm happy to see you, but I wish you'd never come back."

"Where else was I supposed to go?"

"Martin—"

Millie shook her head. "Is a good friend, but…" Memories were trying to come forward, and she couldn't deal with them just yet. "I'm going to go see what Rosemary wants."

Lola snatched up the tray, rattling cups in her hurry. "Wait, I'm coming with you."

They stopped in the kitchen and then made their way through the parlor into what used to be Papa's office. Rosemary claimed it as hers, but Millie still imagined her father sitting there, and would always think of it as his. Her sister was pacing the floor in front of the massive stone fireplace, and other than a flashing glare, she didn't acknowledge that anyone had entered the room.

Several minutes later, after Millie and Lola had sat down on the cream-colored sofa with wooden arms, which Millie remembered being in the parlor, not in here, her sister stopped.

"Lola, leave us."

Millie laid a hand on the woman's knee. "No, Lola is staying," she said. "What did you want?"

"I said—" Rosemary started.

"What did you want, Rosemary?" Millie interrupted. It was as if a fist gripped her spine, filled her very bones with ire, reinforcing the fact that she was done playing her sister's games.

"Fine, she can be the witness," Rosemary said, flipping her nose in the air. "I have some papers I need you to sign, and Mr. Wells said someone had to prove it was you that signed them."

"Why? Because you already tried to forge my name?" Millie asked, and answered her own question.

Rosemary didn't reply, just handed over a stack of papers. "You have to initial by each paragraph, to prove you read them."

Too fuddle-headed, still thinking of all she'd lost, Millie didn't understand what she was reading until the third or fourth paragraph, at which point she started over. Needles were stabbing her again, especially when she read the last page. Disgusted, she looked up at her sister. "I'm not signing this."

"And why not?"

"Because it says here that Papa didn't leave everything to you. Money was split fifty-fifty and the house, this house, is in my name. I'm not giving all that to you."

"Yes, you are," Rosemary insisted. "I shared my half with you. Now you need to share your half with me."

"When?"

"All the money and things you needed to travel to Indian Territory." Pulling her face into a nasty scowl, Rosemary added, "And then you stab me in the back by telling Seth everything."

"I didn't tell him anything," Millie answered. Nothing he hadn't known, anyway, and thinking of him had her spine stiffening. Living with him the past weeks had left many lasting impressions on her, and the one she recalled right now was how he dealt with people. His self-assuredness and inner power. "The amount of money I took is a mere pittance compared with what this says."

"I've kept you fed and clothed since Father died," Rosemary said.

"No, you haven't," Millie said, completely sickened that she'd let all this escape her before. "It states a third account was created for household needs. If you've spent all your money, that's your problem, not mine."

"You either sign those papers or—"

"Or what?" Millie stood, gestured toward Lola. "I think I need some more tea. Would you care to join me?"

Looking somewhat startled, the housekeeper stood, and then after a long hard stare, she started to smile. "Tea?" She nodded, smiling more broadly.

They were almost to the door when Rosemary

shouted, "If you don't sign those papers I'll kill myself."

The statement stabbed Millie between the shoulder blades. Spinning to look at her sister— a long examination of just who Rosemary St. Clair was—Millie was saddened by what she saw. "Well, clean up any mess you make. Lola and I will be having tea."

Lola made a choking noise as she slapped a hand over her mouth.

Whereas Rosemary started screaming, "I'll do it. I'll do it. I'm not kidding."

Millie stepped closer, challenged her sister with a stare she'd seen Seth use, and was amazed at how strong it made her. "No, you won't. You don't have the courage. You've never had the courage to face anything you've done. You've just used a tragic act—what our mother did—to get what you want."

Her sister gasped.

"I know why our mother did what she did. It wasn't because I was a fussy baby or because I was a girl and not a boy, or any of the dozen other reasons you've claimed over the years. She was distraught that Father had been captured. That he was a prisoner of war. She couldn't imagine living without him."

As if thoroughly startled, Rosemary glanced around the room. "How do you know that?"

The long talks with Ilene Ketchum came to mind, how Millie had wished her mother had lived so she could have taught her all the things Mrs. Ketchum had. But she wasn't about to tell her sister any of that. "Our family secret wasn't much of a secret. When you're an army man, you have no secrets." That bit of truth jabbed her heart. Seth's secrets, especially what she and Rosemary had done to him, would follow him forever. That realization struck home, and sickened, Millie glared at her sister. "Do whatever you have to do, Rosemary. You always do. Just know I'm not going to clean it up. I have my own life to see to."

Millie led the way into the kitchen, where Lola stopped, and stared at her. "You still want tea?" the woman asked.

"Yes, I do. Don't you?"

"You're not worried about her?" She pointed a thumb over her shoulder, toward the room they'd just left.

"No. What good would that do any of us?"

"You've changed, Millie," Lola said. "I like it."

"Yes, I've changed, but I don't know what good it's going to do me."

"Anything you want it to, darling."

The word *darling* sliced her heart. Millie closed her eyes and felt the pain. In an odd way she needed it. Needed to remember how Seth had called her that.

"Sit down, girl," Lola said. "I'll make the tea and then you can tell me how you fell in love with Major Parker."

"It wasn't hard," Millie answered, taking a seat. "It wasn't hard."

Rosemary burst through the door just then.

Holding her breath, awaiting the wrath of her sister at having heard what had just been said, Millie wrapped her fingers around the bride's necklace hanging at her neck.

"I'm leaving tomorrow," Rosemary said. "Moving to England, and I want that dress."

Millie glanced down at the velvet traveling suit. "No," she said. "This dress was a gift. Why are you going to England?"

"Moving," Rosemary corrected. "I'm moving to England."

"Why?"

"She has to," Lola said. "It was part of the deal she made with the people she sold her baby to."

Millie shook her head. "You *sold* your baby?" She should have known there was more behind Rosemary's insistence that she go to Fort Sill.

"Well, I couldn't very well take him to England with me, could I?" Rosemary asked.

Millie bit her tongue, gave herself a moment to process an answer. For the first time ever, maybe Rosemary had thought of someone besides herself. The child was better off with the McPhalens. "Nadine will love him as her own," Millie finally said.

Rosemary didn't try to hide her surprise, but her lips quivered for a moment, and Millie wondered if giving up the baby had been harder than her sister had imagined it would be.

"Well, now that you seem to know everything," Rosemary said a moment later, "I need you to give me some money."

"What for?" Millie asked.

"For my move to England." Squaring her shoulders, she continued, "Nadine and Louis have purchased my ticket, but they won't give me the rest of the money until I'm on the steamer. I've ordered gowns and such that must be picked up today. My scheduled departure is tomorrow."

Millie was amazed by her own new abilities, such as how she was clear-headed enough to ask, "What would you have done if I hadn't returned today?"

Running a finger along the edge of the table, her sister said, "I've arranged to sell a few household items, but now that you're here…"

"It won't be so easy," Millie finished, understanding where the leather couch from Papa's office had gone. Another understanding, though, was the one that Millie focused on. "We aren't so different, you know. You and I."

Rosemary frowned. "How so?"

"All our lives," she said, sadness growing inside her, "we've both wanted to be loved. But since neither of us knew what it was, we didn't know what we were looking for." A huge, invisible fist was squeezing the blood out of Millie's heart and she had to know one thing. "You had no intention of ever divorcing Seth, did you?"

Her sister didn't meet her gaze. "People respect a major's wife."

If either of them knew about being a major's wife, it was she, not Rosemary, and that's when Millie knew she could never give it up as easily as her sister was. Being Seth's wife. "I'll give you the money you need," she said, "but I'd like you to promise me something."

Skepticism glowed in Rosemary's eyes.

Millie reached over and took her sister's hand. "Our mother's death was tragic. Father being gone all the time was hard, but we always had a place to live. Food. Clothes. Lola," she added with a smile. Wind's grubby peppermint stick flashed in her mind and she shook her head. "We were always looking for love to come from the outside, but that's not where it's at, Rosemary. It's inside us, and neither you nor I knew how to let it out." Now she was remembering how she felt standing next to Seth, the pride, and how she loved her body when he touched it. "Promise me you'll learn to like yourself. Once you do that, the rest will come. You have to love in order to be loved."

"You've changed," Rosemary whispered.

"I know," she answered, just as softly. "And you can, too."

For the first time ever Millie believed the tears glistening in her sister's eyes were real. Those same tears appeared again the next day when they hugged goodbye on the dock. Leaving Richmond and the life she'd always known had been what Millie had needed, and she prayed the same would be true for Rosemary.

Later in the day, as Millie walked toward the front door, her heart did a little flip-flop, wishful thinking at who might be knocking. Seth was on her mind nonstop, more poignantly after her trunk and traveling bag had been delivered from the hotel in Washington, along with a note saying her other items would be shipped from Fort Sill upon his arrival there.

It wasn't him, of course, as she knew it wouldn't be, and seeing Nadine McPhalen on the stoop, Millie voiced the only thought that formed. "Rosemary isn't here."

"I know," the woman said. "I watched her

board the steamer this afternoon. I've come to talk to you, if I may."

"Of course, come in." Millie stepped aside, and gestured for the woman's light shawl, for the unseasonably warm November didn't require heavier garments. Yet. The weather would change, just like everything else had. Chasing aside the thought, she said, "I'm sorry, I didn't see you at the dock today."

"I wasn't there to be seen," Nadine said. "I was there to see with my own eyes that she left."

A chill rippled Millie's skin. Nadine and Rosemary, though complete opposites, had been friends for years. Cautious, because her willpower to let her sister's mess stay her sister's problem might be challenged, she waved a hand toward the parlor. "Please, make yourself comfortable. I'll just go ask Lola to bring us some tea."

"Could I ask Lola to do so? I have another favor to ask of her."

Swallowing at the thickness in her throat, Millie nodded. "All right, I'll be in the parlor."

"Thank you."

Nadine returned within seconds. Millie had just sat down on the white sofa, the one she and Lola had carried in from the office and repositioned in its rightful place this afternoon. The other woman didn't sit, but paced back and forth, the skirts and slips of her yellow dress swishing loudly.

"Goodness," she finally said, stopping near the sofa. "I don't know where to begin."

Millie drew in a fortifying breath. "Well, Nadine, just say it. There's nothing worse than keeping it bottled up." She knew that so well. So very well.

"Oh, Millie," the woman said, dropping onto her knees in front of the sofa. "I'm so sorry. I hope you can forgive me."

"Forgive you?"

Nadine wrapped both hands around one of Millie's. "Yes. It was wrong of us to have you do such a thing, but there was no other choice."

Her heartbeat was accelerating, pounding at the base of her throat like a woodpecker on a dead stump. "I'm afraid I don't know what you're talking about, Nadine."

The woman's blue eyes took on a startled look. "You don't?"

When Millie shook her head again, she sat down beside her.

"My life is now complete because of you, Millie."

An eerie sensation settled around Millie's shoulders.

"You see, Millie, my husband, Senator Louis McPhalen, is the father of your nephew."

Millie made no outward sign that she'd already known that.

"It's startling, I know. I myself was enraged when I first heard," Nadine said. "Then again, that's what Rosemary wanted. She was delighted to throw it in my face." The woman smiled then. "But it all worked out so splendidly, I might even forgive her. Someday."

Refusing to jump to her sister's defense, despite her old habits, Millie offered a slight smile.

"I can't have children," Nadine said. "After five years of us trying, the doctor said it just isn't going to happen."

A wave of anguish took Millie's breath away, for just this morning her monthly had arrived. She'd hoped it wouldn't, for then she'd have a reason for Seth to listen to her, had even imagined what he'd do when she traveled to Fort Sill to tell him. That had been a dream, shattered by reality, and now the pain renewed itself all over again.

"I told Louis," Nadine said, "that I'd forgive him for his little indiscretion with Rosemary— for we all know she's free with her favors—if he found a way to get me the baby. Rosemary then tried to say the child wasn't Louis's, and who knows, maybe it's not, but that doesn't matter. He's my son now."

A splattering of joy erupted inside Millie. The

child would have a good life with Nadine. "Yes, he is."

"Because of you."

She shook her head.

"Yes, Millie," the woman said firmly. "You. When Louis began negotiating with Rosemary, she threw around her threats like always, and the only one that scared us was the fact that her husband, Major Parker, could return and discover her condition. Louis was aware of the major's plan to visit Washington, and the furthest he could get it postponed was mid-October, due to winter traveling. We were afraid how the major might react to Rosemary's condition, and needed to make sure he didn't arrive before the baby did. We thought you and your sweet disposition might be able to convince him to postpone the trip a bit longer." Nadine squeezed Millie's hand firmly. "And you did. We are so thankful for that. And Millie, we're so sorry to have involved you in all this."

Trying to grasp it all, she asked, "You wanted me to go to Fort Sill?"

"Rosemary said you'd refuse, but eventually she agreed to convince you to do it. To visit your brother-in-law, and have him escort you home after the baby was born."

"My brother-in-law." It had been so long since Millie thought of him in those terms, it didn't seem as if she was thinking of Seth.

"Rosemary said she was divorcing him, couldn't stay married to him after this. Maybe her conscience finally kicked in, or maybe it was the amount of money we offered her. Either way, it worked. We all got what we wanted."

Millie nodded, but inside she was screaming. Everyone else may have gotten what they wanted, but what about her and Seth?

"I didn't know you'd returned until I saw you at the dock today. I'd assumed so, though, because Louis left last week, right after the baby arrived, to attend the Indian negotiations. You see, I'd left town a few months ago. Told everyone I was expecting, and went to stay with my aunt so I'd have complete rest. I was just over in Browns Corner, so when Louis wired that the baby was arriving, I rushed home to present everyone our newborn son."

All the time she thought she was being selfish, she was being used. As was Seth.

"Millie?"

She glanced up, and her heart somersaulted as Nadine waved for Lola to step closer, holding out a tiny bundle.

"Meet your nephew. Louis William McPhalen III."

Millie's hands shook as she took the infant in her arms and folded back the corner of the blanket covering his little face. The blue eyes gazing up at her brought tears to her own eyes. Maybe because they were as dark as Seth's, or maybe because she was falling in love with this little blue-eyed man as quickly as she had the other one she knew. "Hello, there," she whispered. "I've wanted to meet you for a long time."

Nadine rested a palm on the baby's head. "I can't promise that I'll tell him I'm not his birth mother someday," she said. "I honestly don't know if I'll have it in me. But I can promise to tell him about his aunt Millie, and how she traveled all the way to Indian Territory just for him."

A tear ran down Millie's cheek, and she had to sniffle and blink to keep others from following.

"He'll always know what you did for him, Millie. So will Louis and I. Our entire family owes you so much that my thank-you seems a pittance."

Glancing toward the woman, seeing the tears trickling down her face, Millie shook her head. "Holding him is more than I ever dreamed. More than I hoped. Thank you for this," she said, cradling the baby to her cheek. "Thank you for giving my nephew the home he deserves."

One good thing came out of the mess Seth's life was in. The anger burning inside him couldn't be contained, and that made Congress listen, not just McPhalen.

After Seth's return from Richmond, it took

322   The Major's Wife

only one day and his demands were met, including several other stipulations he'd added to the list of benefits the Indians would receive. The meeting gave a way for his anger to escape—somewhat—but the void left in his chest was then larger than ever.

Ironically, a telegram had caught up with him that evening, one that told him it was still unknown where the St. Clair sisters were. He'd burned the note and then, since there were still a few days before his scheduled return trip west, he took a train up to Boston, hoping that seeing his family would help him know if he was capable of feeling again.

His mother was shocked to see him, and happy. As was he, since it had been years. His stepsiblings were almost grown, but other than that, everything felt as if he'd left just yesterday. In Boston, that was. Inside, he felt as if he'd aged fifty years the past week.

It was his third day there when his mother invited him to sit and chat in front of the blazing fire that kept the freezing winds blowing off the bay from frosting over the inside of the house. He remembered working outdoors on days like this, when the ice and rain had turned his fingers stiff. It had been like that the day she'd sat him down and told him he was going to West Point.

Not a single gray hair could be seen in the

black tresses his mother always kept pinned up in a crown, and her blue eyes looked young and vibrant as she told him stories of things that had happened during his absence. Amanda Parker-Wadsworth would never look old, his stepfather, Ralph, had said when Seth had commented on her appearance. Because she didn't act old, and that was what kept her young.

Seth had laughed good-heartedly at the explanation, while another small corner of his heart broke loose, as it always did when Millie appeared in his mind. She'd be a hundred and still twirling around like a youngster, with laughter shining in her eyes. Her antics and delight had made him feel young, carefree, too.

"You've grown awfully quiet," his mother said.

Pulling his thoughts back to the present, he shrugged, and then stood up to add a log to the fire. "Ghosts, I guess." He flashed her a smile. The house was old, and they all talked about the ghosts of generations gone by.

"Past or present?"

Something clicked in his mind, like the snap of a stick in the woods that told you someone was watching, following. He sat, pondering all that weighed heavily upon him, before he answered. "I don't know."

"Tell me her name."

Seth glanced up as a shiver shot all the way to his toes.

His mother smiled in an understanding way. "You are a grown man, one I'm very proud of, but you're still my son, and I've known since the moment you walked through the door that something's troubling you. A mother's intuition tells me it's a woman. One you love very much."

He shook his head. "I can't love her."

"Why?"

"It's too…" A heavy sigh left his chest.

"Too complicated? Too hard to explain?" she asked.

"Yeah," he answered, staring into the flames.

"We have all afternoon."

Drawing in a breath, wishing it could cleanse him, he shrugged. "I could talk all year and not understand it."

"Maybe," she said softly, "it's not for you to understand. Something you just have to accept."

He let out a lackluster chuckle as his insides churned. "I could never accept what happened."

"Why?"

Running a hand through his hair, he wished he could do something, anything, to release the energy bottled inside him. He pushed himself from the chair and crossed the room to stare out the window. There was nothing to see except leafless trees and a dusting of snow covering the ground. Nothing to grab his attention and make him forget.

Coming up behind, his mother rubbed his arms, patted his shoulders. "She's probably as miserable as you."

"No, no she's not," he insisted, yet he had to wonder. Hope.

"I'd beg to differ," Amanda said.

He spun away from the window, angry there was nothing to see. Angry at himself for still caring. Angry…just angry. "You don't even know her."

"Then tell me about her."

"There's nothing to tell."

"Does she have black hair, blue eyes?"

"No," he said, growing lost in the vision in his head. "They're brown. Her eyes and her hair." He swallowed at the lump forming. "Her eyes are unbelievable. They glimmer in the sunlight, in the firelight, like you wouldn't imagine."

"And her smile? Is it like an angel's?"

"Yeah," he said, but then changed his mind. "No, it's more like a pixie's. Whimsical and magical yet, mischievous at the same time."

Chapter Fifteen

And that's how Amanda Parker-Wadsworth, with her gentle, prodding questions, broke through his shell. Before Seth even realized it, he was telling her everything. From how he became a major to the reason he was sitting here talking about the most wonderful woman on earth, and why he couldn't love her.

"I knew a man once," his mother said, "that was so stubborn no one could tell him anything once he set his mind. Everything was black-and-white. No shades of gray. This way or that. No middle ground." She let out a sigh, then giggled. "Goodness but he drove me crazy, and dear heavens, what I wouldn't give to see him one more time."

Seth frowned, wondering who she missed so.

"Your father," she said. "Sean Parker." Smiling, she patted Seth's knee, sitting beside him on the long couch. "I love Ralph and the children we have together as much as I do you and Sam, but that doesn't mean I stopped loving Sean." Tears shimmered in her eyes. "Oh, he was a good man. A wonderful man, and you remind me so much of him."

Pride swelled in Seth's chest, so much a hint of embarrassment warmed his cheeks.

"But land sakes, he was stubborn. Always had to be in charge. Get the last word in."

Seth now wondered if her compliments were insults.

"I have to go upstairs and get something," she said, standing up, "but while I'm gone, do me a favor?"

"Sure," Seth answered, glancing at the wood box. Hauling some in would give him something to do besides think about Millie and how he wanted to go to Richmond. Beg her to forgive him. The box was full, though, so he turned, wondering what else his mother needed.

"While I'm gone, I want you to think about one thing, so you can answer a question I have."

More questions. He should have known. "All right, Mother, what's that?"

"Why are you here?"

"Becau—"

His mother pressed a finger against his lips. "Think about it while I'm gone."

Seth wanted to growl. He was here to see his family. Hadn't seen them in years. Frustrated all over again, he moved to the window, stared at the nothingness.

When his mother returned empty-handed, which made him believe she'd simply wanted to give him time to think, he tried to fathom the answer she wanted.

"So, why are you here?"

He grinned, though it was so false it hurt. "To see my family."

Smiling, she shook her head.

Seth shook his head in turn and asked, "Then why am I here?"

"You're here because what you really want is to go to Richmond and ask Millie to marry you, but just like when you wanted to go to West Point, you feel you can't. That you'll be letting others down if you do that. What you really want is for me to tell you to do it."

His heart slammed against his rib cage. She was right. That was exactly what he'd hoped.

"I won't tell you what to do this time, Seth. This is between you and Millie. You're the only ones who can figure this out."

Frustrated, he stood, walked across the room. In that, too, she was right. "Millie…" He pressed both hands against the fireplace mantel. "There were a million times she could have just told me the truth."

"And a million times you could have told her you already knew it."

He spun around, tried to come up with a reason why he hadn't.

"Love isn't a curse, Seth. It's a blessing."

Bitterness bubbled in his throat. It felt much more like a curse. Always had.

"Does it really matter who was right or wrong?" she asked.

His mind and heart were being torn in two.

"I'm not saying forget the past," his mother whispered. "Just accept it and move on."

Frozen for a moment, Seth's mind flashed to Per-Cum-Ske, the battle in the Wichita Mountains and the aftermath, him staring at the silent faces of friends and family. *We cannot help it. I did my duty.* The leader, who now had three wives, had definitely moved on. So why hadn't Seth?

"Here."

He glanced at the small box his mother held. "What's that?"

"Just a family heirloom I saved for you."

Lifting the lid revealed a woman's ring, a circle of diamonds around a sapphire.

"It's the one your father gave me."

Seth ran a finger over the jewels. "I thought you weren't going to tell me what to do."

"I'm not. You can do whatever you want with that ring. It's just something I wanted you to have."

What he wanted was Millie. Forever. "She opened things inside me I didn't know were closed," he admitted.

"It takes a powerful love to do that."

Seth nodded. More powerful than anything he'd ever known. "What if she can't forgive me?"

His mother shrugged. "It'll take courage to find out, and you were born with more courage than any man I've ever known."

"Maybe when it comes to battling Indians, but…" His spine stiffened. He'd retreated that night from their hotel room, but he hadn't declared defeat. That word wasn't in his vocabulary. Never had been.

"But I can't leave without it, Lola," Millie said. "I know I had it last night when I took a bath." Retracing every step she'd taken, she rounded the bathtub, searching for the bride's necklace. "I laid it here on the bench so it wouldn't get wet."

"I'm sorry, honey," Lola said, pulling her head in the window. "I laid the towel over the edge of the sill to dry. The necklace must have flown out. I searched the rooftop and the ground, but the wind might have carried it off."

Frustration made Millie's insides sting. It was just a necklace, and probably wouldn't sway Seth either way.

"I'll keep looking," Lola said, "and when I find it, I'll send it to you. I promise."

"See that you do," Millie said, leading the way out of the room and down the stairs. She had to leave now or she'd miss her train to Washington, and then the one to Tulsa.

"You're sure you don't want me to come with you?" Lola asked yet again.

"I'm sure. If he won't talk to me on the train, I'll rent a horse and follow him all the way to the fort, where I'll sit on the front stoop, making him step over me day after day."

Lola laughed. "You've become one determined woman."

"I have to be. I've never before wanted anything like I do this." Millie stopped at the front door, and saw the carriage waiting at the end of the walkway. The driver had already loaded her luggage. "I'm going to miss you very, very much."

"Well, don't. I'll be here, keeping this place in order for whenever you return."

"Visit," Millie corrected. "With my husband and children."

"I don't doubt that," Lola said, as they hugged.

Millie held on tight for a moment, wishing she didn't have any doubts. She did, but she wouldn't focus on them. And she wasn't being selfish, either; she was being true to herself. There was a difference. A big difference. Stepping back, she nodded toward the house. "I told Mr. Wells if you need anything he's to see to it, and an account has been set up in your name for household expenses and such. And Nadine will be bringing little Louie over for you to visit. Give him a kiss for me. Oh, and be sure to tell Mr. Evans I say hello."

"Mr. Evans?"

"Yes, Lola, don't try to fool me," Millie said, grinning. It was amazing how easy it was to see other people were in love when you knew how it felt. "I know you've been sweet on that man for years, but wouldn't leave me and Rosemary. This is your time now. The two of you can get married and live right here. He can keep working at the mill while you take care of Papa's house. Waiting for me and my husband and our children to come visit."

Lola's dark cheeks turned rosy. "Oh, you little scamp."

Millie laughed and skipped down the porch steps. "I'll write. Tell you what happens."

"You do that!"

Millie ran the rest of the way to the awaiting

carriage, but little good it did, hurrying so. The train to Washington had barely left Richmond when it screeched to a stop. After a few minutes the porter came along, explaining that a train ahead of them had troubles and they'd have to wait for repairs. In the end, Millie sat on that train for six hours before it started chugging north, and once she arrived in Washington, the train she'd hoped to catch, the one she knew Seth had arranged for their return trip, had already left.

Thwarted, but not enough to give up, she made arrangements for a private car—the train depot in Washington had several to choose from—to be part of the next train headed west, with connections to Tulsa. She was comforted to learn one was leaving the following day, with no layovers and no switching trains. It was a relief after all the delays during her first journey west, and Millie's excitement started to build again. She might still arrive before Seth and the wagons left for Fort Sill.

It was risky. He certainly could tell her to leave. But she'd never know if she didn't try. The cost of the private car was a bit outlandish, but recalling her other rides, including the one with Seth, she figured it would be worth every dime. Especially since it would be five days before she arrived in Tulsa, and she wanted the private space to make sure she looked her best when she met Seth again, and to rehearse exactly what she'd say.

After paying the man for the car rental, which took a goodly amount of the money she'd withdrawn from her account at the bank, she asked, "When can I board?"

"The train leaves town at ten tomorrow night, miss," the railroad agent said.

"I know that, sir," she responded, keeping the desperation that the train might leave without her from her voice. "When can I board?"

"Well, it'll be hooked up and ready to roll by eight in the morning, so—"

"Fine, I'll be here by eight-fifteen."

Frowning, he removed his wire-rimmed glasses and rubbed the lenses on his vest. "That'll make a long day, sitting on the tracks, miss."

"As well the next five after that," she said. "Now, could you tell me where I might find a room for the night? Not too far away, please?"

"Half a block up the road," he said, gesturing to the north. "The Railroad Inn. It's clean and has good food."

"Thank you, I appreciate that. I'm assuming I can leave my trunk here, and just take my bag with me?"

"Yes, miss. I'll see it's loaded in your car."

A smile of satisfaction tugged on her lips.

"Thank you again. You have a wonderful evening."

"You, too, miss."

Feeling lighter than she had in several days, she picked up her bag and almost skipped down the road. Missing Seth still had her heart heavy, but she was determined to find a way to make him listen to what she had to say, and if he couldn't forgive her... She shook her head and kept walking. There was no room for doubt.

As Seth hurried up the walkway of the general's house, Millie's home, his heart was thudding so hard in his throat each beat threatened to strangle him. A November clipper had kicked in, swirling leaves and tugging on his hat. He may have brought it south with him from Boston, for the weather had dropped several degrees since he'd last been here.

He shivered, not from the wind, but wondering if that was a sign, a premonition of the welcome he'd receive here. Chilly. Cold. Unwelcomed.

Needing a moment, he paused, stared at the porch before him. Trellises framed the steps, and vines, withering in the season, fought to hold on as the wind raced through the wooden lattice work. Something caught his attention and he suddenly found a lump blocking his airway.

Stepping closer, he stretched on his toes and

reached as high as he could. His fingertip caught the leather and he untangled it from the wood and vines, and then lowered the necklace to dangle before his face. The bride's necklace. The one he'd placed over Millie's neck before leaving Fort Sill.

Glancing up, he stared at the windows of the second story. Was one of those rooms Millie's? Had she thrown the necklace out, wanting nothing to remind her of him, of their time together?

His hold on the leather tightened.

"Major?"

He turned to the front door. "Miss Burnett," he said, recognizing the black woman. "I'm looking for Millie."

"I assumed as much." She gestured toward his hand. "I see you found her necklace."

"Yes, it was caught on the trellis," he explained. Manners told him he should give it to the woman, but he couldn't. He wanted to be the one to give it to Millie.

"She'll be glad to see it, searched for it for hours on end."

It took less than a second for his heart to leap back into his throat. "She did?"

"Yep." The housekeeper planted both hands on her hips. "Didn't want to leave without it."

A gust of wind caught him, made him wobble, or maybe just her statement had done that.

"Leave? Where'd she go?" *To Texas? With Martin Clark*. Seth hadn't remembered that little piece until just now.

Lola Burnett was eyeing him thoughtfully.

"It's imperative that I talk to her, ma'am. My train for Tulsa leaves tonight."

"Tonight?"

"Yes, I switched trains so I could come here. Talk to her." Neither Per-Cum-Ske nor the men had minded one more day of visiting. Actually, Per-Cum-Ske was so busy trading it might be hard to get him on a train.

"Oh, no," the woman whispered.

"Why? What's wrong?"

"She left for Washington yesterday, to catch the same train as you heading west."

A mixture of joy and frustration filled him. "Yesterday?"

Lola nodded.

Imagining Millie arriving in Tulsa, without him, of all the dangers she might face, had Seth's insides rolling.

"She'll be fine, Major," Lola said. "She's full of strength and determination."

He had to crack a smile at that. The woman was right. As much as he wanted to believe Millie was helpless, needed his protection at all times, she'd already proved him wrong. In actuality, she had all the grit and fortitude of an army man. Of a major's wife.

"She'll be waiting in Tulsa when you get there, Major. I ain't got no doubts."

An amazing reunion flashed before his eyes. Holding up the necklace, he said, "I'm taking this to her."

"She'll be glad to see it, and you."

Glancing around, attempting to hide the joy bursting inside him, Seth wondered if Millie would want to live here instead of the fort. He could do that. As long as they were together he didn't care where they lived. "I hope to see you again someday, Lola."

"I ain't got no doubts on that, either, Major."

They both chuckled and then bade each other farewell, Seth feeling more optimism than he had in decades. However, by the time he got to Washington, he was furious. The train had been stuck on the tracks for over five hours before it started up again. Passengers had mumbled about how the same thing had happened the day before, and Seth had contemplated getting out and walking. He hadn't, and when they finally arrived, he had less than ten minutes to catch his westbound train.

He ran fast and hard across the huge railroad yard, and had to jump to grab the handrail of the already rolling train.

"Glad you made it, Major," Jack Roberts said, pulling the door shut behind him.

"Me, too," Seth admitted, catching his breath before moving down the row of seats.

"Your wife isn't returning with us, sir?" the sergeant asked.

He'd forgotten no one knew what had happened. Just that he'd escorted her to Richmond, to see her family. The sadness on the man's face wasn't lost on him. Everyone had been taken with her, and he could appreciate that. Smiling, he answered, "She caught an earlier train. We'll meet up in Tulsa."

"Oh, that's good news, Major," Sergeant Rex Moore said from his seat. "Real good news."

"Yes, it is, Sergeant," Seth replied, plopping onto the hard bench. "Yes, it is."

Chapter Sixteen

Private car or not, the train ride seemed to be taking weeks instead of days, and Millie was feeling like a bird in a cage. She could venture to the dining car, but hadn't liked stepping between the cars even when Seth had been at her side, so trying it alone was not going to happen. Besides, the porter, Mr. Williams, was extremely considerate in seeing to all her needs. He even sat for a few minutes during his visits, talking about some of the other passengers.

It appeared there were army men and Indians on this train, as well. Leastwise from what Mr. Williams said. Washington had been full of them for the negotiations, so it wasn't surprising. The porter said most of them were going as far as Tulsa, too, where they'd catch other trains.

Millie kept her fingers crossed that Seth hadn't

already left Tulsa, and while doing that, she also prayed he'd listen to her. Let her explain why she'd done what she had. The closer she got to her destination, the more doubt tried to sneak into her mind. She battled it, but it was a hard war. The only thing that helped was recalling who she was. A major's wife, one fully capable of any battle put before her.

She awoke the last morning of the trip in such turmoil she felt as if her head was spinning along with her heart. After taking down the brown traveling suit from where she'd hung it upon boarding the train at eight-fifteen that morning back in Washington, she ran a hand over the soft, lush material. This, too, wearing the outfit, was a conflict she had to resolve. She wanted to look her best, but wearing the velvet while riding across the plains might damage it. Of course, she could put another gown in her traveling bag, but changing along the way, without access to Seth's tent, would be difficult. Then again, if he did forgive her, and she would be welcomed in his tent...

"Oh, goodness," she whispered, plopping onto the bed beside the gown. Maybe she didn't have the fortitude of a major's wife, after all. She certainly hadn't on her first trip west.

A knock on the door brought her to her feet again. That had been the old Millie. The one so unsure of herself she'd let others rule her life. The one who no longer existed.

Millie crossed the car and pulled open the door. "Good morning, Mr. Williams," she said to the tall, slender man with deep, sunken eyes.

"Good morning, ma'am." He carried a tray in and set it on a small table. "We'll be arriving in Tulsa before noon. Would you like me to bring you some warm water to freshen up when I return for your dishes?"

"Yes, please, I'd appreciate that very much. I'm looking forward to arriving."

"The soldiers are happy to be almost home, too," the porter said. "The one major's practically jumping out the window—the one I told you about. He's with the Indian who traded his feathers for a white wig after seeing a picture of George Washington."

She nodded, smiled, mainly because her heart was flapping against her breastbone. There was more than one major in the army, and several in the Indian Territory. She understood that, but there was only one she couldn't wait to see.

The smile remained on her face while she ate breakfast, and after Mr. Williams delivered the promised water, a bucketfull, still steaming, she made sure all the curtains were secure before stripping down to her bare essentials. With a small towel she washed herself, remembering the last time she'd been in Tulsa, and Seth had washed her hair.

Another thought flashed into her mind, making her hand stall near her throat. Everyone back here, from Mrs. Brewster in Tulsa to Briggs Ryan at Fort Sill, knew her as Rosemary. What would they think of her and her deceit?

Bits and pieces of her breath caught in her lungs. Explaining to Seth was one thing, having to explain it to everyone else was a whole different issue. He might be scorned or discredited by what she'd done.

Why hadn't she thought of this before? Why hadn't she taken the repercussions of her behavior into consideration?

"Well, Millie," she told herself aloud, "you are just going to have to face it. That's all there is to it. There's no turning back."

By the time the train sounded its whistle, announcing their arrival in Tulsa, she was so nervous she almost jumped out of her boots. Holding on to the door handle, ready to exit as soon as the wheels rolled to a stop, she glanced around the car. Her trunk was packed, ready to be unloaded, and Mr. Williams promised it would be set near the wall. An extra dress was rolled up inside her traveling bag.

She set the bag down, smoothed the velvet over her uneasy stomach and picked the bag back up.

Only to set it down again to run a hand over her hair and make sure the ribbon securing the end of her braid was tight.

Then she took a deep breath and picked the bag up yet again, just as the whistle repeated and the train started jolting as the brakes caught and released. Mrs. Ketchum had said being an army wife wasn't always easy, and Millie knew she was about to face just how hard it could be.

The last jolt left the car gently rocking, and she opened the door, rushed down the steps. The private car was near the end of the train, and people started exiting the other cars by the dozens. Hurrying around blue uniforms and bare chests, though with the cooler weather more were covered than when she'd arrived two months ago, she kept her gaze on the main street of town. Mrs. Brewster would know if Seth had already left, and the hotel was her destination. Her only focus.

When her foot caught, brought her to an abrupt stop and sent her flying forward and downward at the same time, one thought occurred.

Not again.

A pop echoing over the platform had Seth, as well as several others around him, drawing guns and scanning the area for the shooter. The whole station had gone still, with everyone looking at everyone else.

"There's a woman down," a man shouted.

"Her heel caught in a knothole," another said.

"That happened once before," someone else said.

Seth had to smile, recalling Millie's story, and though it was probably a spectacle to see, his sights were set on the hotel. Mrs. Brewster would know where Millie was. Curiosity had him glancing to where a crowd was forming, around the woman, no doubt.

His feet stopped so fast someone bumped into his back.

"Excuse me, Major," a faceless person said. Faceless because Seth's eyes were on the brown material of the dress the woman on the ground was wearing. He couldn't see much, just a flash of skirt between bystanders' legs, but he recognized the velvet.

He elbowed, shouldered and flat-out shoved men aside until he was the one bending over her, and then a tremor shot through him, hitting every muscle.

Her little shoulders were shaking as she lay belly down on the wood. Someone had already freed her foot, and he took her arms, turning her over slowly. "Millie?"

The smile on her lips grew, but then faded as her big, adorable brown eyes locked with his. "Seth?"

"Are you hurt?" he asked, willing himself not to pull her into his arms.

She closed her eyes, pinched her lips together as she shook her head. "No," she said, opening her eyes again. "Just my pride."

"I thought you were crying," he admitted.

"No, I was laughing. I couldn't believe it happened to me again." She sat up, folded one knee to examine her boot. "My heel caught in the knothole and broke off, again." Her eyes came back to him and that charming little grin appeared on her lips. "The opposite boot this time."

"Here, let me help you up." His body was alive, pounding and throbbing, all because his fingers were touching her.

Gazes locked, they stood there for a few minutes before he let her loose. They still had to talk. He had to set things straight before he could kiss her. That was the little voice in his head, and he listened to it, wanted to make sure he did things right this time.

She bent down, picked up a bag, and that made him frown. "That's your traveling bag."

"Yes, I just got off the train and was—"

"Just got off the train?" he repeated, sure he hadn't heard right.

"Yes, I missed our scheduled train, and—"

"You missed our scheduled train?" he interrupted, checking his hearing again.

"Yes."

He spun, glanced at the engine still letting off steam. "You were on that train?"

She nodded.

Comprehension hit him, made him say, "You were the rich woman in the Pullman car."

Her eyes grew wide, glancing at the train and then back to him. "You were the major with the Indians?"

"Yes."

"We were on the same train?"

"Yes," he repeated, wanting to pull her forward into his arms. The urge was growing so strong he folded his fingers around one of her wrists. "Millie, we need to—"

"Seth, I want to—" she said at the same time.

"Come on." He took the bag from her hand. "Let's go to the hotel, where we can talk."

She nodded, spinning around to walk beside him, but when they took a couple steps, her uneven gait had him stopping. Scanning the crowd, he caught sight of Rex Moore.

"Sergeant Moore?"

"Yes, Major?"

"Please retrieve…" He paused, almost saying "my wife's." "Please find the lady's heel and have that board replaced."

"Yes, sir." Tipping his hat, the man added, "Good to see you, ma'am."

"You, too, Sergeant Moore," she replied.

"Major, would you like the wagons prepared to leave in the morning?" The man's grin showed his teeth.

Seth's insides reached a new plateau of excitement. "Yes, Sergeant, tomorrow morning will be fine," he replied. Holding her arm, he kept his pace slow to accommodate her high-low steps. It reminded him of another walk they'd taken, back at the fort, and a part of him wished he could go back to that day, start over.

"Seth, I'm sorry, I—"

"Excuse me for interrupting, but I'd prefer we wait to begin our discussion at the hotel."

She nodded, and the haze of sorrow overtaking her eyes had him rubbing the inside of her arm.

"Just so we aren't interrupted," he whispered.

A shine replaced the haze and a glow covered her cheeks. She nodded again, while bowing her head bashfully. Seth was fighting the desire to scoop her into his arms and carry her the rest of the way to the hotel. He almost did, except for her bag in his opposite hand.

"Oh, Major, I had my dates mixed up. I expected you yesterday," Mrs. Brewster said, opening the door as they approached. She frowned then. "Goodness, dear, what happened? Are you hurt?"

"No, Mrs. Brewster," Millie said, "I broke my heel. It caught it a knothole."

"Oh, that happened once before." The woman moved toward the desk, gathering a key. "Don't know to whom. A woman traveling through, I think."

Seth, meeting Millie's gaze, returned her smile, enjoying their shared knowledge. "Thank you, Mrs. Brewster," he said, taking the key the woman held out.

"Would you like lunch in your room? I could—"

"We'll let you know," he said, already leading Millie up the stairs.

Millie. A beautiful name indeed. Stopping at the door of the same room they'd used before, he unlocked it, swung it open. She walked in and stopped in the middle of the room, glanced around as if nervous.

He knew the feeling. Turning, he shut the door and set her bag on the floor, then twisted the key in the lock.

As he turned back, she said, "Seth, I…" Her eyes fluttered shut as she took a deep breath.

Watching her breasts rise as she drew in air, he also noticed how one shoulder was a good two inches lower than the other. "Why don't you take your boots off? That can't be comfortable."

"It's not," she admitted, cheeks aglow.

While she sat on the bed, he moved to the window. He'd known it was going to be hard, but this was painful, keeping his hands off her. His lips off hers.

"I don't even know where to start," she said softly.

He turned, found her standing near the foot of the bed, stocking footed.

"I'm so sorry, I know my actions—"

Shaking his head, he moved toward her, until his finger touched her lips. "I'll tell you where to start."

Her expression grew even more serious as she nodded.

Trailing his finger from her lips to beneath her chin, he said, "Are you still engaged to Martin Clark?"

Frowning, she shook her head. "No." Her cheeks grew red. "I lied about that, too."

Seth held his breath at the joy erupting inside him.

"I lied to you about so many things. I—"

His finger went back to her lips. "There's only one thing I want to know. If it was a lie or not."

Her eyes had grown teary and her lips quivered beneath his touch as she nodded.

He removed his finger. "When you said you loved me, was that a lie?"

"No," she whispered. "That was the truth. Still is. I love you very, very much."

The rushing of his blood had him light-headed for a moment. His palm cupped her cheek. "That's all I need to know."

She wobbled and he caught her waist with his other hand.

"I do, however, have something to tell you." He drew a breath while waiting until her eyelids opened, before he said, "Once, not that long ago, I promised I'd never hurt you, and yet that's exactly what I did. I knew you weren't Rosemary from the beginning, yet I never said anything. I'm ashamed of that. I should have told you, but I was afraid."

"You were afraid?" she whispered.

"Yes, very. I still am." Seth took a breath, knowing he had to come clean before they could start over. "I didn't want to fall in love with you. Didn't want to love anyone."

"Why?"

He ran his finger down the side of her face, wiping at an escaping tear. "Because losing someone you love is very painful."

"Yes, it is," she whispered. "But never knowing love is worse."

The sincerity in her eyes was so profound his breath burned his lungs.

"I never knew love until I met you," she said. "Never imagined how splendid life could be."

Her gentle smile was contagious. "We are quite splendid together, aren't we?"

She let out a tiny giggle. "I think so."

He'd never experienced such a reprieve. Such joy. "Me, too."

Her gaze, still holding his, grew serious. "How did you know I wasn't Rosemary?"

Seth knew now exactly what it was. Had discovered it back in Richmond. Framing her face with both hands, he caressed the delicate skin. "Your eyes. No one has eyes like yours. They melted my heart the first time I saw them. They're gorgeous, and so…" He found himself choking up. "So full of kindness and generosity, and love." He tilted her head back, wanting so badly to kiss her. "I love you, Millie."

Millie wondered if her heart was going to beat its way right out of her chest, and her throat was so full of emotions words couldn't filter through. Which didn't matter because Seth leaned down just then and kissed her so tenderly she swooned.

His hands went to her waist, held her close, as his gentle kiss filled her entire being with pure and precious love. He'd kissed her before, but somehow, this kiss did more. It made her whole, the one thing she'd never been before.

When his lips slipped away, she wobbled

slightly, and had to look down to find him when her eyes opened.

Seth was on one knee, looking up at her. "Millie St. Clair, will you marry me?"

Covering her gasp with one hand, she sucked in another gulp of air, afraid she might faint as she had back in Washington. She hadn't expected this. Well, not yet. She hadn't told him everything. Hadn't apologized a hundred times over, and told him about little Louie, or that Rosemary had moved to England, and that as Millie, she'd never, ever lie to him again.

"Darling, if you don't answer me pretty soon, I'm going to keel over from the desire to hold you. Love you."

She cupped his handsome, wonderful face with both hands, and giggled. "Don't keel over," she said. "I've done that, it's not fun."

"Millie," he growled teasingly.

"Of course I'll marry you."

He stood and the love in his eyes was more intense. "Say it again."

"Yes, I'll marry you," she repeated.

"Again."

"Yes, I'll marry you."

"Louder."

She threw her head back, laughing as a great storm of joy erupted inside her. "Yes!"

she shouted, and then said softly, "I'll marry you, silly."

He was laughing, too, and paused only long enough to kiss her quickly, briefly. "I love you, Millie. I love you."

"I love you, too." She stretched up on her toes, wanting a kiss that would last so long she'd become lost in him, as she had while wrapped in his arms those wonderful nights they'd shared before.

"Oh, no," he said, catching her wrists with his hands.

Startled, she searched his face, looked for a teasing glint, but didn't find one. Love was in his eyes, and happiness, but seriousness, as well. A stinging sensation curled around her spine. "What's wrong?"

Walking backward, he led her to the window. "See that building over there?"

Focusing wasn't easy with her body throbbing so, but she scanned the area, a side street of town, full of houses and… "You mean the church?"

"Yes, we are going there," he said. "Getting married, and then we'll return here…" he kissed the side of her neck "…and spend some time in that bed."

A moan rumbled in her throat and desire flared inside her. His tone said that what would happen in that bed would be more intimate, more long lasting than it had ever been. "All right," she said. "When?"

"Right now." He scooped her into his arms. "I can't wait any longer."

It wasn't until he'd unlocked the door and pulled it open, a difficult task with her still in his arms, that Millie grabbed the doorjamb. "Stop."

He groaned, and she giggled.

"What?" he asked.

"I don't have any shoes on."

"I'll carry you the entire way."

He didn't, at her insistence, for she wasn't getting married barefoot—or stocking footed. However, she didn't make him put her down until they entered the shop across the street, where the woman carried on about how lovely the traveling suit fit, and told Millie about the morning Seth had purchased it. The pinkish glow on his cheeks made her love grow deeper, if that was possible, and wearing yet another pair of boots Seth bought for her, she ran with him across the street and the field leading to the church, hand in hand, laughing all the way.

The preacher was there, as was his wife, and in a private ceremony that Millie knew she'd hold as one of her most treasured memories until she was too old to remember, Seth and she became husband and wife. She cried when Seth vowed his love, and when he slipped the bride's necklace over her head. But when he slid a ring on her finger, a sweet sob locked itself in her throat and remained there.

Afterward, while returning to the hotel, she held her hand up, stared at how the sun glistened in the jewels. "It's the most beautiful thing I've ever seen."

"You are the most beautiful thing *I've* ever seen," he said, kissing her temple as they walked.

She leaned against him, cherished how his arm tightened around her waist. "I'll treasure it forever."

"I'll treasure you forever."

"You're silly," she whispered.

"No, I'm in love. And happier than I've ever been."

She stepped in front of him, making him stop, and reached up to lay a hand against his cheek. "Me, too."

He kissed her then, in that all-consuming way she'd been hoping he would. To the point she barely recognized that halfway through his kiss he'd scooped her up and started walking again.

She rested her head on his shoulder as he carried her through the hotel lobby and up the stairs, and laughed aloud when he plopped her onto the bed.

"Finally," he growled.

She giggled and then held her arms open when he returned from locking the door.

As he took her hands, crawled onto the bed beside her, she whispered, "Welcome home, Major."

Their union was a turbulent combination of love, passion and infatuation, as well as a blending of lives, old and new, past and present. It left Millie breathless, spent and eager, knowing there were now years ahead of them. Years upon years.

With her head on his shoulder, twirling a fingertip in the fine hair on his chest, she whispered, "Seth?"

"Yes, darling?"

"What am I going to do once we get to the fort?"

"What do you mean?"

"They all think my name is Rosemary. How am I going to tell them it's Millie?"

He tugged her onto his chest with both arms, settled her there, lying fully atop him. "We'll tell them the truth. That you traveled to the fort for me to sign the divorce papers, and we fell in love."

She loved him all the more for making things sound so simple, yet had to say, "That's not exactly—"

"That's how I remember it."

He kissed the end of her nose and then sighed, understanding she needed more of an answer.

"How many people called you Rosemary?"

Searching her mind, she finally said, "Well, no one really. They either called me ma'am, Mrs. Parker or the major's wife."

"Mrs. Parker," he whispered, kissing her again.

A lovely sigh left her chest, for it was a wonderful name. "What if they hear you call me Millie? What if—"

"You worry too much," he said, kissing her chin this time. "No one knows what happened. We can leave it that way if you want. Even the few that do know will never say anything."

She bit her bottom lip.

"What is it?"

It was a silly thing to worry about when everything else was so perfect, but she had to admit, "I want to be me. Millie."

"Oh, darling," he said, kissing her lips lightly. "You've always been Millie. Your sister would never have traveled out here, not by train or wagon. She'd never have befriended Briggs's maidens, or Per-Cum-Ske's wives, or even Ilene Ketchum." He kissed her again. "But most of all, she'd never have become the perfect army wife."

Millie's heart swelled, and all she could do was whisper, "I love you."

"I know, and I love that about you, too," he said, running both his hands down her back.

"We could tell everyone Per-Cum-Ske traded your name for a new one."

That made her laugh. "I heard about the white wig."

"You did? From whom?"

His hands were working their magic again, sparking miniature fires wherever they touched, and it was a moment or more before she could answer. "Mr. Williams, the porter."

"I can't believe we were on the same train, all those days." He held her hips firmly against his. "All those nights."

The feel of him pressing against her belly had her desire sparking again. "You're making me fuddle-headed," she admitted, nuzzling his chest with her chin. It would be like this forever. One look and she'd be racing up the stairs to the bedroom at the fort as fast as Per-Cum-Ske's wives did to their tepees.

"Oh, no," she said, propping herself up on her elbows.

"What?"

"Mrs. Ketchum. I forgot her list. All the things—"

"I remembered them," he said. "They'll be on the wagons in the morning." He lifted her then, pulled her forward until her breasts were within easy access of his lips.

"Seth," she groaned, the sensations making

her arch into him. "We were talking about my name, what I'm going to tell people."

"No," he mumbled, since his mouth was full. "*You* were talking."

She had to agree, but could barely nod, and then, within no time, forgot all about her name. What mattered was who she was—the major's wife.

* * * * *

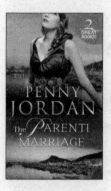

The Regency Ballroom Collection

A twelve-book collection led by Louise Allen
and written by the top authors and rising
stars of historical romance!

Classic tales of scandal and seduction in
the Regency ballroom

Take your place on the ballroom floor now, at:
www.millsandboon.co.uk

Join the Mills & Boon Book Club

Want to read more **Historical** books?
We're offering you **2 more** absolutely **FREE!**

We'll also treat you to these fabulous extras:

- **Exclusive offers and much more!**
- **FREE home delivery**
- **FREE books and gifts with our special rewards scheme**

Get your free books now!

visit www.millsandboon.co.uk/bookclub
or call Customer Relations on 020 8288 2888

Discover more romance at

www.millsandboon.co.uk

- ♥ WIN great prizes in our exclusive competitions

- ♥ BUY new titles before they hit the shops

- ♥ BROWSE new books and REVIEW your favourites

- ♥ SAVE on new books with the Mills & Boon® Bookclub™

- ♥ DISCOVER new authors

PLUS, to chat about your favourite reads, get the latest news and find special offers:

- 🅕 Find us on facebook.com/millsandboon
- 🐦 Follow us on twitter.com/millsandboonuk
- ♥ Sign up to our newsletter at millsandboon.co.uk

WEB_SD

The World of Mills & Boon®

There's a Mills & Boon® series that's perfect for you. We publish ten series and, with new titles every month, you never have to wait long for your favourite to come along.

By Request
Relive the romance with the best of the best
12 stories every month

Cherish™
Experience the ultimate rush of falling in love
12 new stories every month

Desire™
Passionate and dramatic love stories
6 new stories every month

n o c t u r n e™
An exhilarating underworld of dark desires
Up to 3 new stories every month

M&B/WORLD4a